Paul Thomas, born in Yorkshire a[...]
New Zealand, is a novelist, scriptwriter, j[...]
sports biographer. He has written a bestselling series
featuring maverick Maori cop Tito Ihaka, which includes
Dirty Laundry (aka *Old School Tie*, 1994), *Inside Dope*
(1995), *Guerrilla Season* (1996) and *Death on Demand*
(2013). *Inside Dope* was the winner of the Ned Kelly
Award for Best Novel, and *Death on Demand* won the
2013 Ngaio Marsh Award for Best Crime Novel.

FALLOUT

Paul Thomas

BITTER LEMON PRESS
LONDON

BITTER LEMON PRESS

First published in the United Kingdom in 2015 by
Bitter Lemon Press, 47 Wilmington Square,
London WC1X 0ET

www.bitterlemonpress.com

First published in New Zealand by Upstart Press Ltd., 2014

A CIP record for this book is available
from the British Library

ISBN 978–1–908524–49–2
eBook ISBN 978–1–908524–50–8

Typeset by Tetragon
Printed and bound in Great Britain by
CPI Group (UK) Ltd, Croydon, CR0 4YY

To the memory of
my mother and father

Acknowledgements

I would like to thank my sister Susan for her legal expertise and Ross Vintiner for sharing his insights into the nuclear ships issue.

Thanks also to the Christchurch Writers' Festival for its support of New Zealand crime writing.

1

Since becoming Auckland District Commander and developing an appreciation for wine – the two were related – Finbar McGrail hadn't been sleeping as well as he used to.

His late, grimly Presbyterian mother had been fond of saying 'the sleep of the righteous is sweet', a paraphrase of Proverbs 3:24. While McGrail was confident that promotion hadn't disabled his moral compass, he had to acknowledge that he'd gone from having an occasional glass of wine to not needing an occasion to open a bottle, and from dutifully saying his prayers to no longer bothering to touch base with God before calling it a night.

First the formalities were dispensed with: the kneeling beside the bed, head bowed (because although heaven is commonly thought to be up there somewhere, presumably above airliners' cruising altitude, believers know that God is everywhere, even under one's bed), hands clasped, eyes shut, the constipated expression of rapture tempered by obeisance. Once he started saying his prayers after, rather than before, getting into bed, it was a short step to mouthing the words, as opposed to saying them out loud, and an even shorter step to thinking them. And once the process was internalised, it was difficult not to get distracted or deflected. It was almost as if his mind had a mind of its own.

Eventually McGrail gave up the struggle and fell into the habit of thinking about work for however long it took for his wife's current book to make her eyelids droop. When she said goodnight and turned off the bedside light, he would roll onto his side and go to sleep, albeit not without a twinge of guilt, like someone who has let another day go by without ringing his aged parents.

As often as not these days, McGrail would wake up in the early hours. Rather than wait for the fog of sleep to roll back in or engage in that erratic, tangential mental activity that seems productive, even inspired, at 3 am but turns out to be inconsequential at best when retrieved in the morning, he'd slip out of bed. After making himself a cup of cocoa, he'd go into his study to chip away at his email backlog, which was seldom less than a hundred messages.

Before he went back to bed, McGrail would look at a photo that he still kept in his bottom drawer even though his children had left home. It was a head-and-shoulders shot of a teenage girl trying to put on an exasperated 'Do I really have to do this?' expression but unable to keep the smile off her face. McGrail knew a lot about this girl, whose name was Polly Stenson. For instance, he knew that she'd had her braces removed a fortnight before the photo was taken. The orthodontist had met the challenge he'd been set two years earlier: to have Polly's teeth straight and unencumbered by her seventeenth birthday.

The date print-out, in orange lettering on the bottom right-hand corner of the photo, said 15.8.87. It was taken on the last afternoon of Polly Stenson's short life.

McGrail had been in New Zealand a fortnight, having left Northern Ireland even though – in fact because – he was a rising star in the Royal Ulster Constabulary. The Stenson murder was the first case for Auckland Central's new Detective Inspector, of whom much was expected.

Polly was murdered at an election-night party held at the spectacular Remuera home of merchant banker Tim Barton and his wife Nicky. Barton had called it a 'Win-Win' party because, as far as people like him were concerned, it made no difference who won the election. That was understandable: it seemed to McGrail that the only real economic disagreement between the two major parties was over which of them was the more laissez-faire.

McGrail was taken aback by the ostentatious displays of wealth and unashamed extravagance he encountered during the investigation. He and his wife had decided to emigrate to New Zealand after extensive research and the process of elimination led them to the conclusion that their people – the Protestants of Ulster – had more in common with New Zealanders than any other nationality.

McGrail was under the impression that New Zealanders were stoic, understated, laconic to the point of taciturnity, suspicious of self-promotion and public display, inclined to pessimism and quick to say 'I told you so' when their gloomy prognoses were borne out. The glaring difference was that New Zealanders didn't seem to take religion anywhere near seriously enough to kill or maim their neighbours over denominational differences. (That was an aspect of life in Northern Ireland that McGrail was keen to put behind him: he had thought about emigrating for years, but the tipping point was finding out that his name was on a Provisional IRA hit-list. While hit-lists were a dime a dozen in Belfast – there were pub darts teams who had them – the Provos had already put a black line through some of the names on theirs.) If McGrail had wanted nouveau-riche vulgarity, he would have gone to America, or even Australia. Thankfully it didn't last. After the Black Tuesday sharemarket crash later that year, New Zealanders reverted to type. For a while, anyway.

The investigation was a nightmare. Over the course of the evening at least three hundred people had passed through the Barton mansion, but that was a woolly estimate since there were no formal invitations or guest list: Barton had just put the word out to his friends, who passed it on to their various overlapping social circles. Barton's twenty-one-year-old son Johnny and teenage daughter Lucy had hosted their own sub-parties.

There was no proper security and therefore no one with a sober recollection of comings and goings or who was likely to notice odd or jarring behaviour. Security, such as it was, was provided by Johnny's rugby team, who were given the narrow brief of repelling any uncouth elements that might try to crash the party. Predictably, most of the rugby players got drunker and did so faster than the other attendees.

Polly and Lucy went to the same girls' private school, although Polly was a bit of an outsider. Her father was middle management; she was a scholarship girl, bright and athletic. Although her friends had done their best to corrupt her, Polly stuck to her unfashionable principles relating to booze, drugs and what was a seemly level of sexual activity for a girl her age.

By midnight, most of the girls and their dates – Polly was one of the few in the group who didn't have a boyfriend – were too tipsy or distracted to look out for their friends. But then why would they? If you weren't safe in that grand house in one of Auckland's most prestigious streets surrounded by hundreds of people, including MPs from both major parties and an array of Rich Listers and movers and shakers, where on earth would you be?

The Barton place was on three levels. The ground floor was the living and entertainment area. Downstairs was the kids' domain: the only adults who ventured below were the cleaning ladies. Upstairs was the parents' quarters, complete with his-and-hers studies, library, gymnasium and sauna. It was well understood that upstairs was a child-free no-go zone.

The adults had congregated on the ground floor. The younger generation had split into groups: despite the time of year the rugby players yahooed around the pool; Lucy and friends mainly stayed downstairs; the little band of dope smokers had made their furtive way to the tennis court.

Polly had arranged to sleep over at another friend's house; a cab was booked for 2 am. Around 11.30 pm, without saying where she was going or why, she went upstairs. She had a brief exchange with Tim Barton, telling him she felt like getting some fresh air. He later said she seemed fine: she'd obviously had a few drinks but wasn't drunk, disoriented or looking for trouble.

Outside she bumped into a friend's boyfriend who'd been out on the tennis court where the joints were circulating. She told him she was taking time out from the tiresome boy-girl interaction downstairs. He advised her to get stoned, knowing there was zero chance of that happening. That was the last anyone saw of her.

Just before 2 am the girl she was going to stay with went looking for her. It wasn't an exhaustive search. The friend was feeling woozy and aware that the sooner she got to sleep, the less awful she'd feel the next day. She quickly reached the convenient conclusion that Polly had got sick of being the only girl downstairs whose knickers weren't under siege and cabbed it back to her own place. The friend went home and crashed; her parents hadn't felt the need to wait up. It wasn't until 10.30 the following morning when her mother Barbara rang to remind Polly of their deal – she could go to the party and sleep over at her friend's on the condition she spent Sunday studying – that anyone realised she was missing.

Barbara rang Nicky Barton, who went straight downstairs. There were several girls sleeping it off down there, but Polly wasn't one of them. At around 11.15 Tim Barton got out of bed and shuffled down the corridor and through the state-of-the-art gym to the sauna, where he hoped to sweat out his hellish hangover. He was so stupefied that his first thought on noticing that there was someone tucked in under the wooden seat was: how shit-faced would you have to be to crash under there?

Polly had been strangled. There was nothing to indicate a struggle: her clothes were intact, her torso and face unmarked. She hadn't been sexually active or sexually assaulted.

Suspicion fell on the rugby players. They ticked a lot of boxes: aggression, inebriation and a reputation for Neanderthal behaviour towards women. The theory was that Polly, bored and curious, had decided to explore. (Her fingerprints were found in the master bedroom.) One or more of the rugby players had seen her go upstairs, followed her, put the hard word on her and reacted violently when rebuffed.

The players proclaimed their innocence. No one remembered seeing any of them go upstairs, but then no one remembered seeing Polly go upstairs either. Part of the problem was that the stairs were well away from the party's epicentre. Secondly, even though there were three toilets on the ground floor, there were lots of people taking on lots of fluid, resulting in steady traffic up to the toilet at the top of the stairs.

The theory unravelled. Johnny Barton was the only member of the team whose fingerprints were found upstairs. Then there was the inconvenient fact that just before midnight the rugby team had chased the pot smokers off the tennis court so they could practise some moves. The practice session, which went on for over an hour with frequent beer breaks, was run by the team's Samoan contingent, two deeply religious teetotallers. They were adamant that the entire team – bar Johnny, who'd been inside chatting to a High Court judge – had been present and correct, although their handling skills had left something to be desired. Even if there had been circumstantial evidence pointing to a player, it would have been difficult to make it stick given the time of death was between midnight and 1 am.

The first rule of police work is never overlook the obvious. McGrail accepted that 'drunken rugby brute gone nuts' was the obvious scenario, but never subscribed to it. The crime scene would have been messier, the victim would have been roughed up, the killer would probably have drawn attention to himself with his behaviour or demeanour.

It didn't look or feel sexual to McGrail. It looked and felt as if murder had been the object of the exercise, rather than the by-product of attempted rape or a psychotic reaction to rejection.

It was conceivable that a burglar had infiltrated the party and was helping himself to Barton's wife's jewellery when Polly poked her nose into the master bedroom. He hid her body in the sauna to delay discovery and left empty-handed rather than advertise his presence by stealing anything.

Or Polly could have interrupted someone going through the filing cabinets in Barton's study. He was renowned for playing hardball and there was commercially sensitive information in the cabinets, but nothing was missing and there were no unidentified fingerprints in the study. Barton scoffed at the notion that a guest might have tried to steal jewellery or information: he wasn't in the habit of hosting his enemies or people who needed to steal.

In Northern Ireland McGrail had worked on many cases involving terrorism (or criminal activity disguised as terrorism) on the part of the IRA, its offshoots and the various Protestant paramilitaries, so he was no stranger to political pressure or outside interference. But he was to be amazed at the level of oversight exercised by his superiors all the way up to the Minister of Police. He was even more amazed by the brazen lack of cooperation from some guests, and his superiors' preference for a softly-softly approach which only encouraged the non-cooperators to carry on being uncooperative. And once it became apparent that there wouldn't be a swift resolution, the pressure, if anything, increased. Only now the pressure was on to downgrade the investigation.

Nine months after Polly's murder, McGrail went to see her parents for the last time. They lived on the border of Meadowbank and Glen Innes, an area he'd heard described as 'middle class but not by much', in a house that was nice enough but a world removed from the Barton residence with its harbour views and palatial scale, its art collection and temperature-controlled wine cellar and abiding impression of having been created and furnished not on the basis of what was sensible or necessary or even desirable, but to ensure that all and sundry understood money was no object.

McGrail brought the Stensons up to date, outlining in his dispassionate, expressionless way the difficulties and frustrations arising from the circumstances of that night and having to deal with people who seemed to think their wealth and status freed them from legal and moral obligations. He admitted that after nine months' intensive work, he and his team had no leads, no witnesses, no suspects, no credible theory and therefore no clear path forward. That didn't mean they were giving up, but the investigation would be scaled down, which meant fewer resources.

He wasn't expecting them to protest: desolation had overtaken them, driving out all other emotions. It was even possible, he thought, that they feared catharsis might compromise the emptiness they now accepted as their destiny, or fretted over what might come to light in the event of a breakthrough. The victim's family and friends always ask why, although the answer is usually mundane or sordid or just another example of the randomness of fate. There was no explanation for this poor child's destruction that would make any sense to her parents.

Gordon Stenson was greyer and thinner, mild to the point of passivity, his eyes sunk in black, bony recesses. 'So you don't have a theory, Mr McGrail? I mean you personally?'

'Not really,' replied McGrail. 'As I said, I don't believe it was sexually motivated. I have an instinct that she was killed because she was in the wrong place at the wrong time rather than because she was Polly Stenson, if you follow me. But why that should have been the case, I've no idea.'

Barbara Stenson was five years younger than her husband. Now they looked the same age and he looked five years older than he actually was. 'Would it be fair to say, Inspector,' she said, 'that you've stopped looking and are really just hoping for something to drop into your lap?'

'That would be overstating it,' said McGrail, 'but there's an element of truth to it. I'd just add that quite a lot of crimes are solved because something drops into our lap.'

She handed McGrail an envelope. 'There's a photo of Polly in there – perhaps you could look at it from time to time. She deserves to be remembered by more than just the two of us.'

McGrail examined himself in the mirror above the basins. Well, he thought, that could have been worse; I could've told the Minister what I really think of him.

He had just had dinner at the Northern Club with the Minister of Police, the Commissioner of Police and the Minister's new best friend, a South African management consultant and self-styled 'change engineer' who had been brought in to conduct what his profession called a 360 review of the police service with the object of eliminating waste, increasing efficiency and delivering a better return on taxpayer investment. In other words, he'd been brought in to find the dead wood that McGrail and his fellow district commanders couldn't or wouldn't identify.

The report ran to 245 pages, most of which was padding. There was a review of the status quo that McGrail could have generated in an afternoon, if it had occurred to him to waste an afternoon telling people what they already knew. There were many statements of the obvious, blithe assertions and lofty sentiments, mostly relating to culture, accountability and empowerment, and incessant use of management jargon, presumably to obscure the lack of intellectual rigour. The bottom line for McGrail, who liked to think he was sharp-eyed when it came to spotting atrophy and decay, was that there was apparently a lot more dead wood in the Auckland district than he'd noticed.

When the Minister asked McGrail for his thoughts, he began by acknowledging that Mr Pienaar and his associates seemed to recognise that the people who would be restructured, reoriented, downgraded, taken out of their comfort zones or just plain sacked if the recommendations were implemented wouldn't be happy about it.

The Minister nodded approvingly. 'There's no attempt to gild the lily,' he said. 'I like that. Some of my colleagues prefer these things sugar-coated, but no one could accuse me of that.'

'But —'

The Commissioner interrupted. 'Ah yes, the but. With Finbar, there's always a but.'

The Commissioner, who had a deceptively genial demeanour, sounded even more peevish than usual. McGrail wondered if that was because he realised his life was about to take a turn for the worse as a result of Pienaar's report, or because the alcohol component of the meal had been restricted to a single bottle of Pinot Gris, a beverage he was on record as dismissing as 'a breakfast wine'. The Commissioner probably also suspected that the discussion was about to get prickly, requiring him to perform a delicate balancing act, and drag on for some time, thereby keeping him from his hotel room and the bottle of single malt scotch that he never left home without.

McGrail resumed, as if he hadn't noticed the interruption: 'But I believe they seriously underestimate the scale and intensity of the reaction. In my opinion, full-scale implementation would trigger industrial action.'

'There's no point in half-measures,' said Pienaar crisply. 'The report's very clear on that.'

'Indeed it is,' said McGrail. 'The Australians have a saying, "Crash through or crash". That's a pretty bold approach if there's a decent chance you'll come a cropper.'

The corners of the Minister's mouth turned down. He glanced at the Commissioner, who raised his eyebrows as if to say 'what did you expect?'

'I obviously have more faith in your policemen and -women than our friend here,' said Pienaar, addressing the Minister, 'because I can't see them going on strike. But if they did —' He shrugged. 'That would be a strategic confrontation you couldn't afford to lose, even if it meant deploying the army.'

McGrail's chuckle was devoid of any trace of amusement. 'This country doesn't really have a tradition of sending the army into the streets. Besides, our army doesn't have your army's experience in, shall we say, crowd control.'

'You're behind the times, Superintendent,' snapped Pienaar, 'in more ways than one.' He turned back to the Minister. 'You can't make an omelette without breaking some eggs. Sure, there's going to be opposition, but if you back off, in ten years another minister will be sitting here having this exact same conversation. Look what happened in Britain: for years they caved in to the unions and the place went to the dogs. Finally Maggie Thatcher had the balls to say "Enough is enough". She faced down the miners and the printers and turned the country around.'

'I'm not sure what history's verdict on Mrs Thatcher will be,' said McGrail. 'What I do know is that the police's role was crucial to the outcomes of both those disputes. Which I suppose is my point: you're going out of your way to pick a fight – and a bitter fight, let there be no doubt about that – with an organisation that symbolises and ensures the rule of law. I wouldn't presume to give the Minister political advice, but I fail to see how that's either good government or smart politics.'

It was all downhill from there. Oh well, thought McGrail as he dried his hands, only a year till retirement. If I can't survive that long, I'm not as clever as people think I am.

He exited the toilets. A man was standing in the corridor, as if he was waiting for McGrail. 'Superintendent McGrail?' He had most of the distinguishing features of a typical Northern Club member: Pakeha, well-fed appearance, no longer young, expensive suit, midwinter tan.

'Yes.'

'I was pretty sure it was you, but not a hundred per cent. It's been quite a while.'

McGrail couldn't place him, despite his memory for faces. 'You have the advantage of me.'

'Nineteen eighty-seven, to be precise.'

'That is a while ago. The year I arrived here, in fact.'

'Yeah, I remember someone saying it was your first case. I was there the night Polly Stenson was murdered.' He extended his hand. 'Andy Maddocks.'

They shook hands. 'You were a friend of the Barton lad.' Maddocks nodded. 'You must excuse me – I conducted or sat in on a lot of interviews.'

Maddocks shook his head, smiling. 'I would've been amazed if you'd remembered me.' He paused, the prelude to an awkward change of gears. 'Look, could I get you a drink?'

'That's very kind,' said McGrail, 'but it's been a long and rather trying day. And I wouldn't want you to take this personally, but I don't have fond memories of that case.'

Maddocks reddened. 'Superintendent, there's something I have to tell you – for my own good. I've been sitting on it all these years, and I need to get it off my chest. I'd really appreciate it.'

'Is it to do with Polly?'

'Yes. It's not that big a deal, but it might clear up a couple of things.'

'In that case, lead on, Mr Maddocks.'

They found a quiet corner. McGrail had a port, Maddocks a glass of Pinot Noir.

'I didn't lie or withhold information when I spoke to you,' said Maddocks. 'At that stage I didn't know what I'm about to tell you. Johnny Barton told me a couple of months later – after swearing me to secrecy. He had a bit of a soft spot for Polly. He liked the fact she wasn't a follower, like most of his sister's friends. She said to me once, "What Johnny doesn't seem to get is that I can't afford to be." Anyway, Johnny being Johnny, his way of showing it was to tease her – mostly good fun, but sometimes it got a bit mean. Like that night. You remember Tina Best? She and her husband Roger were at the party.'

'Vaguely.'

'She was the mother of a mate of ours. I guess these days you'd call her a cougar.' Maddocks peered at McGrail, wondering if he needed to elaborate.

'She fancied younger men?'

Maddocks nodded. 'Well, she certainly fancied Johnny. A few weeks before the party, he'd gone round to their place to drop off something for Roger and Tina threw herself at him. According to him – and Johnny had his faults, but he didn't bullshit about women; he didn't need to – she was pretty much besotted with him. He'd ring her up, it didn't matter what she was doing, she'd drop everything and go and meet him. He used to knock her off in car parks, in the back seat of her Merc. One time he went over there when they were having a dinner party; she came out and gave him a blowjob in the garage.' Maddocks reddened again. 'Sorry, it's a bit bloody grubby.' McGrail was unblinkingly non-judgemental. 'Anyway, Johnny spent most of that night out at the pool with his rugby mates. About eleven thirty he went off to hook up with Tina – although we didn't know that – and bumped into Polly, who was bored and thinking of going home. On the spur of the moment he decided to do a number on her. He told her to go upstairs, wait in the walk-in wardrobe in the main bedroom with the door slightly open, and in a few minutes she'd see something that would knock her socks off.

'Off she went, but as Johnny was talking Tina into popping upstairs for a quickie, his parents appeared. Nicky, his mother, said to Tina, "Just the person I'm looking for; I need a second opinion on some curtains" or whatever, and more or less dragged her away. Tim told Johnny, who was doing law, that there was some judge he wanted him to meet. So he got hauled off to talk to the judge with his old man right there making sure he didn't slide off. This went on for about half an hour, by which time all Johnny wanted to do was get back outside and get wasted. He didn't even bother looking for Polly – he just assumed she'd think she'd been taken for a ride and be highly pissed off with him.'

'Did Johnny take this to mean that his parents knew or suspected what he was up to with Mrs Best?'

'Yeah, the next day Tim told him to stick to girls his own age. It turned out Tim and Roger had some big hush-hush deal on the go, and if it got derailed because of Johnny putting his dick where it didn't belong, he could kiss his inheritance goodbye. That's why Johnny swore me to secrecy.'

'How did his father know?'

'Didn't say,' said Maddocks. 'Johnny asked, of course, but Tim gave him the old, "You'd be surprised what I know".'

Within a couple of months it was all academic. The October sharemarket crash put paid to whatever was in the works, the Bests sold up and moved to Australia, and Johnny set out on his journey to rock bottom.

Maddocks knew the story because one of his mates had married Lucy Barton. With his parents' encouragement, Johnny had taken a year off law to do a rich boy's whirlwind overseas experience. In London, though, he fell hard for a girl who was out of his league. Part model, part muse, she had posed for society photographers and a fashionable painter, and rock stars, the likes of Bryan Ferry, had written songs about her. She ran off to Paris with a married novelist. When he came home with his tail between his legs, Johnny saw a window of opportunity and rushed over to France. She still wasn't interested, but she did introduce him to the expat bohemian scene. He wasn't artistic or intellectual or cultured or worldly or fizzing with anarchic vitality, but he had one thing that not many in that circle possessed, and that was money. He discovered that having lots of drugs on hand and being generous with them was a good way to make and keep friends. Thus began a slow descent into addiction.

A decade later, when his trust money had run out and

the 'just to tide me over' remittances had dried up and after several unsuccessful interventions, his father hired a team of ex-US Army Special Forces guys who specialised in extracting people from cults. They kidnapped Johnny from a commune in Mexico, took him to England and left him in the care of the woman who unhooked Eric Clapton from heroin. When Johnny was clean, his parents brought him home.

'Where is he now?' asked McGrail.

'Right here,' said Maddocks. 'Talk about going from one extreme to the other: he went back to varsity, finished his law degree and set himself up in a practice, with a little help from his parents. I bump into him now and again: he's turned into Tim lite – smug, conservative, very much part of the eastern suburbs social scene, but without Tim's business nous. Not that money's an issue.'

'Am I right in thinking the father died not so long ago?'

'Yep, dropped dead on the seventeenth tee at Middlemore. His mother sold the family home, much to Johnny's disgust. She's got an apartment in the Viaduct. The Bests split up – surprise, surprise. I heard Tina's back in town, but I don't know whether that's true.'

'Could you find out?'

Maddocks stared. 'Are you going to follow this up?'

'I've waited twenty-seven years for a break on Polly Stenson's murder,' said McGrail. 'It's not much, but it's something. You bet your bottom dollar I'm going to follow it up.' He produced a slim notebook and a fountain pen from his jacket pocket. 'Let's go back to the beginning.'

2

All was in readiness. The highly decorated (and priced) bottle of Central Otago Pinot Noir had been breathing for a couple of hours. The fire, craftily tended and force-fed, had worked itself into a yellow-orange fury generating so much heat that the room had been opened up and outer layers discarded. The lamb shanks had been slow-cooked into submission. The panel of pundits had squeezed every last drop out of the bleeding obvious and hedged their bets. The players were about to take the field.

Their Saturdays revolved around ten-year-old Billy's rugby, which had become Tito Ihaka's rugby since he'd been roped in to help with the coaching. After a post-game McDonald's they would shop for dinner, usually one of the wine-soaked casseroles that Denise Hadlow, Billy's mother and Ihaka's girlfriend, considered her speciality. 'One-pot cooking,' she called it whenever Ihaka wondered out loud if it was about time they had a roast with all the trimmings. 'Think about that when you're doing the dishes.'

They would browse in the DVD hire shop, where the challenge was to find something that was suitable for Billy and which Ihaka was prepared to sit through in stoic silence. (As long as it passed the appropriateness test, Denise didn't mind what Billy chose, no matter how dumb or noisy it was.) They divided their time, as the Sunday supplements say, between her Point Chevalier townhouse and his Sandringham bungalow, but All Black test nights were always spent at Ihaka's place because it had a fireplace. Ihaka wasn't a great one for rules, either his own or other people's, but he was adamant that a roaring fire was part of the ritual. You simply couldn't watch the All Blacks without one.

Billy had scored three tries that morning and been so clearly the best player on the field that the parents had abandoned their usual practice of giving the player of the day award to the boy with the bloodiest nose or whose roughneck enthusiasm had more or less made up for his brain explosions. If the Blacks nail it, thought Ihaka, it would be the perfect end to a perfect day. Correction: it would be the perfect prelude to the perfect end to a perfect day.

Billy was practising the haka, muttering the words to himself. Ihaka had taught him the words and actions, not realising that Billy would see it as their patriotic duty to accompany the All Blacks. Denise told them to take their places on the sofa, she was about to serve up.

'Just ducking to the loo,' said Ihaka, and left the room.

His mobile, which was on the arm of the sofa, started ringing. Being a modern parent, Denise encouraged Billy to answer her phone if she wasn't around; he had no reason to think Ihaka, who was pretty easy-going about that sort of thing, had a different policy. 'Hello. This is Billy speaking.'

There was a short silence. A woman said, 'I'm sorry, I've got the wrong number.'

'Um, it's not my phone,' said Billy.

'Oh, I see. Well, I was trying to get hold of Tito Ihaka.'

Ihaka reappeared. 'He's here,' said Billy. He held out the phone. 'It's for you.'

There were a few things Ihaka could have said, but he restricted himself to 'Funny that' because he didn't want Billy to think he was pissed off with him for answering his phone and it would be easy to give the kid that impression. Secondly, Billy probably couldn't answer the burning question, 'Who the fuck would ring at this time?' Third, he was making a conscious effort not to swear in front of Billy and, by and large and somewhat to his surprise, succeeding. He'd expected that, deprived of the F word and its variations, he would struggle to communicate, express an opinion, pass comment on the daily round and let off steam over minor misadventures like splashing water on himself when doing the dishes. It actually wasn't that hard.

He took the phone. 'Ihaka.'

'Hi, it's Miriam Lovell.'

She was a freelance journalist in whom Ihaka had, briefly, taken an interest. His affair with Denise had taken off in a storm and quickly encountered turbulence. Under the impression that it had in fact crashed and burned, he'd entered into negotiations with Miriam over the ground rules for what they agreed would be a low-key, one-step-at-a-time relationship. Then Denise had second thoughts. By the time Ihaka got around to informing Miriam that their relationship wouldn't be progressing beyond the hypothetical stage, she'd worked it out for herself.

Ihaka couldn't help flicking a wary glance at Denise, who was bringing in his dinner. She mouthed, 'Who is it?' He put on a dumb show to indicate that he'd walked into an ambush.

'Oh hi,' he said leadenly. 'How are you?'

'Is this a bad time?'

'Well, yeah, as a matter of fact. The test match is about to start.'

Ihaka heard Denise ask Billy, 'Who is it, sweetie?'

'A lady.'

Ihaka kept his eyes on the TV screen: the All Blacks were coming out onto the field. He sensed Denise's narrow-eyed scrutiny and Billy's rising anxiety. He thought of leaving the room, but that would guarantee an interrogation.

'So not exactly life and death, then?' said Miriam.

'We'll have to agree to disagree on that.'

'OK, I get the message. I'll be brief: I need to see you. Don't worry, this isn't about you and me – I've well and truly moved on. It's something that directly affects you, personally and professionally. How are you placed tomorrow morning?'

The teams were lining up for the national anthems. Billy was looking at him beseechingly: no point in doing the haka if Ihaka's attention was elsewhere. Denise came back in with her and Billy's meals, looking disgruntled. He had to get off the phone. 'Yeah, that's OK,' he said.

'Imperial Lane, ten thirty,' said Miriam. 'Don't be late.'

As Ihaka switched off his phone, he remembered that there had been talk, to which he'd raised no objection, of a Sunday-morning outing. Come to think of it, he'd suggested going to Devonport on the ferry, which Billy was all for.

The All Blacks and Billy prepared to do the haka.

'Who was that?' asked Denise, trying to keep it casual.

Ihaka decided this was one haka he really should participate in. He took his place beside Billy. 'OK champ, let's do it right.'

It wasn't easy getting Billy into bed. He wanted to watch the post-match interviews and the replay of the match highlights. Ihaka suspected that if the All Blacks had lost,

Billy would've claimed he was too upset to go to sleep and needed to be distracted with a game of Monopoly or allowed to stay up to watch whatever they watched. He was normally pretty good at charming or cajoling Denise into cutting him some slack, but not tonight. You're wasting your breath, pal, thought Ihaka: as far as Mum's concerned, two's company, three's a crowd. Not necessarily in a good way.

They put Billy to bed. Two, maybe three seconds after they got back to the living room, Denise asked, 'So who was that on the phone?'

Ihaka explained. It was the first time Denise had heard the name Miriam Lovell.

She sat at the far end of the sofa, legs tucked underneath her, arms folded, giving the distinct impression that Ihaka's notion of the perfect end to the perfect day was already a lost cause. 'Let me get this straight: you're giving us the flick to go and meet your ex?'

He shook his head. 'That's as straight as a dog's hind leg,' he said. 'She's not my ex, and it's not like I've got much choice. She said it's important.'

'And what are we, trivial? Of course she said it's important; she wants to see you.'

'Actually, I got the impression she'd really prefer not to see me. She's come across something she thinks I should know about so —'

'Like what?'

'That's what I'm going to find out. I could've asked her to spell it out, but then I could've been on the phone for another five or ten minutes and I didn't want to spoil the evening.'

'Really? Well, if that was the plan, I have to tell you, you came up short.'

'What's the big deal? I mean, a fucking two-minute phone call —'

'A fucking two-minute phone call to set up a date that means you won't be coming to Devonport with us. Which, incidentally, was your idea – or have you already forgotten that? Just as you've obviously forgotten how much Billy's looking forward to it.'

They'd had rows before, of course, but not because he was breaking an arrangement to meet an ex. Ex-what? Ex-acquaintance if the truth (or near enough to it) be told, but Denise wasn't buying it. Ihaka could have kicked himself: he should have seen this coming and headed it off at the pass. Easier said than done, though, with Billy's big, brown, anxious eyes on him.

Denise tended to heat up quickly and cool down almost as quickly. Experience had taught him that the best way of dealing with these flare-ups was to call a time out: stop it getting out of hand, give her a chance to calm down. In twenty minutes she'd be acting as if they hadn't exchanged a single cross word and, what's more, she didn't give a shit about the thing that twenty minutes earlier she was drawing a line in the sand over. That was the ticket: park it for a while, take the heat out of it, then quietly work out a compromise like grown-ups.

'Listen,' he said, 'this is silly. Why don't we —?'

'Silly?' Now there was a dangerous glint in her eyes. 'If you think it's silly for me to be upset by this shit, then fuck you.' She stood up and walked past him, looking straight ahead. 'I'm going to bed.'

Just like that, said Ihaka to himself. Masterfully done.

He did the washing-up. The bedroom was in darkness and Denise had her face turned to the wall. She didn't stir or speak when he got into bed. It would be the first time they'd shared a bed without getting to the verge of sleep in each other's arms.

Ihaka wasn't a light sleeper. When he woke up, Denise and Billy were gone.

Imperial Lane was an architect-designed cave. Miriam Lovell was already there, dabbing at the crumbs on her plate and wishing she hadn't bolted her trim latte. Her hair was shorter, blonder and tamer, but the overall look – Ihaka called it 'lipstick vegetarian' – was intact. He didn't have to wonder what he ever saw in her.

'Well, this is cosy,' said Ihaka.

'Cosiness is a suburban concept,' she said. 'In the city only the cool survive. But the coffee's good, and I thoroughly recommend the raspberry friands.'

Ihaka carefully lowered himself onto a spindly metal chair. 'I'm pretty sure friands are on my list.'

'Which list?'

'The stuff you shouldn't eat if you don't want to be a fat shit list.'

She gave him the once-over, tilting her head. 'Is it my imagination, or have you lost a gram or two?'

'I'll take that to mean I'm a shadow of my former self. You don't seem to have let yourself go.'

'I'm reasonably disciplined when it comes to exercise and intake,' she said. 'Sadly, I can't say the same about other aspects of my life. I'm referring to my work habits,' she added hastily. 'My thesis will soon be old enough to stay up later than me.'

She was writing a PhD thesis on communism in the trade union movement during the 1960s and 70s. She knew more about the working life of Ihaka's late father Jimmy, a union firebrand and renegade Marxist, than he did.

'So the boy who answered your phone —?'

'Billy. Belongs to a friend of mine.'

'Would he, by any chance, be the same boy whose game of cricket was so much more attractive a proposition than meeting me for brunch?'

It occurred to Ihaka that history was repeating itself, only in reverse: he'd put paid to his relationship with Miriam by going to watch Billy play cricket when he was meant to be meeting her in a Herne Bay café. (Getting Billy to invite him was Denise's way of signalling that, while she might have told Ihaka to get the fuck out of her life, she didn't mean it, like, literally.)

Ihaka nodded.

'So is your attachment to this child something that should concern the authorities?'

He raised his eyebrows. 'Thank you for caring. His mother doesn't seem to think so.'

'Ah, *cherchez la femme*. We come to the nitty-gritty.'

Ihaka pushed his chair back. 'This is it? This is what I rearranged my day off for?'

Miriam's chin came up. 'Oh, don't be so pompous. I'm entitled to a bit of fun, aren't I?'

'Can I make a suggestion?' he said. 'Why don't you tell me whatever it is you think I need to know? Once that's out of the way, we can see how we're going and either have a friendly catch-up or just go our separate ways.'

Miriam took a deep breath. 'Spoilsport. Well, a couple of months ago, when I was having a moan to one of the old union guys I've got to know, he said, "I wonder what happened to Ethan's diaries; there'd be some meaty stuff in there." He was talking about Ethan Stern, an American who was a political studies lecturer at university and used to hang out with the comrades. He was one of those rather head-in-the-clouds left-wing intellectuals who believed that if the politically aware working class and the enlightened middle class linked arms, we'd have a people's paradise in no time. Apparently, though, he was an assiduous diarist, and if they still existed, his diaries would be pure gold from my point of view: primary source material that hadn't been cherry-picked by academics and churned up by a horde of post-grads. Stern died years ago, but I traced his widow, who's doing the old hippie thing down on the Coromandel. She told me that after Ethan's death she'd packed up all his papers, including the diaries, and sent them off to the pol studs department.' She eyed Ihaka suspiciously. 'Am I boring you?'

'Well, maybe a bit.'

'Trust me, it gets better,' she said. 'I was very excited. If I could find those diaries, finishing the thesis would be a piece of cake, plus it would be infinitely better than it was looking like being. I got hold of the woman who'd been the head of department's secretary at the time and, wonder of wonders, she remembered the cartons arriving. As you'd expect, they got bunged in a corner awaiting a permanent home and promptly forgotten about.

'It was a convoluted process – the department's not in the same street these days, let alone the same building – but to cut a long story short I found the cartons in one of the main library's storerooms. I'm sure you, being a detective, can appreciate what a thrill that was.' She waited for Ihaka's salute, one dogged sleuth to another.

'It must have been very satisfying.'

'Indeed. And I'm sure you can imagine how deflating it was to discover the diaries had been removed.'

'Oh shit.'

'Oh shit, indeed. Seeing I'd gone to all that trouble, I thought I might as well go through what was there. It was mostly lecture notes – all I can say is thank God I didn't have to sit through the lectures – but I did come across this long article he'd written for some academic journal. They'd sent it back with a note saying he needed to do this, that and the next thing before they'd publish it, but he'd taken umbrage and told them to get stuffed. He'd written on the back of it, basically used it as notepaper. After I'd read a couple of pages, it occurred to me that maybe this was stuff he'd decided not to put in his diary for whatever reason: there were some pretty forthright comments about his departmental colleagues and certain well-known trade unionists.' She took a folded A4 page from her handbag. 'Have a look at this.'

It was a photocopy; half the page had been blacked out.

'What happened to the rest of it?'

'A little nugget for my thesis,' said Lovell. 'Of interest only to academics.'

It took Ihaka a few seconds to get the hang of Stern's handwriting:

6. 13. 87.

Jimmy Ihaka never ceases to amaze me. An extraordinary combination of idealism, bloody-mindedness, and mischief-making. Impossible to dislike, impossible not to admire, but he really can be a pain in the ass. You'd think on this of all issues he wouldn't rock the boat, but oh no. The leadership of the Moscow faction hates him with a passion. Sometimes they forget I'm not a card-carrier; I guess they're just venting their frustration, but after some of the stuff I've overheard I really wouldn't be that surprised if Jimmy met with an 'accident' one of these days.

'You'll note the date,' said Lovell.

Ihaka nodded slowly. 'Just days before the old man died.'

'Quite a coincidence, wouldn't you say? He had a heart attack, right?'

'So I've always understood.'

'Was there a post-mortem?'

'Wouldn't know. I guess it was kind of taken for granted – he'd had a couple of scares and heart problems ran in the family.'

'Well, you might want to look into it because here's another coincidence: a few days after your father died, Stern went jogging in the Waitakeres, as he did every Friday morning. Except this time he slipped down a bank, went head-first into a tree, and that was the end of him.'

3

The ex-policeman lived in a basement granny flat at the back of a professional couple's house in the Wellington suburb of Wadestown.

Most nights their two-year-old woke up between 2 and 3 am and howled till he was blue in the face. An ugly little face in the ex-policeman's opinion, although it would be fair to say he had a jaundiced view of the child's appearance, personality and, indeed, existence. The bawling had the desired effect of waking the parents, and the side effect – also desired, in the ex-policeman's agitated imagination – of waking him.

The lady of the house, a lawyer whom the ex-policeman suspected of frightening ambition, got up at six. He would lie awake wondering why she made such a production of getting ready for work, having a Clayton's breakfast (yoghurt and a cup of hot water embellished with a handful of fragrant leaves) and saying goodbye to her son and husband, a Cabinet Minister's press secretary.

Every morning she went walkabout up there, high heels click-clacking on bare floorboards. Was it nervous energy? A workout while you get ready for work regime for incredibly busy people? Was she strategising on her smartphone with an equally up and at 'em colleague? (Probably not, given that virtually every other noise they

37

made invaded his consciousness; he sometimes heard him fart and her complain.) Or was she one of those driven yet fluffy-minded individuals who can mislay their car keys while boiling a jug of water?

The granny flat was dark and pokey and cold. His children were quite matter-of-fact about their unwillingness to overnight there. He couldn't really blame them: one had to sleep on the sofa, which wasn't a great place to sit, let alone sleep. The other had the second bedroom, which resembled a cell in the monastery of a ferociously austere order. And there was the sleep disruption: he had to put up with it, but there didn't seem much point making them.

His kids weren't particularly spoilt, at least compared to some of their friends, but it was a come-down from what they were used to. And given his sometimes problematic relationship with them – it was officially his fault the family was no longer together – it made no sense to squander his limited capacity for emotional blackmail on lost causes.

On the plus side, the flat was as cheap as accommodation gets in Wadestown, an agreeable suburb with harbour views for some less than ten minutes from downtown. And it was within walking distance of the rented house where the kids lived with their mother, his estranged wife. Most mornings he would go over there to walk their Labrador, the only living thing that was always pleased to see him.

The ex-policeman tried to avoid self-pity. It was like vertigo: an impulse to do what your rational self knew was pointless and self-destructive. But when he contemplated what he'd become, the distance from his children, the wreckage of his marriage and career, and the scant if not non-existent prospects of redemption, it was impossible not to succumb now and again.

Whenever that happened, he'd remind himself of Tito Ihaka's parting words. Ihaka, his best friend in the police and the agent of his downfall, had ended their final conversation thus: 'Look on the bright side, Johan: you've got away with murder.'

Shortly after Johan Van Roon arrived at Auckland Central straight from Police College, a shy, pale, lanky first-generation Kiwi, the son of Dutch immigrants, Detective Sergeant Ihaka took him under his wing. Van Roon repaid Ihaka's gruff, erratic patronage with loyalty bordering on devotion.

But Van Roon was too capable to remain a detective constable. Once he and Ihaka were on the same level, they could be mates; Ihaka was, nominally, godfather to Van Roon's fourteen-year-old daughter. When Ihaka was denied promotion and subsequently banished to the Wairarapa, Van Roon was outraged: his friend and mentor, the best cop he knew, had been cut down and marginalised by a cabal of small minds and big egos for refusing to bend the knee and play their petty political games. Consumed with bitterness, blinded by disillusionment, Van Roon lost his way.

An information swap arrangement with Doug 'Prof' Yallop, a clever and manipulative underworld grey eminence, evolved into a hijacking operation. Van Roon rationalised it as separating thieves from their ill-gotten gains. When Blair Corvine, an undercover policeman and mate of Ihaka's, picked up a whisper that one of the rip-off crew was a cop, Van Roon bailed out. Shortly afterwards he was promoted to detective inspector and posted to Wellington. He was out of Auckland and going straight, but he'd set uncontrollable forces in motion: Corvine was shot and left for dead; the shooter and third member of the hijacking crew, a bikie gangster named Jerry Spragg, lost his mind as a result of a savage prison beating.

Then the previous summer, out of the blue, Superintendent Finbar McGrail had asked him to pass on the message that Ihaka's presence was required in Auckland.

An alarm bell went off. Corvine's intelligence and his interactions with his handlers at Auckland Central had been investigated; no evidence was found to support the rumour of police involvement in the hijacking operation or to suggest that a breach of security had blown Corvine's cover. But McGrail was acute and subtle: he would know that Ihaka would assume the investigators' first and over-riding priority had been to protect the organisation; he'd also know that, once back in Auckland, Ihaka would poke around in the undergrowth to see what crawled out. That was just the way he was.

So when Ihaka rang wanting the address of Corvine's safe house, a highly classified piece of information known only to a handful of senior officers, Van Roon knew it was game on. He dispersed his criminal proceeds, about $200,000 in cash. Some was in safety deposit boxes; some was buried in Otari-Wilton's bush where he walked the dog. He went out at night in a car he kept in a lock-up garage in Lower Hutt, burying the money in $20,000 batches at remote locations in the Wairarapa.

But Yallop was his real vulnerability. If the squeeze went on, Yallop had the perfect get-out-of-jail card: he could finger a corrupt cop. And if the need arose, he would play that card in a heartbeat. That was just the way he was.

Then Yallop got in touch to say Ihaka had been around asking questions about Corvine and Spragg. Just out of curiosity, so he said, but, as they both knew, Ihaka didn't do idle curiosity. Yallop's point was that if Ihaka was half as good as Van Roon had made him out to be, he might have to be dealt with. As in taken out; as in put in the ground.

Even as Van Roon was stuffing his pockets with stolen cash, he would have sworn that he simply didn't have it in him to kill another human being in cold blood. After that conversation with Yallop he had an epiphany: what had been unthinkable was now unavoidable. As long as Yallop lived to tell tales, Van Roon was exposed; if Yallop was silenced, he was untouchable. They could search his house and property, go through his financial records, follow the paper trail, scrutinise every transaction, run down every number in his phone records and turn the Auckland underworld inside out without finding a scrap of incriminating evidence. And now here was Yallop talking about putting out a contract on Ihaka. Two irresistible imperatives: save himself, save his mate.

He called in sick and drove through the night to Auckland with a Walther PPK/E semi-automatic, which he'd surreptitiously pocketed during a raid on a P lab, taped to the underside of the driver's seat. By then he had persuaded himself that it was his duty to eliminate Yallop. Yallop was a sociopath with no respect for anyone or anything, not even the notion of honour among thieves; a hands-off operator who got others to do his dirty work then taunted the cops when they couldn't pin anything on him. 'Catch me if you can,' he boasted, but as soon as Ihaka put some heat on, Yallop's first instinct was to have him killed. Even if Ihaka hadn't been a mate, Van Roon couldn't look the other way while a fellow cop took a bullet. Besides, all professional criminals understood that killing a cop was a declaration of war. Sure, this was a pre-emptive strike, but the first rule of war is that there are no rules.

Killing Yallop was surprisingly easy. When the time came there were no second thoughts or shaking hands. He steeled himself to do it, he did it, then drove south on the back roads untroubled by his conscience. That came later. North of Taupo he nosed the car down a grass track into a state forest and slept on the back seat for a few hours. At four in the morning he slipped into Hatepe, a village on the southern side of the lake. A friend of a friend had a holiday home there which Van Roon had rented the previous year. He knew where the keys were. He got a kayak out of the lock-up, carried it down to the lake, paddled out to deep water and dropped the pistol over the side.

Ihaka figured it out as, deep down, Van Roon had known he would. From what he heard later, the Commissioner had favoured a low-key resignation with the whole thing swept under the carpet. McGrail persuaded him that the most damaging outcome would be if it leaked later that they'd had good reason to believe one of their senior men had gone rogue but had opted not to pursue it. So they came after him in a roundabout, unofficial way because, while there was an institutional desire to nail him, there was an even stronger institutional desire to keep a tight lid on it.

They came at night and politely but methodically searched his house. They spun an unlikely yarn about a drug dealer stashing dope in the area and went up and down his street looking in basements and garden sheds. They searched in Otari-Wilton's bush and on Tinakori Hill, where he also walked the dog. All they came up with was that he'd recently stopped renting safety deposit boxes through a shelf company.

They checked CCTV footage from service stations up and down the North Island for the twelve hours either side of Yallop's murder, to no avail because he'd had extra fuel in jerry-cans to get to Auckland and back without stopping at a pump. By then he'd dumped the car, and the false number plates he'd used were under several tonnes of landfill.

He spent days on end being browbeaten by Ron Firkitt, a detective sergeant out of Auckland Central with a well-deserved reputation as a harsh and relentless interrogator. But Firkitt had never come up against anyone as well prepared as Van Roon: he anticipated every angle of attack, saw every question coming. And of course he knew the tricks of the trade.

It was stalemate: they didn't have a case, he didn't have a future. He could have hired a hard-nosed employment lawyer and gone after a big pay-out, but McGrail warned him off. If it came to that, said the Ulsterman, the reasons for his departure from the force would become public knowledge, one way or another. Did he want his kids to have to deal with that?

So he went quietly, which his wife Yvonne interpreted as an admission of guilt. The investigation had put an intolerable strain on a relationship which was already in decline. Time was she would have begged him to stay home rather than disappear on another mysterious nocturnal mission. Lately though, she'd just tell him to come in quietly and use the downstairs toilet, not even bothering to pause whatever she was watching on TV.

He moved out of the family home, which was sold with all proceeds going to Yvonne to offset his much reduced contribution. (He'd set himself up as a private investigator and security consultant, but the phone wasn't ringing off the hook.) She took his pliancy to mean he had stolen cash hidden away. But she didn't object when he left a wad of notes on the kitchen table after dropping off the kids. She didn't say thank you either.

Last time they spoke Yvonne had mentioned – 'Oh, by the way' – that she was seriously thinking of moving back to Auckland. He questioned whether it was a good time for the kids to be changing schools; she said she'd discussed it with them and they were all for it. He couldn't really object, she said, because there was nothing to stop him doing likewise. It wasn't as if there was anything much keeping him in Wellington. Like a proper job.

Walking the dog in Otari-Wilton's bush was as close as Van Roon got to being at peace. He stuck to the steep tracks, which didn't get much traffic in summer let alone at this time of year when the mud sucked at your tramping boots and if you didn't tread carefully you could find yourself tobogganing down a stony hillside on your arse. It was just him and the dog and bush sounds: branches creaking in the wind, tui babbling to each other through the mist, the clumsy take-off of a startled kereru.

His mobile rang.

'Van Roon.'

'Mr Van Roon, this is Caspar Quedley. Does that name mean anything?'

Christ, talk about a blast from the past. He hadn't heard that name for the best part of twenty years. Quedley was an Auckland PR man who'd been involved in one of Ihaka's cases. He had a reputation for being well-connected and charming, but like a lot of Auckland charm his was skin-deep and what lay beneath was as attractive as gangrene. While Quedley had managed to stay out of jail, he was portrayed in such an odious light in a magazine article about the case that his clients took flight. He'd shut up shop and gone to ground. Van Roon hadn't heard of him since.

Van Roon said, 'There can't be too many Caspar Quedleys out there.'

'I've never come across another one. Look, I know this is short notice, but are you free for lunch?'

'Short notice is a relative concept. What's it in aid of?'

'I've got a project you might be interested in,' said Quedley. 'All above board.'

'What are you up to these days?'

'Same sort of thing, only more discreet and more ethical.'

'Really?' McGrail had been true to his word in terms of hushing up the reasons for Van Roon's abrupt resignation, but if Quedley was half the operator he used to be he would have heard the rumours. 'So why are you talking to me?'

'We can cover all that at lunch.'

'Well, if you've done your homework, you'll know I'm not in a position to be choosy. In fact, you don't need to buy me lunch: a cup of coffee would do it.'

'Oh, I think we can stretch to a bowl of pasta and a glass of Eytie plonk. You know Bella Italia in Petone?'

'Yes.'

'One o'clock. Now I've got to go, they're about to close my flight.'

Although Van Roon had never met Quedley, he remembered him from photos as a handsome rascal. Quedley still stood out in a crowded restaurant, even one the size of an aircraft hangar. For a start, he was the only person there wearing a tie. The rest of his outfit consisted of a navy-blue suit, dark cashmere overcoat and white silk scarf. His hair had turned silver-grey and was swept back off his forehead, accentuating the receding hairline. He didn't look like a local; he looked like a distinguished visitor from the old country who'd heard this was the only place in Wellington where he could get meatballs the way Mama used to make them.

They shook hands. Quedley handed his overcoat and scarf to a nonplussed waiter and ordered antipasto and a couple of Peronis, 'unless my guest isn't drinking, in which case one will suffice'.

Van Roon shrugged. 'I cancelled my appointments.'

Quedley smiled to show he got Van Roon's little joke. 'I'm guessing you're too young to know who Eddie Brightside is. Or was.'

'Is this small talk, or have we skipped that?'

'I'm a reformed character, Mr Van Roon. I don't bother with the bullshit these days.'

'Suits me. OK, no, never heard of him.'

'Back in the mid-eighties Eddie Brightside – inevitably known as Fast Eddie, although in his case it was appropriate – was quite an identity in this town. I suppose "likeable rogue" would be one way to describe him. He had a knack of attaching himself to high-powered people and persuading them they couldn't do without him. If you're thinking here's the pot calling the kettle black, then touché because there'd be a few people who'd say much the same about me. Anyway, having invested a lot of time and effort in getting to run with the big dogs, he up and disappeared – hasn't been seen or heard from since. Until yesterday: someone who knew Brightside reasonably well back in the day swears he saw him at a Hawke's Bay vineyard. Your assignment, should you choose to accept it, would be to check it out and, if it stacks up, find the prick.'

The beers and antipasto arrived. Quedley suggested

they share a whole baked fish. Van Roon nodded; he'd never been that interested in food, and now that money was tight and he was fending for himself, most nights he ate out of a can.

'When did he disappear?'

'August 1987.'

'I assume it was a missing persons case?'

'That's where it gets a bit murky.' Quedley took an A4 envelope out of his leather satchel. 'The life and times of Eddie Brightside. You'll be pleased to know it's not the usual PR company backgrounder, a half-hour Google job by a trainee with an attention span as short as her skirt. There are still a few gaps and some rumour and specula-tion, but that was our Eddie – he cultivated the image of an international man of mystery. The business arrangement is five K up front, a further two and a half on completion, all reasonable expenses paid on presentation of receipts. And if you do a good job and the client wakes up without a hangover, there might be a bonus. All conditional on you getting on to it pronto and staying on it full-time for three weeks, or until you find Brightside, or establish that he's left the country.'

'Why are you so keen to find him?'

'Let's get one thing clear: I couldn't give a fuck. I met Brightside a few times; he struck me as an obvious con-man, so I wasn't surprised when he did a runner. Someone saw through him or someone from his dodgy past turned up, so he skedaddled. That's what con-artists do – they travel light and always know where the nearest exit is. The client is someone Brightside persuaded to invest in an Australian entrepreneurial stock that went south like a lead shit. He has a long memory when it comes to dud financial advice and can afford to hold a grudge.'

'So if I find Brightside, what then?'

Quedley grinned. 'You won't be required to sodomise him with a red-hot poker, if that's what you're worried about. Frankly, I don't know what the client has in mind; I imagine it'll depend on Brightside's circumstances.' He could tell Van Roon was sceptical. 'Perhaps I didn't adequately convey how loaded the client is. Put it this way: your fee's peanuts. He'd think nothing of dropping that much on a hand of poker.'

'Who's the guy who thinks he saw Brightside?'

'An old hack called Barry McCormick who was in the Press Gallery for donkey's years. He's retired now, lives up on the Kapiti coast. I haven't seen him for a while, but when we talk on the phone he still seems to have his marbles.'

'What about his eyesight?' asked Van Roon.

'I don't hear a guide dog farting in the background.'

'An old journo spots someone who disappeared, I assume reasonably sensationally, back in '87: why didn't he go to the media?'

'Because, unlike me, the media wouldn't pay him,' said Quedley. 'I'm an information trader, among other things; I've got a few old lags around the place keeping their eyes and ears open on my behalf. I buy a lot of ho-hum stuff to keep them motivated, and every once in a while it pays off.'

'So this guy who's been underground all these years surfaces at a vineyard? Does that seem likely to you?'

'As you say, it's been a fair old while. He could be excused for thinking that if he hasn't been spotted by now, he never will be. What happened was, Baz was trawling round the vineyards sampling free wine – ex-journo for you; old habits die hard. At this particular place there was a couple up at the counter buying a case. Baz couldn't believe his eyes: he's a hundred per cent certain it was

Brightside. He went over and, knowing Baz, would've said something like "Eddie fucking Brightside, as I live and breathe". Brightside – or his doppelganger – hustled the woman out to the car park, where they jumped into a Honda Civic and took off like the hounds of hell were on their tail. Baz thinks he got the number.' Quedley patted the envelope. 'It's in here, along with his contact details.'

'Last question,' said Van Roon. 'Why me?'

Quedley nodded, as if he'd been expecting it. 'First off, you come recommended – by Ihaka.'

Van Roon's eyes lit up. 'You talked to Ihaka?'

'That's how I got your number.'

'What did he say?'

'He said you were good. I'm afraid that's all he said.' There was a flicker of sympathy in Quedley's eyes. Van Roon shrugged and took an interest in the antipasto. 'Secondly, the client values his privacy. What that means is he has an intense aversion to anyone outside the inner circle knowing what he's up to. You're a one-man band, which is good for security, and by all accounts you can keep a secret. Third, again by all accounts, you did a bloody good job of covering your own tracks, so this should be right up your alley. The old poacher turned gamekeeper principle.'

'How much do you know?'

'About your situation? Let's say the broad outline. You see, the main reason for coming to you is that I also had a spectacular fall from grace. I woke up one morning to find I'd metamorphosed into persona non grata. My clients couldn't dump me fast enough; most of my so-called friends turned their backs on me; life in the material sense turned to shit. I know what it's like: you're in a hole, and you don't have to be down there too long before you start to lose the will and the energy to haul yourself out of it. I got a lucky break which got me back on my feet. This isn't charity – I wouldn't be here if Ihaka hadn't given you a tick – but I happen to believe that everyone's entitled to a second chance.'

'In that case, you've got yourself a bloodhound.'

'Good,' said Quedley as the waiter arrived with the fish. 'Email me your bank account details and I'll process the payment first thing tomorrow.' When the waiter left, Quedley passed over the envelope. 'Actually, I reckon this will be the easiest money you've ever made. My theory is that back in '87 Brightside skipped the country on a false passport. If that was him at the vineyard, I bet he drove straight to Napier airport and fucked off back to wherever he's been all these years.'

4

Well, this should tell us something, thought Tito Ihaka as Detective Inspector Tony 'Boy' Charlton beckoned him into his office.

They'd never got on, these two. Even when they were both detective sergeants, their dealings had been awkward and sometimes counter-productive because they were such different animals, professionally and personally. As a cop, Charlton was disciplined, politically savvy, risk-averse, never short of a buzzword, always up with the latest big idea that was going to change policing as we know it, and not above claiming credit to which he wasn't entitled. As a person, Charlton was disciplined, fit, presentable, socially adept, a family man and six years younger than Ihaka.

So they were never going to be soulmates, but their relationship took a turn for the toxic when Charlton was appointed to fill the vacancy at Auckland Central created by Finbar McGrail's promotion to District Commander. Not only had Ihaka been overlooked, but the usurper was now his boss, a galling state of affairs that Charlton seldom missed an opportunity to aggravate. Nothing if not perverse, Ihaka didn't let the fact that Charlton was on his case, if not out to get him, cramp his style. In due course, Ihaka pushed his luck so far that not even McGrail could save him from being banished to the wilderness, aka Wairarapa.

It took McGrail five years to find a way to get Ihaka back. Even then Charlton resisted until any further resistance would have amounted to laying down a challenge that McGrail couldn't afford to ignore. Charlton still didn't like it – never would, in all probability – but he was an ambitious man and recognised there was no percentage in being seen to prolong a feud whose origins were increasingly obscure.

McGrail had instructed them to find a way of interacting that didn't generate acrimony, or at least kept it to a minimum. Avoiding public conflict was a good start: when they had an audience, Ihaka resisted the urge to be provocative and/or insolent, and Charlton refrained from being patronising or pulling rank for the sake of it.

So far, so good, but neither was convinced the uneasy truce would hold. One of the very few things they agreed on was that once a shithead, always a shithead.

Now Ihaka was going to ask Charlton for indefinite unpaid leave, with immediate effect and without telling him why: because he wanted to investigate the possibility that his father hadn't died of natural causes. In the past Charlton would have knocked back a more reasonable request on principle – the principle being that if it came from Ihaka, it couldn't be reasonable. Ihaka was about to find out if anything much had changed.

Charlton's expression was blandly polite. He tugged an earlobe. He shifted in his seat, leaning sideways and resting his chin on the heel of his hand. 'When you say you're not sure how long you'll be out of commission…'

'I was thinking we could start with a week,' said Ihaka.

'That might be as much as I need. If not, it would roll into the next week. And so on.'

'You mean two weeks might become three? And three might become four? And so on?'

'That kind of thing.'

'And when do you propose to commence this indefinite disappearing act?'

'Pretty soon. Soon as possible really. Say tomorrow.'

Charlton's eyebrows arched. He changed position again, transferring his chin to his other hand. 'I see. Well, I think all I need to know now is why? What's up?'

'Personal stuff.'

'Uh huh.' Charlton nodded, pursing his lips. 'Would that be the favourite uncle in intensive care after being gored by a bull, the favourite nephew kidnapped by pirates in the South China Sea, or the family home being eaten by termites?'

Ihaka stiffened. Charlton's sarcasm was like a precise poker thrust into a dying fire that causes the embers to flare back into life. 'Take your pick.'

Charlton sat up straight, drumming his fingers on the desk. 'OK. As you know, sergeant, we're flat out right now, so indefinite leave as of tomorrow is a non-starter. I suggest you come back in a week's time with a more specific proposal, and we can revisit it.'

'Is that a no?'

Charlton shook his head. 'It's a not this week, and not on those terms.'

Ihaka stood up. 'No point in having power if you can't abuse it, eh?'

'Sergeant, I'm aware that you pride yourself on not learning from experience, but don't start World War Three just because you didn't get what you want when you wanted it. I'm trying to be reasonable here. If I was in your shoes, I'd be thinking that was an encouraging sign and responding in kind.'

'Fair enough. Next week then: same time, same place, different outcome.'

Curiously, Ihaka's relationship with Detective Sergeant Ron Firkitt, Charlton's hulking right-hand man, the doer of his dirty work, the Igor to Charlton's Doctor Frankenstein (as many at Auckland Central put it behind their backs), had progressed beyond an uneasy truce. Curiously, because their antipathy had been so sincere, it made Ihaka and Charlton seem like the cowboys in *Brokeback Mountain*. They had actually come to blows. Or rather a blow; a blow delivered without warning but with considerable force and precision that was the trigger for Ihaka's exile, and which Firkitt had sworn to avenge.

While Firkitt was liable to turn a blowtorch of scorn on anyone who suggested that he'd mellowed, the consensus was growing. No one in their right mind would choose him for a desert-island companion, but he was certainly less confrontational than he used to be.

The credit for this transformation – some called it a miracle – belonged to Firkitt's GP. The previous summer the doctor had pointed out that he'd been dispensing the same advice – quit smoking, lay off the junk food, drink less, sleep more, exercise regularly – for fifteen years and getting the same response: Firkitt would act surprised, as if he hadn't seen that coming, and promise to take it on board, then just carry on doing all the bad stuff and steering clear of the good stuff. His GP had no intention of participating in this exercise in futility for another fifteen years, not that it was likely to come to that. If Firkitt was ignoring his advice because he thought it was bullshit, he should find himself another GP; if he couldn't or wouldn't change his ways, he should stop wasting money on doctor's fees.

The GP was aware that when Firkitt's ex-wife had issued a not dissimilar ultimatum a decade or so earlier, his response was to help her pack. He was therefore astonished when Firkitt declared he'd got the message. He'd have a blow-out that night and when he woke up the next day feeling like shit, he'd finally be ready to go on a health kick.

No one believed that, of his own free will, Firkitt could go without a cigarette for more than a few hours, let alone give them up altogether. But he'd gone cold turkey, hadn't taken a drag since the aftermath of the showdown with his GP. He'd also given up hard liquor and embraced healthy eating and regular exercise, even joining the 'homo harriers club', as he'd previously referred to the jogging group that set off from Auckland Central every lunchtime.

The event that cemented the rapprochement had taken place a fortnight earlier. At 8.30 pm Ihaka was tidying his desk – i.e. sweeping food wrappers, paper cups and documents he wouldn't get around to reading into the wastepaper basket – when Firkitt appeared. He would appreciate Ihaka's advice on something, he said, but it would mean going for a bit of a drive.

Under normal circumstances Ihaka would have pointed out that it was getting late, he'd had a long day, he was buggered and surely to Christ it could wait till tomorrow. In all likelihood he would have commenced this spiel and flagged where it was heading by telling the other party, 'You must be fucking joking.' But Firkitt was making an effort: asking for advice didn't come easily to him. And, up till that moment, Ihaka had assumed the word 'appreciate' wasn't in his vocabulary.

So he'd followed Firkitt over the Harbour Bridge out to Glenfield where they pulled up outside a darkened building in the main shopping centre. A sign identified it as 'Fergie's Gym: Home of Boxing on the North Shore'. Firkitt had a key. He opened up and they went inside.

'What's the story?' said Ihaka.

'You'll see,' said Firkitt.

Firkitt locked the door behind them and switched on lights. He led Ihaka down a corridor, through the reception area and into the gym proper, which consisted of a weights room and a large space with a raised ring in the centre. The extractor fans had been turned off and a miasma of body odour hung in the air like mould.

They walked around the ring into a changing room. Firkitt opened a locker, took out a plastic shopping bag and tossed it to Ihaka. It contained shorts, sports shoes, a T-shirt and a mouthguard.

'They should fit, more or less,' said Firkitt.

'What, so you're a fucking charity now?' said Ihaka.

'I told you I was going to get you back,' said Firkitt. 'Tonight's the night: you and me in the ring, Marquis of Queensberry rules. A fair fight, which is more than you fucking deserve.'

Ihaka laughed. 'You seriously want us to get in that ring and carry on like a couple of silly old fucks in the Fight for Life?'

'Speak for yourself,' said Firkitt, 'but yes, you bet I'm serious. Get changed, fatty, we're on in five.'

Ihaka stood there looking at his kit, hearing Firkitt getting changed on the other side of a bank of lockers. He had half a mind just to walk away, until he remembered that Firkitt had locked them in. What the fuck? He had always known that one day there would be some sort of reckoning.

He'd assumed it would be an ambush, as opposed to formal hand-to-hand combat, but it was Firkitt's call. If he wanted to slug it out, so be it.

Ihaka emerged from the dressing room shivering from the chill and feeling slightly ridiculous. Firkitt was already in the ring, putting on boxing gloves. There was a pair of gloves on the canvas in the opposite corner.

Ihaka climbed up to the ring and manoeuvred himself through the ropes. 'We can't go on meeting like this,' he said.

'Get your gloves on,' said Firkitt. 'I haven't got all night.' He watched Ihaka fiddle with the gloves' Velcro tabs. 'I know your idea of a fair fight is king-hitting a bloke when he's having a slash —'

'Yeah, well, racial abuse brings out the worst in me.'

Firkitt nodded. 'I'm not proud of that. But you should be bloody ashamed of pissing on me.'

'Just for the record,' said Ihaka, 'I didn't actually piss on you. I pissed in the trough and it just happened to flow your way.'

'I'm going to enjoy wiping that fucking smirk off your face,' growled Firkitt. 'The way I see it, the abuse and the pissing cancel each other out, which leaves the elbow in the chops. So we're going toe to toe, I'm going to give you a good old tickle-up, then we'll be all square.'

'You didn't think of this on the way to work,' said Ihaka. 'You've been planning it for a while. In fact, I'll bet you've been training for it.'

Firkitt grinned wolfishly. 'I wondered how long it would take you to work that out. Yeah, I've been training here for the last few months. The guy who runs the joint used to train fighters. You might say he's taken an interest in my little project. You might also say I'm quietly confident of giving a good account of myself. You right there, mate? You're looking a bit dubious. OK, these are the rules: a three-minute round, a minute's break, then it's non-stop till we've had enough. Or till one of us has had more than enough, and the other bloke takes pity on him.'

It was a genuine heavyweight match-up, but Firkitt had a height and reach advantage. He looked ominously lean and well-conditioned, and had devised a format that maximised his fitness advantage. I could be in the shit here, thought Ihaka. He can have the first round; he's entitled to that. Then I'll have to think of something. Very fucking quickly.

'Ready?' said Firkitt. There was an egg-timer on the floor in his corner. He pressed it with his foot, hammering his gloves together. 'Ding dong, come out fighting. Or not. It makes no fucking difference to me.'

Firkitt crabbed across the ring on surprisingly light feet. Before Ihaka got his guard up, his head was snapped back by a stiff straight left. He covered up; Firkitt dug a left hook into his side and a heavy right into his midriff, then stepped back to observe the reaction.

In their strategising sessions, the ex-boxing trainer had drummed in two messages: first, fatties tend to run out of puff pretty quickly; second, they hate copping it in the bread-basket. Firkitt had actually reached the point of not being entirely sure which he was looking forward to more: beating the shit out of Ihaka, or never again having to listen to the trainer recite Smokin' Joe Frazier's mantra: 'Kill the body and the head will die.'

But Firkitt was already rethinking his strategy. He'd expected that when he went to the body, his gloves would sink into soft, sucking flesh and Ihaka would bleat as if he was giving birth. Neither of those things had happened. In fact, it looked like the prick actually didn't mind getting smacked in the guts that much. Either he wasn't as fat as he looked, or his fat had unusual properties, because those body shots had pretty much bounced off. Firkitt decided to go for the head, which was what he'd really wanted to do all along.

Ihaka's strategy was to stay out of hospital; his tactic was to exert himself as little as possible. He stood in the middle of the ring, gloves in front of his face in the peek-a-boo guard, elbows tucked in, watching Firkitt circle. If Firkitt wanted to get in close and deal to him downstairs, that would bring his head into range. But since that early flurry, Firkitt had stayed outside, using his reach, moving clockwise then counter-clockwise to switch the angle of attack, peppering Ihaka with left jabs and right crosses. He blocked a lot of them with his gloves or arms, but too many still got through.

As the egg-timer went off, Firkitt whacked Ihaka with a hard overhand right. As he headed to his corner, he gave Ihaka a wink and asked, 'Having fun yet?'

Ihaka flopped over the ropes, sucking in air. His head was full of harsh noise, a chorus of complaint from every joint and organ. His arms felt like anchors. His face throbbed with pain. He felt moderately beaten up.

All he'd managed by way of counter-attack was a few ineffectual flaps, more airy gestures than punches. Fuck this for a joke, he thought. If I can't put a stop to it, I'll be a lump of raw meat by the time the cunt's finished with me.

After what seemed like ten seconds, Firkitt called out, 'Here I come, ready or not. Remember, it's last man standing.' He sounded positively jolly, like a Father Christmas at a children's party.

Ihaka took a couple of plodding sideways steps and leaned back heavily against the ropes, peering at Firkitt between his raised gloves.

'The old rope-a-dope, eh?' said Firkitt. He let fly with a flurry of punches, most of which Ihaka blocked. 'Won't work, pal. I hit the heavy bag or the speed ball most nights, spar three times a week. I can do this all fucking night.'

As Firkitt stepped forward to throw more leather, Ihaka pressed back even further against the ropes, then catapulted forward. A straight left crunched into his mouthguard; he felt blood pop from a crushed lip. Then he had a grip on Firkitt's biceps. He hoisted him off his feet, swung him around and threw him against the ropes. As Firkitt rebounded off the ropes, Ihaka planted his feet and speared a ramrod right into the centre of his face.

Firkitt lurched like an off-balance roller skater. His arms windmilled, his legs gave way and he slid down the ropes. Before he could get back up, Ihaka was on top of him, a knee on his chest, left hand on his throat, right fist drawn back and cocked, ready to drive his head into the canvas.

'I've had enough of this shit,' said Ihaka. 'The way I see it, we're all square, so we can call it quits right here. You want to keep going, fine, but the Marquis of Queensberry can go fuck himself. It's anything goes, including knocking a man's block off when he's down.'

Firkitt stared up at him for a few seconds, then lowered his head back onto the canvas. 'When you put it like that...'

Ihaka extended his right hand. They bumped gloves. He got to his feet, hauling Firkitt up with him. 'Honour satisfied?'

'I reckon so,' said Firkitt.

As they walked to the changing room Firkitt said, 'You took your lumps – most guys would've dropped their bundle. Ever done any boxing?'

'Well, since you ask,' said Ihaka, 'one of the cuzzies fought pro for a while. I used to mix it up with him now and again. While ago now, though.'

'What happened to him?'

'He had just enough sense to get out before his brains turned to mush. These days he's an assistant to an assistant manager at a Pak'nSave in South Auckland, comes in at about a hundred and forty kg. If you're going to shoplift there, you'd want to be a fucking fast runner.'

5

EDDIE BRIGHTSIDE

A Backgrounder Prepared For Strategic Solutions Ltd
Strictly Private and Confidential

1. ADVISORY

Of necessity much of what follows is unsubstantiated; some is gossip, rumour and hearsay, or extrapolation thereof. It includes material that could be regarded as defamatory, assuming Mr Brightside is still alive (there is no compelling reason to think otherwise) and inclined to pursue legal action (which, under the circumstances, seems highly unlikely). Nevertheless we recommend that this document is circulated on a strict need-to-know basis.

2. INTRODUCTION

The difficulties we encountered in compiling this back-grounder reflect the subject: Brightside was a chronically unreliable source of information about himself and his activities.

From boyhood Brightside had what one source described as a 'creative' approach to the truth. For example, he told fellow pupils at Auckland Grammar School that he was given the second name Fletcher because he was closely related to the Fletcher family who had built their construction company into one of New Zealand's largest conglomerates. When his friends wondered why, in that case, the Brightsides were not better off, he explained that his grandfather on his mother's side had been the 'black sheep' of the Fletcher family. After being disowned (and impregnating Eddie's grandmother), he went to Latin America to become a soldier of fortune and was never heard from again. Brightside warned his classmates not to raise the subject in the presence of his mother, Elizabeth, as she was still highly sensitive about it.

In fact, there was no such black sheep in the Fletcher family and photographs show that Elizabeth Brightside bore a distinct resemblance to her legal father. Furthermore, she herself stated that she got the name from Fletcher Christian, the leader of the 1789 mutiny on the British naval vessel HMS *Bounty*.

We have heard Brightside described as a 'compulsive liar and name-dropper', 'consummate bullshit artist' and 'a Walter Mitty figure' who had difficulty distinguishing between fantasy and reality. However, just as many sources insisted there was nothing pathological about it: in their view Brightside was a calculating operator (and self-promoter) who tailored his spiel to his audience and agenda of the moment.

Adding to the difficulties arising from his tendency to tell different people different things is the fact that he 'dropped off the radar' at various times while he was overseas. The only sources of information regarding his whereabouts and activities during these hiatuses are his own, sometimes conflicting, accounts.

Finally, the very nature of the intelligence world makes it difficult, if not impossible, to verify or disprove what Brightside led people to believe: that he was or had been involved in that world.

3. CHILDHOOD

Edward Fletcher Brightside was born in Auckland on May 25th 1949. His father Eric was a journalist at the *Auckland Star,* a gregarious individual, partial to a drink and a punt. These proclivities were far from uncommon in his profession and do not appear to have impacted on his work or family life. Elizabeth Brightside was a mother and housewife.

When Eddie was 12, his father walked out on the family and moved to Sydney. In light of subsequent events it is tempting to speculate on the psychological impact this had on young Brightside: it may, for instance, have been the inspiration for the black-sheep grandfather yarn, and possibly the model for his own disappearance. Within months of his father's desertion, Brightside began to reveal the propensity for telling tall tales that some later acquaintances would regard as his most marked characteristic. At the time his mother interpreted it as a coping mechanism: creating a fantasy life to compensate for his diminished reality.

While Eric had not been a wastrel, he was the sole breadwinner, so his departure meant his family faced the prospect of significantly reduced circumstances. (Elizabeth's parents were able to provide limited assistance.) She went out to work, initially as a shop assistant. From this point on, Elizabeth worked full-time, mainly in administrative and basic accounting roles in small businesses. Perhaps as a consequence, her son was notably more self-reliant than most of his peers.

Brightside did not shine at Auckland Grammar, either academically or athletically. He did, however, have the knack of ingratiating himself with high achievers. While the Brightsides eked out a frugal existence in Eden Terrace, most of Eddie's friends lived in Remuera or Epsom and were comparatively well-off. He thus had plenty of opportunities to see how 'the other half lived'. On the other hand, his lively personality and 'gift of the gab' made him a social success and the object of some admiration and envy.

Brightside left school in 1967 with School Certificate and University Entrance. Although his mother wanted him to go to university, he was anxious to start earning money and took up a traineeship with the Bank of New Zealand.

4. UNIVERSITY

In 1969 Brightside surprised his mother and friends by leaving the BNZ to become a full-time university student. Claiming a keen interest in politics, a development that had escaped their notice, he enrolled for a Bachelor of Arts degree majoring in Political Studies and History. He was soon actively involved in student politics. While not all students were politically engaged and those of a conservative persuasion were probably inclined to keep their heads down on campus, the wider student movement was overwhelmingly left-wing and anti-government, and its leaders and spokespeople, the likes of Tim Shadbolt, stridently so.

The defining and galvanising cause was opposition to the Vietnam War in which New Zealand was a minor participant in line with its obligations under the ANZUS Treaty.

In January 1970 American Vice-President Spiro Agnew visited New Zealand, staying at the Inter-Continental Hotel in Auckland. An estimated 700 protesters gathered outside the hotel, which was located on the edge of the university campus (and whose large lower-floor bar was a popular student watering hole). Emotions ran high; the confrontation between protesters and the large police contingent spilled over into Albert Park, and the skirmishing that took place there led to accusations of police brutality.

Brightside was one of the protest organisers, but may have played a double game. He later claimed that he was approached by the New Zealand Security Intelligence Service (NZSIS) and/or the police seeking information on the protesters' aims and tactics. In some versions of the story he refused point-blank; in others he pretended to cooperate, but provided misinformation. However, he told the woman with whom he was romantically involved at the time of his disappearance a rather different story: that he was arrested for possession of marijuana, but escaped without charge by offering to be an informant.

Here we see the first instance of what would become a pattern: vagueness about his exact role and motivation, leaving different people with contrasting impressions.

Brightside's links to the student movement proved helpful when he showed up in Wellington fifteen years later. While not a close associate, future Cabinet Minister Phil Goff was among the rising stars in the Labour Party who knew Brightside from their student days and were able to 'put in a good word'.

Although he had passed all his papers and was on track to complete his BA, Brightside dropped out of university mid-way through his third year. In July 1971 he left for Australia, telling his mother that he had issues with his father that he needed to resolve one way or the other. However, he told friends that BAs were 'a dime a dozen' and that his father had been in touch, offering to pay his airfare and arrange a job for him in Sydney.

5. AUSTRALIA

Notwithstanding what he had told his mother and any psychological scarring caused by Eric's desertion, Eddie's reunion with his father seems to have been entirely amicable. Through Eric's contacts (he was working for the tabloid *Daily Telegraph*) Eddie got a job at a leading Sydney public relations/advertising agency. Following the right-of-centre Liberal-Country Party Coalition's loss in the December 1972 federal election, the agency secured the Liberal Party as a client and Brightside became part of the team working on the account. Although he had exaggerated his qualifications (for instance, claiming to have completed an honours degree in Political Studies), he impressed both his colleagues and Liberal Party officials as 'a natural' – a sharp, skilled operator with finely tuned political instincts.

(Incidentally, given the uncertainty over where Brightside's political sympathies actually lay – he was nothing if not a chameleon – it is worth noting that Liberal Party officials who worked with him during this period were surprised by his later involvement with the New Zealand Labour Party, having been under the impression that he was robustly right-wing.)

Brightside played an active role in the December 1975 federal election campaign in which the Liberal-Country Party Coalition, led by caretaker Prime Minister Malcolm Fraser, trounced the Labor Party, led by deposed Prime Minister Gough Whitlam. Brightside would later claim to have had a hand in devising the strategy of using the Coalition's Senate majority to delay the passage of budget bills and thereby force an early election. The failure to secure supply was the trigger for Governor-General Sir John Kerr's dismissal of the Whitlam government in November 1975.

Given some of the speculation that followed Brightside's disappearance, we should draw attention firstly to the Australian left-wing conspiracy theory that the US Central Intelligence Agency (CIA), perhaps in collusion with Australia's domestic intelligence agency, the Australian Security Intelligence Organisation (ASIO), had a hand in Whitlam's downfall; and, secondly, to the fact that Brightside often implied that he had contacts in the CIA, ASIO and the Australian Secret Intelligence Service (ASIS).

In March 1976 Eric Brightside drowned while swimming at Coolum beach, Queensland. He was bodysurfing in strong waves and was probably dumped on his head, knocked unconscious and swept out to sea. Eddie was the sole beneficiary and was thought to have done well from the sale of his father's terraced house in Paddington. He would later claim to have given half this windfall to his mother; she insisted that she received 'a couple of thousand dollars'.

On a brief visit to New Zealand, Brightside told friends he was going to spend a year or so travelling overland from Singapore to London. He flew out of New Zealand in July 1976. Eight and a half years would elapse before his return.

6. UK/USA

There is no hard information to hand regarding Brightside's whereabouts and activities between July 1976 and August 1978, when he surfaced in London. Wellington acquaintances recall him claiming to have been in Beirut, Lebanon during the early stages of the civil war which lasted from 1975 to 1990.

Through his Australian Liberal Party connections, Brightside obtained a position with the Conservative Party organisation, then gearing up for the general election that would sweep Margaret Thatcher into power in May 1979. As in Australia, he was highly regarded for his political instincts and mastery of the logistical and organisational aspects of campaigning.

On the basis of glowing references from the Conservative Party high command, Brightside flew to the United States in July 1979 to take up a position with Republican presidential hopeful Ronald Reagan's campaign organisation. It is testimony to Brightside's political acumen that he chose to work for former movie star Reagan, at that time widely dismissed in UK political circles as lightweight, extreme and unelectable, rather than more highly regarded candidates like Senator Howard Baker, former Texas Governor John Connally and former United Nations Ambassador and CIA Director George Bush Senior.

In November 1980 Reagan gained a landslide victory over President Jimmy Carter, winning 449 Electoral College votes to Carter's 49. Thus Brightside had worked on three triumphant election campaigns in three different countries. While his roles and influence within the various campaigns remain a matter of some conjecture and were almost certainly less than he sometimes implied, this was nevertheless a unique distinction. It explains why he was seen in Wellington as something of a political guru, even by those who distrusted him because of his association with parties of the right or were put off by his glib manner and brash personality.

During the campaign, Brightside became friendly with Gerard 'Gerry' Waitz, the multi-millionaire Wall Street hedge-fund operator and a leading donor to the Reagan campaign. It was at Brightside's suggestion that in 1981 Waitz made the first of his many visits to New Zealand, purchasing a beachfront property on Waiheke Island. In 1983 Waitz bought the famous Morgan homestead and surrounding property in Wairarapa. (It is understood that he has resumed spending time at the property since the fall of Helen Clark's Labour government in November 2008.) Given the American's track record of contributing to political causes, Brightside's access to Waitz was another factor in his favour when he was seeking to establish himself in Wellington.

In 1981 Brightside spent several months working for a Washington DC political lobbyist. He then disappeared from view. We have no hard information on his whereabouts and activities in 1982–84, although he sometimes mentioned that he had visited a number of Latin American countries, including El Salvador, where a bitter civil war between the US-backed junta and leftist insurgents was under way.

7. WELLINGTON

Brightside arrived unannounced in Wellington in February 1985. With his impressive CV and international connections he had no trouble securing a position with one of the many consultancies which 'set up shop' in the capital around this time. Despite his past involvement with right-wing parties, he presented himself as a non-partisan political strategist enthused by the Labour government's programme of social reform and economic restructuring.

As noted above, his University of Auckland ties gave him 'a foot in the door'. Labourites who believed a second term of office was crucial in order to consolidate their legislative achievements were impressed by Brightside's track record in successful election campaigns; his charm, worldliness and breezy self-confidence helped win over some of those who were initially suspicious. Over time he was also able to capitalise on his links to big business, a by-product of his friendship with Waitz.

The degree of Brightside's access to and influence on Labour's inner circle would become a matter of speculation and dispute. Broadly speaking, there were several schools of thought.

Those who believed Brightside oversold himself characterised him as a glorified court jester whom certain ministers enjoyed having around but didn't take very seriously. Others saw him as 'not one of us' – i.e. an unprincipled opportunist to be kept at arm's length. The dissenting view was that his counsel was sought and listened to, and he was seen as a useful go-between to the business community and the Reagan Administration as the nuclear ships row worsened. There is no doubt that he was on friendly terms with a number of ministers, particularly those who enjoyed discussing American politics late into the night over a few drinks.

8. DISAPPEARANCE

The last known sighting of Brightside was on the evening of Thursday, 27 August 1987. He had a quick, late dinner at a Chinese restaurant with his girlfriend, a Press Gallery reporter. She recalled him being distracted and somewhat off-hand, as he had been for the previous two weeks. Their usual practice after eating out was to spend the night together at Brightside's city apartment, but he ruled that out, saying he would have to work through the night. He was not at liberty to discuss the project in question which, given their respective roles, was not an uncommon situation. Brightside told her he would be out of town on business over the weekend, but would be in touch the following Sunday night or Monday morning. When she had not heard from him by Tuesday morning and was unable to contact him, she began ringing around his friends and associates.

A month earlier Brightside had renewed the lease on his apartment, suggesting his disappearance was not long in the planning. He cleared out his bank accounts. He left a note in his apartment – 'To Whom it may Concern' – saying he had decided to pursue unspecified opportunities overseas and did not want to go through a tiresome round of explanations and farewells. To those inconvenienced by his abrupt departure or who felt let down, he offered an apology and an explanation of sorts: 'That's the nature of this beast.'

All of Brightside's friends and associates that we were able to contact and who consented to be interviewed insisted they have not heard from him since his disappearance. His mother, now ninety and living in an Auckland retirement village, was not responsive when we tried to interview her.

9. CONCLUSION

The most baffling aspect of Brightside's disappearance is this: if he did what he said he was going to do – pursue overseas opportunities – why has he not been heard from or heard of since 1987? Internet searches generate no references post-dating his disappearance.

Six months after Brightside disappeared and at the behest of a former associate, an Immigration Department official checked whether his passport had been used in the interim. It had not (and, we understand, has not been used since). On the face of it, this would indicate that Brightside was still in New Zealand in early 1988, and indeed still is. However, he may have acquired a second passport while he was overseas. Given his supposed contacts in the intelligence world, it is entirely possible that he had a false passport and has been living under that assumed identity ever since.

Brightside's disappearance triggered a welter of speculation. Some believed he was spooked by his twenty-five-year-old girlfriend's desire to cohabit. The relationship had been going for ten months, and she made no secret of her intention to be married with children by the time she was thirty.

Others took Brightside at his word: it was simply the nature of the beast. He was an opportunist who avoided emotional connections or commitments; an opportunity had arisen elsewhere and he reacted in typical 'fly by night' fashion.

A theory popular in left-wing circles was that Brightside had been recruited by the CIA and sent to New Zealand to ingratiate himself with senior ministers and persuade them to revisit their anti-nuclear stance. Proponents of this theory pointed out that Brightside turned up in Wellington a matter of days after the Government refused to allow the USS *Buchanan* to visit, a decision that signalled the beginning of the end of the New Zealand-US military alliance. According to this theory, after Labour's re-election in August 1987 the Americans decided the situation was irretrievable and extracted Brightside to avoid the fallout that would have ensued had his role come to light. The obvious counter-argument is that, if that was the case, a conventional, low-key departure would have caused much less speculation.

Although there is no hard evidence to support any of the theories arising from Brightside's disappearance and subsequent invisibility (one of which, obviously, is that he is dead and has been for some time), we believe the most likely scenario is that he left the country on a false passport within a matter of days and has, for reasons unknown, lived under an assumed name, most likely in the USA, ever since.

Caspar Quedley's package also contained a photo labelled 'Eddie Brightside, 1986'. Brightside had an impressive head of yellow-blond hair that flopped over his ears and onto his forehead, and a roundish face whose soft shapes and lack of definition suggested cheerful hedonism or perhaps a character deficit. He was smiling for the camera, but it was a cool and distant smile of private amusement that had nothing in it for the photographer or anyone else out there.

There was no logo, no letterhead, nothing whatsoever to identify the authors, just an elegantly handwritten note across the top of the first page:

I know you've handled lots of confidential/sensitive info in your time, but you heard the man. Do not copy, do not show to anyone. Burn after reading. Seriously. QC.

Van Roon tossed the document aside and leaned back on the sofa, closing his eyes. He really didn't know what to make of Eddie Brightside or Caspar Quedley or the assignment. The only thing he was reasonably sure of was that whoever was after Brightside, it wasn't because they were still pissed off over some dud investment advice thirty-odd years ago.

6

Tito Ihaka didn't believe in any of it. He didn't believe in God, Satan, heaven, hell, previous lives or reincarnation – coming back as a dolphin or a giant of the forest or, for that matter, a sewer rat. He didn't believe in karma, destiny, extra-sensory perception, UFOs, the Abominable Snowman, elaborate conspiracy theories or the notion that you could be whatever you wanted to be as long as you kept telling yourself you could be whatever you wanted to be.

He believed that shit happened. He believed in randomness and coincidence and being in the wrong place at the wrong time. He believed there were bad people out there. Some were bad because their upbringing and circumstances pushed them in that direction; some were just born that way. Whichever it was, most of them were never going to change. He understood that you had to be in to win. He also understood that your chances of winning Lotto were roughly the same as your chances of being killed by a piece of space junk falling back to earth.

So he didn't attach any significance to the fact that as he was sitting there contemplating going over Detective Inspector Tony Charlton's head, he got a call from the Auckland District Commander's secretary summoning him to mahogany row.

By the time he got there, he still hadn't decided whether he should try to persuade Finbar McGrail to override Charlton's veto. It wasn't that he was wary of getting further offside with Charlton; since the knock-back, irritation and frustration had hardened into truculence. Nor was he worried that some colleagues would see it as hypocritical given his long track record of rubbishing anyone who resorted to weaselly manoeuvring. There was a bloody big difference between using your connections to get unpaid time off to find out how your old man really died, and brown-nosing your way onto some bullshit War on Drugs junket or into a bigger office.

No, his uncertainty was around McGrail's reaction. There was a view that McGrail had turned into a political animal since becoming Auckland District Commander. Even if that was true, he'd still got there the hard way: strictly on merit, without greasing up to the hierarchy or pretending to be Mr Nice Guy to score cheap points with the troops. And even if McGrail was open to the idea of interceding, Ihaka would still have to put up a compelling case; airy-fairiness like 'family matters' or 'personal issues' would cut even less ice than it did with Charlton. But what really worried Ihaka was that McGrail might come back at him with several reasons why looking into his old man's death would be a waste of time.

Things got off to an encouraging start. McGrail came out from behind his desk, bestowing a rare uncalibrated smile and an even rarer avuncular pat on the back. He examined Ihaka's face. 'I heard you were sporting a few bumps and bruises, Sergeant, but they seem to have cleared up. What happened?'

'I slipped in the shower.'

'Yes, I heard that too. I also heard DS Firkitt had a

domestic misadventure around the same time. I couldn't help but wonder if they were in any way related.'

Even if there was such a thing as a good time to try to bullshit someone with an exceptional inbuilt lie detector, this wasn't it. 'Yeah,' said Ihaka. 'We cleared the air.'

'What with – baseball bats?'

'No, it was almost civilised. We boxed. You know: gloves, mouthguards, a good clean fight – no low blows, no rabbit punches.'

'And?'

'As I said, we cleared the air.'

'No more bad blood then?'

Ihaka nodded. 'I think it's sorted. Not saying it's going to be all sweetness and light, but for now we're cool.'

'Now I've heard everything,' said McGrail, shaking his head. 'Still, I don't suppose mediation was ever going to do the trick. What did DI Charlton make of it?'

'Don't know,' said Ihaka. 'I guess Firkitt told him, but he hasn't mentioned it to me. We've got our own issues.'

'He said ominously. That sounds like one step forward, two steps back.'

'Other way round. The Charlton thing's not a big deal, but I never thought me and Firkitt would be where we are.'

'Peace in our time,' said McGrail. 'Well, let's hope so anyway.' He steered Ihaka towards the meeting table that took up half the office. It was bare except for a thick manila file. 'I'd be obliged if you'd peruse that file, Sergeant. No rush; coffee and sandwiches are on the way.'

Ihaka sat down, dragging the file towards him. A glance at the cover told him that it related to an unresolved 1987 murder investigation headed by a certain DI F. McGrail. A glance at McGrail told him it wasn't just another cold case.

'Still rankles, eh?'

McGrail's expression went from bleak to quizzical. 'Good word, Sergeant; possibly not one I would have expected to hear from you.'

'I joined a book club,' said Ihaka. 'It's done wonders for my vocab.'

'Really? You've joined a book club? Your reinvention proceeds apace.'

'Yeah, right,' said Ihaka, flipping open the file.

McGrail sighed. 'I'm getting old; I wouldn't have fallen for that a few years ago.' He went back to his desk. 'But yes, it still rankles.'

The heavy emphasis caused Ihaka to look up, but McGrail was already bowed over a document, fountain pen poised correctively.

Half an hour later Ihaka pushed the file aside. 'Jesus, what a fucking nightmare.'

McGrail joined him at the meeting table. 'There's been a development. Minor, one would have to say, but a development nonetheless.'

He gave Ihaka an abridged version of what Andy Maddocks had revealed at the Northern Club. 'So at least we now know why the poor girl was upstairs,' said McGrail. 'What do you make of it, Sergeant? What are those renowned instincts telling you?'

'Shit, I don't know. Maybe she heard something she shouldn't have heard, or saw something she shouldn't have seen.'

'We considered that, of course, but didn't really follow it through. I've reviewed the file very carefully since that conversation with Maddocks and came to the same conclusion as you did after a quick skim.' When Ihaka didn't respond, he added, 'That's a compliment, by the way.'

'You know me,' said Ihaka. 'I just say the first thing that comes into my head.'

'The first thing that comes into most people's heads is idiotic but, as you've demonstrated many times, you're not like most people. My second conclusion was that we approached it the wrong way. We were trying to find a killer, which was like looking for a needle in a haystack. We should have been trying to find out what it was that Polly saw or heard that got her killed.'

Ihaka shrugged sceptically. 'Much better. Like looking for a four-leaf clover in Cornwall Park.'

'I disagree. We asked, "Did you see anything suspicious?" "Did you notice anyone acting in an unusual manner?" We might as well have asked, "Did you happen to see anyone who looked like a homicidal maniac?"' McGrail was hunched forward, prodding the tabletop with his index finger. Christ, thought Ihaka, he'll be loosening his tie next. 'Instead of starting with the murder and working back, we should have tried to find out what was going on that night, because whatever Polly saw or heard upstairs, there was probably an inkling of it downstairs.'

'Such as?'

'The Barton boy had arranged a rendezvous upstairs with Mrs Best. It didn't happen because his parents knew what was afoot and made it their business to stop it. Perhaps someone else had the same idea: upstairs was out of bounds, so it was the ideal place for an assignation. And bear in mind there were some prominent people at that party.'

'Well, yeah, I can see it might be embarrassing for a big shot, especially a married one, to have some kid walk in when he's up to the apricots where he shouldn't be. I can see him putting the hard word on her, or trying to bribe her to keep her mouth shut. I can't see him strangling her.

I mean, you're loaded, you've got friends in high places, a teenager catches you on the job, what are you going to do? You're going to pull up your tweeds and walk out of there like nothing happened. Then it's your word against hers, and who's going to believe her?'

'Well,' said McGrail, 'I suppose I was thinking of something potentially more damaging than bog-standard adultery.'

'Oh yeah? Were there any little kids there that night?'

'What?'

'Because if we're talking about Mr Pillar of Society busted molesting a kiddie, I can see he might go a bit overboard. Or the family pet: "MP dorks host's dachshund at posh party". Not an ideal headline if you're hoping for promotion in the next cabinet reshuffle.'

'For God's sake, man.' McGrail flushed hotly, his voice rasping with indignation. 'This is no laughing matter. For twenty-seven years barely a week has gone by that I haven't thought about Polly Stenson. When I walk out of here, I'll do so with very few regrets, but this case will stay with me until I've forgotten I ever was a policeman.'

Ihaka held up his hands. 'Sorry, I should have got the message the first time. What do you want me to do?'

'Offload whatever you've got on and give this case one last shake. Then at least I'll have the comfort of knowing the answer wasn't staring me in the face.' Ihaka was counting on McGrail noticing his slight grimace. 'You don't seem too enthusiastic, Sergeant. Is there a problem?'

'Not for me there isn't. Charlton will be hacked off, though. See, he just knocked back my request for unpaid leave. He's going to think I've gone over his head.'

'I assume you presented a reasonable case.'

'Personal matters.'

'Ah. That covers a multitude of sins.'

'I know, but this is real and about as personal as it gets. And, well, shit, you know the background.'

'You're a closed book at the best of times, and Charlton's the last person you'd be inclined to open up for. I would hope,' McGrail added gently, 'that I'm not the second to last.'

Ihaka relayed his conversation with Miriam Lovell.

'Have you established whether there was a post-mortem?'

'Mum's sure there wasn't,' said Ihaka. 'He'd had heart trouble and there was a family history of it, so I guess it was just taken for granted he'd had a heart attack. You feel you owe Polly; I feel the same about this. The least I can do is check it out.'

'Oh, I think this can work for both of us, Sergeant. Officially, you'll be pursuing the new lead in the Stenson case, but I'm sure there'll be lulls here and there.'

'Suits me down to the ground but, as I said, it's not me you have to worry about. Doesn't matter how you sell it, Charlton's going to spit the dummy.'

'Well, Tito, I can't say I give a damn what Charlton does.'

'Did you just call me Tito?'

'I believe I did.'

Ihaka was faintly embarrassed at how chuffed he was. 'First time ever.'

'Yes, I suppose it is,' said McGrail, as if he couldn't quite believe it himself. 'Seeing we're breaking new ground, perhaps you could return the favour.'

'You want me to call you Finbar?'

'I was thinking more of Sir.'

McGrail held Ihaka's confused stare.

'But I've hardly ever called you Sir.'

'Well, precisely.'

CALGARY
PUBLIC
LIBRARY

Village Square Library
Self Checkout

April 21,2018 12:50

39065145355622   5/12/2018
Fallout : Maori detective Tito Ihaka my
stery

39065140453406   5/12/2018
Bone deep : [a Doc Ford novel]

Total   2 item(s)

You have 0 item(s) ready for pickup

Ihaka floundered, lost for words.

McGrail, frowning: 'So it's a matter of principle?'

Ihaka groaned. 'That makes it sound like a big deal, which it's not. Not with you, anyway. It just doesn't come naturally.'

'And leg-pulls don't come naturally to me,' said McGrail, poker-faced. 'But it was rather a good one, if I say so myself.'

'Fuck.' Ihaka put his elbows on the table and buried his face in the crook of an arm. In a muffled voice he said, 'There's a few things I wouldn't mind calling you right now.'

'But you won't, will you?'

Ihaka lifted his head, starting to see the funny side. 'No sir, I won't.'

He rang Miriam Lovell for contact details. After she'd provided them, she said, 'I assume that means you're taking it further, which in turn tells me there was no post-mortem.'

'Two out of two.'

'What are you going to do?'

'Ask questions,' said Ihaka. 'Try to get a feel for whether there's anything to it. Follow my nose. I do this sort of thing for a living, remember?'

'Plant evidence, beat confessions out of innocent people…'

'Every job has its perks,' he said. 'What about you? What are you up to?'

'That's a rather personal question.'

'I just have this feeling you're holding out on me.'

Miriam laughed. 'So the boot's on the other foot?'

Then she hung up.

* * *

Since he was off the roster and determined not to be late for a kiss-and-make-up date with Denise, Ihaka left work early. He was walking out of Auckland Central as Charlton was walking in. Charlton circled, unsmiling, hands shoved in his pockets. 'You ever heard the expression "Be careful what you wish for"?'

'All the time,' said Ihaka. 'And I've noticed when people say it, they get this strange look on their face, like their haemorrhoids are firing up. I've worked out it's because they think they've said something really fucking profound.'

'Enjoy your moment of triumph, Sergeant. And I use the word "moment" advisedly.'

'What did McGrail tell you?'

'He said new information relating to a cold case has come to light and he's tasked you with following it up,' said Charlton. 'He also acknowledged that the timing wasn't ideal, given that I've just turned down your leave request.'

'But you don't believe him.'

Charlton acted affronted. 'Excuse me? Of course I believed him. I believed every word he said. But our esteemed leader is a man of few words when it suits him, and I was more interested in what he didn't say. I still am.'

'For what it's worth, I didn't go over your head.'

Charlton chuckled, like an indulgent parent listening to a child tell a convoluted but hopelessly transparent fib. 'Is that right? I think you've got me mixed up with someone who believes in fairy tales. As I said, make the most of it – and be careful what you wish for.'

He stopped pretending that he wasn't taking it personally, frosting Ihaka with an arctic stare. Then he brushed past Ihaka and went inside.

* * *

Ihaka no longer believed food was about combinations which had stood the test of time: burgers, fish and chips, bacon and eggs, sausages and mash, roast and two veg. Back in the day he would freely admit that restaurants were wasted on him. When he did eat out he had a few non-negotiable requirements: that there was steak on the menu; that they cooked it the way you wanted; that they left your bottle of wine on the table so you could have another glass when you felt like it, as opposed to when the waiter could be arsed bringing the bottle back; that the waiter didn't expect you to pay attention when he or she went through the specials of the day which no one ever ordered.

What gave him the shits were restaurants that operated on the basis that the more complicated the dish the better. Where things came on a bed of this and with a drizzle of that. Where you had to ask what half the things on the menu were, and what you'd told your dining companion was probably some sort of pasta was actually a type of seaweed. Where most dishes had so many things going on, they were like sex positions in the *Kama Sutra* – so elaborate they took the fun out of it. If you were hungry, you didn't want sixteen competing flavours, you wanted a simple, satisfying feed. Likewise, if you were champing at the bit, who the fuck wanted to contort like a gymnast? The missionary position would do just fine, thanks.

One time, in this so-called fine dining restaurant, he'd let himself be talked into choosing adventurously. When he ordered the quail starter and duck for the main course, the waiter raised a snooty eyebrow and lowered his pen and notepad. 'You do realise, sir,' he said, 'that's two fowl courses?' Ihaka considered various responses before set-tling for, 'Do I look like I give a fuck?'

Then he and Denise discovered Depot in Federal Street, in the shadow of Sky City. At first Ihaka baulked at the idea of shared plates, which was at odds with his whole approach to eating. If other people wanted to share what was on their plate, he'd consider the offer on its merits; if they were expecting reciprocity, however, they were shit out of luck. But he was swayed by Depot's easy-going atmosphere, the lack of preciousness, and the breezy but professional service. And once he realised that the food was delicious and the smaller shared plates meant that you could actually eat more without drawing attention to yourself, he was sold on the joint.

Tonight he was on time but Denise was already there, halfway through a glass of sparkling wine. She seemed very pleased to see him; in fact, she'd arranged for Billy to sleep over at a friend's house so they could reconcile the daylights out of each other, if they were so inclined. He ordered a beer and they spent five minutes happily haggling over the menu before reaching their usual compromise of over-ordering.

Once the conversation moved away from beef cheeks and pulled pork to the recent unpleasantness, it quickly became apparent that, as far as Denise was concerned, the reconciliation was predicated on two assumptions: that he accepted, and would shortly acknowledge, that he'd fucked up; and that he'd promise there would be no repeat of said fuck-up.

'Listen, how about I just tell you what Miriam had to say?' he said. 'Then I think you'll see it differently.'

Denise went blank. 'Miriam?'

'The woman I met the other day. She's doing a PhD on trade union militancy in the seventies and eighties. You know my old man was up to his neck in that stuff, right?

Well, when Miriam was doing her research, she came across something that sort of suggests Dad's death mightn't have been the run-of-the-mill heart attack everybody assumed it was. There might've been foul play.'

Denise's hand flew to her mouth. Not because she was shocked; when she removed her hand, Ihaka realised she was having trouble keeping a straight face. 'Oh, Tito, no,' she said. 'No, come on.'

'No what?'

'You don't seriously expect me to believe that?'

'I'm not saying I believe it,' he said. 'But I sure as hell want to check it out. I mean, if it was your old man —'

'I didn't go to my father's funeral,' said Denise, as if she'd struck a blow for common sense. 'But that wasn't what I meant. I meant you don't seriously expect me to believe that's why what's her name wanted to see you?'

He shrugged. 'Well, I was kind of hoping you would.'

'This thing you want to check out,' she said. 'Where did she come across it?'

'In an old diary. And a week after the old man died, the guy whose diary it was had a fatal accident.'

Her face twitched again. 'I'm sorry, but this is just too out there. Honestly, Tito, you don't have to do this.'

'Do what?'

'Come up with this…' Her hands fluttered as she tried to think of a less confrontational term than 'bullshit'. 'With this stuff. Look, let's just keep it simple: we both say sorry, you promise you won't see this bitch again, and we put the whole thing behind us.'

'First of all, she's not a bitch.' That was probably the last thing Denise wanted to hear, but Ihaka was approaching the point of not giving a shit. 'Secondly, I didn't make this up. Third, while I have no plans or any great desire to see

87

Miriam again, I'm not going to promise I won't, because she has information and knowledge I might need to access.'

Having mentally scripted the encounter to ensure the happy ending she knew they both desired, Denise was flabbergasted by Ihaka's improvisation. She went to Plan B: 'I can't believe you could do this to Billy.'

'Denise, I'm not doing anything to Billy.'

'He's desperate to see you. All I've heard from him the past few days is, "Mum, when's Tito coming?"'

'My relationship with Billy is a by-product of my relationship with you. Billy understands that. Right now we're struggling, and it's not going to make Billy happy if we're struggling in front of him.'

'So how do we fix it if we're not seeing each other?'

'I didn't say we shouldn't see each other,' he said. 'But I guess we need to think about what's got us here, and what needs to change to get us back to where we were before.'

Denise looked away, saying something under her breath.

'What was that?'

She turned back, giving him a look that made Charlton's parting stare seem tender. 'But we know what needs to happen for us to get back to where we were,' she said hotly, 'and you've just made it crystal fucking clear you're not prepared to do that.' She reached for her handbag. 'Why don't you just drop the bullshit and come right out and say it's over?'

'Because I don't want it to be over.'

She stood up. 'Is that right? So if neither of us wants it to be over, how come it is?'

Ihaka watched her leave, vaguely aware that a waiter was placing several dishes on the table. He ordered a carafe of the house Pinot Noir and turned his attention to the food. There was a lot to get through and no one to help him.

7

Having wasted time he didn't have procrastinating, Johan Van Roon rang a former police colleague who could trace the owner of the Honda Civic which had transported Eddie Brightside – or a lookalike – away from the Hawke's Bay winery. Assuming he was so inclined.

In his previous life Van Roon had helped the ex-colleague in ways big and small, but now he was a pariah, and one of the first things a pariah loses is the ability to call in favours. As far as those who owe him are concerned, his disgrace cancels out their obligation.

But whether out of pity or conscience the ex-colleague didn't hang up. He complained all right, but that was a good sign. If he hadn't bitched and moaned, Van Roon would have known it was a futile exercise.

'Jesus Christ, talk about a one-armed paperhanger. I'm up to my eyeballs. You've got no idea.'

Van Roon didn't bother pointing out he actually had a pretty good idea. 'Not a good time?'

'That's the understatement of the year. Plus I could get myself in the shit.'

'I know,' said Van Roon. 'Believe me, I wouldn't be asking if it wasn't important.'

'Important how?'

'It's my livelihood. There's bugger-all work around, and

there'll be even less if I can't deliver.' The silence stretched out. 'You still there?'

'Leave it with me. It won't happen today, though. As I said, this place is a fucking madhouse. You're sure the number's right?'

'It came from a civilian.'

'Well, you know how it works: shit in, shit out. Give us a couple of days.'

'Thanks a lot, mate.'

'Then we'll be all square, right? Don't ask me again. Don't make me say no.'

That afternoon Van Roon drove up to Raumati Beach to see the retired journalist Barry McCormick.

As he came out of Pukerua Bay onto the coast road, the cloud thickened and sagged and the anaemic winter sun faded like a dying light bulb. Within the grey dome the only daubs of colour were the breaking waves foaming amidst the driftwood and the dark-green scrub on Kapiti Island. The base from which Te Rauparaha and his warriors had set out like Vikings on their campaigns of plunder and utu looked desolate and bereft of value, strategic or otherwise.

McCormick had given detailed instructions: park on the street, walk down the drive, then follow the pedestrian thoroughfare snaking between the properties jostling for proximity to the beach; when you reach the sand, double back across the patch of rough lawn and up through the rock garden and Norfolk pines to the deck.

His place was an old bach, a do-it-yourself job that was never quite finished, full of scavenged furniture and anachronisms, where once kids with caramel skin and bleached hair bolted food before careering back to the beach whooping like Apaches. Or, when the weather drove them inside, played cards and board games that ended, often prematurely, in a crossfire of triumphalism and accusation.

McCormick himself was a leftover from the era of filterless cigarettes and long socks: crew-cut and darkly weathered, his spindly arms and legs out of kilter with a wobbling paunch. Only his unblinking magpie scrutiny and crammed bookshelves hinted at an existence beyond cold beer, lawn bowls and the TAB.

They examined each other across a lino-topped table. McCormick asked, 'How do you sleep?'

Van Roon shrugged. 'Not as well as I used to.'

'The sound of the sea, son,' said McCormick. 'Nothing like falling asleep to the sound of waves. You sleep like a baby.'

'Beachfront property's a bit out of my league,' said Van Roon. 'Besides, I bet your rates would buy a heap of sleeping pills.'

'Christ, you're a romantic soul, aren't you? You're the ex-cop, right?'

Van Roon nodded. 'I retired.'

'Course you did, son. You gave up being a Detective Inspector to run errands for Caspar Quedley.'

'I didn't come up here to talk about my career.'

'No, I don't suppose you did,' said McCormick. 'But you want my help, and neither of us has got anything better to do.' He tilted his head interrogatively. 'I heard you were corrupt. I heard you drilled someone in cold blood, just to shut him up.' McCormick sat back looking pleased with himself.

Not as clever as he thinks he is, thought Van Roon; not many are. His gaze drifted away over McCormick's shoulder. It was raining heavily now, sheeting in off the sea, pelting the sliding glass doors. 'Say for the sake of argument you heard right, you'd be silly to get on the wrong side of me, wouldn't you?'

'That's a point,' said McCormick with a satisfied chuckle, as if he'd managed to extract valuable information without Van Roon even being aware of it. 'So what can I do for you?'

'Are you absolutely sure it was Eddie Brightside?'

McCormick folded his arms, an assertion of authority. 'Let me tell you something, son. You hear people say they never forget a face. What they mean is they have a pretty good memory for faces. Not me. I literally never forget a face. If I see a face that rings a bell, I'll go talk to the person to find out if I'm right. I've been doing it for fucking years and I've never struck out. A few weeks ago I saw this woman on Lambton Quay: career woman in her forties, tidy enough but no show-stopper. I knew I'd seen her before, but couldn't place her at all. Turns out when she was a student, she did a bit of waitressing at this restaurant in Thorndon I went to a couple of times.'

'So what?'

'So what? She took my order for fancy-pants beef stew twenty-odd years ago and I remembered her face, that's fucking what.'

'Doesn't necessarily follow. The fact that you thought you'd seen her before and the fact you went to that restaurant around the time she worked there doesn't prove anything. It just establishes the possibility.'

McCormick looked like the neighbourhood misery-guts catching some kids looking for a lost ball in his vegetable garden. 'If you're going to be a smart-arse, you can sling your hook, Mister Van whatever the fuck your name is.'

'I introduced myself ten minutes ago. Memory not what it used to be?'

'Don't you worry about my memory, sonny boy,' growled McCormick. 'I remember stuff that happened before you were born like it was yesterday.'

'Then you'd remember Brightside's girlfriend.'

'Louise Fraser? Course I bloody remember her. I worked with her in the Gallery.'

'Obviously that wasn't her at the winery?'

'Obviously.'

'What happened to Louise?'

'She's still around, far as I know,' said McCormick. 'Last I heard she was a policy analyst at the Human Rights Commission.'

'Did you recognise the other one? Maybe you sat behind her at a Charlie Chaplin film in Lower Hutt once upon a time.'

McCormick squinted, his eyes hostile slits beneath what was left of his eyebrows. 'You've got a bloody funny way of trying to get people to give you a hand. As it happens, I had seen her before – I never forget a face, see? But I've no idea who she is or where I saw her.'

'Was it recent?'

McCormick shook his head. 'Back in the good old days.'

'So she was probably in the political-slash-journalism world?'

'Doesn't necessarily follow,' said McCormick with passable mimicry. 'It was pretty social back then, and there was more overlap. Things weren't so – what's that word? – compartmentalised. Let me ask you a question: why do you think you're doing this? I mean, what did Quedley actually tell you?'

'That he's got a client who wants to track down Brightside.'

'Why?'

'Because Brightside talked him into a bad investment.'

McCormick's laugh rose to a cackle. 'Jesus wept, in those days every bastard was giving every other bastard dud share tips.'

'Well, you know Quedley, you tell me: why does he want me to find Brightside?'

McCormick tried to look clueless, but came across as shifty. 'Shit, don't ask me. All I know is Caspar operates on the iceberg principle: you only get to see the tip.'

Tele-marketers who ring in the middle of dinner get a warmer reception than Van Roon got from Louise Fraser. It took some fast and earnest talking to convince her that his Eddie Brightside update would be worth hearing. He offered to buy her a drink at the venue of her choice, but she wanted to get home to her cat. If it was all that urgent, he could drop by.

Fraser's apartment building was off Vivian Street, a neighbourhood of backstreets and inner-city disorderliness, terraced houses and hopeful boutiques sandwiched between offices and workshops. After the inevitable peep-hole scrutiny and much clicking and clanking, the door was opened by a middle-aged woman in yoga pants and a sweatshirt cradling a ginger cat. Van Roon's instant impression was that the woman had once been pretty, and had always been complicated. The cat looked as supercilious as every other pampered, overweight feline he'd come across.

She invited him in. The apartment was tiny – real estate agents would have debated the merits of 'compact' and 'cosy' before going with both – but managed to be stylish without being clinical.

'What's it called?' he asked, feigning interest in the cat.

'His name is Simon.'

'Named after?'

'Why should he be named after anyone?'

'When people give pets proper names, as opposed to Rover or Fluffy or whatever, they usually have someone in mind. In my experience.'

'Do you remember Monty Python?'

'I've seen clips on YouTube,' he said. 'Seemed a bit dated.'

'You're too old to patronise my generation,' said Fraser. She and the cat sat down on a retro two-seater sofa. 'Simon's named after an electric elk mentioned in passing in one of their less crowd-pleasing skits, in which an absurdly pretentious theatre critic reviews a play that explores the human condition via the British Rail timetable.' She gave him a receptionist's smile, the sort that comes and goes in the blink of an eye. 'Sorry you asked?'

'It went over my head,' said Van Roon. 'But it didn't take long.'

'Well, anyway, life's too short to fritter away in idle chit-chat. I gather you're going to tell me a ghost story.'

'Your former colleague Barry McCormick is certain – like one hundred per cent certain – he saw Brightside in Hawke's Bay a few days ago.' He told her McCormick's story. 'Do you believe it?'

'Let me say first of all that one hundred per cent certain is a tautology.' She said it with a faint smile, as if to let him know it was more for her amusement than his discomfort. 'As for what Mac saw or didn't see, I wouldn't dismiss it out of hand. Knowing Mac I've no doubt he believes the person he saw at that winery was E.F. Brightside. And that's about all I can say.'

'OK, assuming McCormick's right, what do you make of it?'

The question seemed to bemuse her. 'I don't know what to make of it. Actually that's not true: I don't make anything of it. I haven't seen, heard from or heard of Eddie for almost thirty years and, as far as I know, nor has anyone else. He stopped cropping up in my thoughts and feelings a long, long time ago. Anyway, why do you care? What's it to you whether it was him or not?'

'Personally, not a thing. It's a job: I'm being paid to find out.'

'Surely you jest?'

Van Roon shook his head. 'I'm just the hired help. I don't know who the client is, but apparently back in the eighties Brightside advised him to invest in some shares that tanked big-time. Seems he's still pissed off about it.'

'Oh, for crying out loud.' Fraser offloaded Simon so that she could use more expressive body language; he left the room without a backward glance. 'Of course Eddie dabbled in the stock market – practically everybody did. It was a crazy time and proof, if any were needed, that a little knowledge is a dangerous thing. No one personified that more than Eddie: he'd buy shares on the say-so of some deadbeat he met in a bar. But I never heard him dispensing investment advice, for the very good reason that no one who knew him would've paid any attention to it.'

'Well, maybe the client didn't know him well enough. You must have a theory on why he took off. Everybody else did.'

'You mean those hysterical spy scenarios? My theory's much more mundane. I think Eddie was impaled on the horns of a dilemma and while he was trying to decide what to do, an opportunity came up overseas. It was a win-win situation: by grabbing the opportunity, he extricated himself from an uncomfortable and perhaps impossible situation.'

'And what might that have been?'

Fraser sighed. 'There was another woman. Well, I did warn you it was mundane. I went through a brief phase of thinking there are worse fates in life than getting married and having children. Some of Eddie's friends inflated that into me scheming day and night to drag him to the altar. It was nothing of the sort, but given his other girlfriend was probably at him to dump me, you can understand why he might have felt trapped.'

'You know for a fact he was seeing someone else?'

'You mean am I one hundred per cent certain? No.' She stood up. 'If I'm going to talk about this and you're going to listen, we'll need some recreational drugs. In this apartment that means alcohol.'

'Don't worry about me,' said Van Roon. 'I'm driving.'

Fraser pulled a stage frown. 'Are you a teetotaller?'

'Well, no, but —'

'If one glass of Pinot Gris puts you over the limit, you're not the grown man you give every appearance of being.'

She came back from the kitchenette with a bottle of white wine and two glasses. She filled the glasses, passed one to Van Roon and took a grateful gulp from the other. He got the feeling it wasn't her first of the evening, and that the bottle wouldn't go back in the fridge when he left.

'Thank you.'

'You're welcome. I think he had another girlfriend because that's the sort of guy he was. Based on what I've observed over time, men who, for whatever reason, attract women like moths to a flame aren't inclined to look gift horses in the mouth – if you'll pardon the metaphorical mishmash. Secondly, the very last thing you'd say about

Eddie was that his life was an open book. Not only was he cryptic, if not downright evasive, about what he'd done overseas, he was often cryptic about what he'd done that afternoon. Bear in mind this was back in the dark ages before mobile phones, when you could drop off the radar for a few hours here and a night there, which he tended to do. The fact that I was in the Press Gallery and he was working for the government meant we couldn't really live in each other's pockets even if we'd wanted to, which I didn't.' She paused. 'I don't suppose the name Gerry Waitz means anything to you?'

'Mega-rich American,' said Van Roon, 'who Brightside got to know when he worked in the States. Owns a property in the Wairarapa.'

'My, my,' said Fraser, arching her eyebrows, this time without irony. 'We have done our homework. I can see the search for Eddie Brightside isn't a whim.'

Van Roon shrugged. 'It's not the hunt for Osama bin Laden either. What about Waitz?'

'Soon after Eddie and I became a couple, we had a weekend at Waitz Manor. It's a lovely place – great big country house with rolling lawns and rose gardens. Even has a maze. Waitz turned out to be a generous host and, somewhat to my surprise, quite sophisticated. I suppose I was expecting a born-again evangelical in cowboy boots and a ten-gallon hat who smoked a ten-inch cigar at breakfast and kept red wine in the fridge, but he wasn't like that at all. He was, however, incredibly right-wing. The nuclear ships row was hotting up and Waitz couldn't make up his mind whether David Lange was a commie fifth-columnist conspiring to undermine everything we hold dear or simply the biggest fucking fool under the sun, although he was tilting towards the former. It wouldn't have been so bad if he'd been interested in discussing the issue, but he wasn't; not remotely. He seemed to think that putting us up for the weekend and plying us with food and wine gave him the right to rant ad infinitum and obliged us to listen in respectful silence.

'Well, I did my best for Eddie's sake, but eventually I just couldn't take any more of it so I had him on. Silly thing to do really, him being so black and white – and sexist, although he tried to pretend otherwise. We yelled at each other for a few minutes, then he jumped up roaring that he wasn't going to be harangued in his own house and stalked off with his Barbie doll of the month in tow. He was still in a huff the next morning, so I got Eddie to take me to Featherston and caught the train home. It was my first and last visit. Whenever Waitz was in the country Eddie had a standing invitation, but I had a trespass notice so there were quite a few weekends when I was here and he was there. At least, that's where he said he was.

'Not long before the vanishing act, I was out with a colleague, an older woman who, it would be fair to say, had done extensive research on the male of the species. I drank too much and therefore talked too much, including giving her a full and frank rundown on the state of my relationship with Eddie. She said, very matter-of-factly, "Well, I'm sorry to be the bearer of bad news, but he's obviously fucking someone else." When she spelt it out, I had to admit there were an awful lot of telltale signs. She also pointed out that I only had his word for it that he really was spending those weekends at Waitz's place.' Fraser put on a Mae West drawl: 'For all you know, sweetie, he could be shacked up with some tart down in Oriental Bay.'

'I presume you had it out with him?'

'Actually, no. I hardly saw him over the next two or three weeks. He was working on the election campaign and Waitz was around – so he said. I suppose I was in that hopeless state of not wanting to ask the question because I was afraid I wouldn't like the answer. And then he was gone.'

'You were quoted as saying he'd been distracted and offhand.'

'As people on the horns of a dilemma tend to be.'

'But it still came as a shock?'

Fraser leaned back, staring at the ceiling. 'That's what I told people. To be honest, though, even when things were hunky-dory, I had this vague sense, a foreboding I suppose you'd call it, that one day I'd look around and he'd be gone. And one day he was.'

8

Tito Ihaka drove across the Hauraki Plains to Coromandel Peninsula through drizzle as fine as a spray of perfume.

Ethan Stern's widow lived in a solar-heated cabin on a hillside a couple of kilometres inland from Coromandel township. Ihaka parked in front of a carport housing an old lawnmower, an older Japanese hatchback and a brand-new mountain bike. When he got out of his car, pinpricks of moisture settled on his shoulders like microscopic insects whose lifespan is measured in minutes. He smelt fresh-mown grass. A strip of lawn ran down the side of the cabin to a vegetable garden big enough to feed a commune.

In Ihaka's experience, semi-rural fringe dwellers didn't bother keeping up appearances. You expected neglect and overgrowth, mounds of tyres and the rusting shells of long-abandoned vehicles rising like atolls from a sea of weeds. He reminded himself that he'd visited such properties in a professional capacity; the occupants were, as they say, known to the police. P-heads mostly, too fucked up to care that their kids were feral or the lawn hadn't been mowed for a year and a half, so feckless they'd let their property turn into a rubbish dump rather than go to the tip. Jeanine Stern wasn't like that. She wasn't known to the police.

The front door opened and two dogs catapulted out, one a ball of white fluff that fizzed and yapped around

Ihaka's ankles in a not unfriendly manner, the other a dark, rangy animal with a tail like a question mark, the sort of dog Ihaka had heard described as 'all ribs and cock'. This one kept his distance, pacing to and fro, eyeing Ihaka sullenly.

Dogs didn't bother Ihaka. The way he looked at it, they had more reason to be scared of him than vice versa. Perhaps the larger dog sensed that, because he wheeled away and trotted back inside. After a flurry of indecision, the fluffball followed, leaving Ihaka and Stern to get acquainted.

She was tall and bony – sharp shoulders and hollowed-out, angular features – with an American accent and grey hair that looked as if it had been cut by someone, perhaps Stern herself, in a tearing hurry and a foul mood. Holed, shapeless jeans and a tatty grey pullover reinforced the impression of an ascetic personality and lifestyle. He wondered if that was a philosophical choice or an adaptation to circumstances, and whether she would've gone in a different direction if her husband hadn't broken his neck, becoming an earth mother in a flowing floral dress with a trail of hippie hair and the contours of her body softened by childbirth.

They went in. She offered a range of herbal tea options, all of which he declined. When she apologised for not having coffee in the house, he assured her that he never drank the stuff after midday, which wasn't remotely true but seemed to relax her.

Ihaka sat on a bar stool at the kitchen bench while she carried on making soup, piling greens and root vegetables into a huge pot on the cook top. It smelt a lot better than vegetable soup as he knew it.

He asked what had brought her here.

'A friend of mine who lives over the Black Jack Road found it. I'm not hard core like her – like, I want to be able to go to the movies without it being a day trip – but I'd always had a hankering to live in the country. You remember *Green Acres* – Eva Gabor and Arnold the pig? That was my favourite TV show when I was a kid.' Stern burst into song, grinning goofily and conducting herself with a wooden spoon, throwing out her arms on the last line. 'Green Acres is the place for me, farm livin' is the life for me, land spreadin' out so far and wide, keep Manhattan, just give me that countryside.' She resumed stirring, head down. 'Not that I grew up in Manhattan. Sorry about that. When you live by yourself in the country, you get a bit hazy about how normal people behave around each other.'

Ihaka shrugged. 'Who's normal? Besides, you've got a nice voice.'

She made a pull-the-other-one face. 'I guess you're not that into music. As I was saying, I'd always liked the idea of going country. One reason for coming to New Zealand was to get the hell away from the political scene we were in. When you start feeling guilty if you haven't been roughed up by the cops for a few days, it's a pretty good indicator that you're taking life – and yourself – a tad too seriously. The other big attraction was the clean, green, under-populated thing. We were planning to get a place within striking distance of Auckland so Ethan could either commute or rent someone's spare room while I stayed at home with the babies. Well, after the accident babies weren't a happening thing and proximity to Auckland wasn't a consideration, so Aotearoa was my oyster. I've been here more than twenty years now. You know what's funny? When my Auckland friends come down here, they go on about the lifestyle, the stress-free existence, how living in

Auckland's such a pain in the ass. Then they get back in their great big four-wheel-drives and go home. And I'm listening to them thinking, actually, I could use some of that bright lights, big city action. But here I am, and I'm pretty sure here I'll stay.' She paused. 'Now I get that your friend – Miriam is it? – is doing a PhD, which explains her interest in the obscure and long-forgotten, but what brings you down here?'

'Just curiosity, really. I'm Jimmy Ihaka's son.'

'You're looking at me as if that name should mean something.'

'He was one of the trade union guys your husband knocked around with.'

'Well, there was no shortage of them. I doubt I'll be much use to you – not that I'm too clear on what it is you're after. I sat out Ethan's slow dance with the working-class heroes. As I said, for me, coming to New Zealand was a way of going cold turkey on politics. It was meant to be a joint venture, but Ethan couldn't help himself.'

'I guess that's not so easy when you're a Political Studies lecturer.'

'I'm talking about activism, extra-curricular stuff. By the way, did Miriam manage to find Ethan's diaries?'

'Well, that's sort of why I'm here,' said Ihaka. 'That and curiosity. You put your husband's papers in cartons and sent them to the Political Studies department, right?'

'Uh huh.'

'Well, Miriam found the cartons in some storeroom, but the diaries weren't there. Someone beat her to it.'

'You make it sound kind of sinister. She wasn't the only person interested in those diaries. I tried to tell her that, but once she'd got a lead on them she was off in a cloud of dust.'

'Who else was?'

Stern frowned and looked away. The daffy songstress had left the building, replaced by the quasi-recluse who two decades ago had come to the conclusion that hell is other people. She put a lid on the saucepan, turned down the heat and tidied the bench that didn't need tidying. 'I did hear you right: you're a cop?'

'Yep.'

'So is this like an investigation?'

'No, this isn't a police matter; it's strictly personal. I'm just trying to find out a bit more about my old man. He died a week before Ethan; I was nineteen. He was a pretty passionate union man, but I never knew much about that part of his life. I'm interested in the diaries because Miriam seems to think he'd feature quite prominently.'

The personal thread and almost simultaneous bereavement seemed to disarm her. 'Sorry, I was having an acid flashback to my student radical days. Rule number one: never trust a pig.'

'I haven't been called that for a while,' said Ihaka.

'Actually, I like pigs,' she said. 'There was Arnold, of course, and I've had a couple here. You know, they're really quite intelligent.'

'So I've heard. I like pigs too, but I'm picking you're a vego.'

'Don't go there,' she said firmly. 'If I dwell on the fact you're a cop and a carnivore, I might freak out completely. Where were we?'

'You were saying Miriam wasn't the only one interested in the diaries.'

'Right. Not long after Ethan died – like a few days – I got a call from some union guy. They'd let Ethan sit in on some confidential discussions and he wanted to know what had happened to his notes. I told him I'd had quite a lot on my mind, what with my husband going for a jog and never coming home, and hadn't given the fricking notes a moment's thought.'

'I don't suppose you'd remember the union guy's name.'

'Strangely enough, I do: he was Mister Small. As he was talking, I was thinking, you must be the opposite of Mister Big.' She shook her head. 'Shows you how spaced out I was, but that's why I remember it.'

'Which union was he?'

'Give me a break. Then a couple of days later this post-grad student – whose name I don't remember, assuming I ever knew it – knocked on my door. His story was that Ethan had told him there was material in the diaries that might be useful for his doctorate and he was welcome to it. Sinister would be overstating it, but I did think it was kind of odd. For a start, he didn't look like the post-grads I'd come across, who were either buttoned-down, earnest to a fault, or space cadets from the outer rings of the counter-culture. This guy looked like he actually worked for a living. As for Ethan saying "help yourself", I was thinking, "Really? Are we talking about the same guy here?" Ethan was a bit obsessive at the best of times, but those last few months he had a real bee in his bonnet. He'd come home from hanging out with his union buddies and start scribbling away. When I'd suggest he could maybe spend a few minutes reacquainting himself with his wife, he'd say he had to get it down while it was still fresh in his mind.'

'I don't get it. Why hadn't he —?'

'Taken notes at the time? I assume he figured that would've been pushing his luck because whatever they were talking about was meant to stay within those four walls. Anyway, I told this guy I just hadn't had a chance to go through Ethan's stuff. That night a woman who worked with Ethan dropped by to see how I was bearing up. When I mentioned I was getting hassled, she said why not just pack up all Ethan's stuff and send it to the department? It seemed a sensible solution, so she came back the next night with some cartons, we chucked everything in and put them in the trunk of her car, and that was the last I saw of them.'

'Who was she?'

'Her name was Julia Prince. We didn't stay in touch; I've no idea what became of her.'

'What do you think Ethan was planning to do with it?'

She shrugged. 'Publish it in some academic journal or political magazine, I guess. Ethan was more ambitious than he let on. He wanted to stir things up, make a bit of a name for himself.'

'So what was the big story? You must've had some idea.'

'All he told me was it would cause a stir and cost him some friends. I took that to mean it wouldn't show the movement' – making speech marks with her fingers – 'in a positive light. Some of Ethan's friends were real black and white: if you said or did anything to undermine the cause, you were a capitalist imperialist lackey. They really did talk like that. Actually, once upon a time, so did I.'

Stern walked Ihaka to his car. The drizzle had stopped, but the wind had swung around to the south. She looked almost offended when Ihaka urged her not to linger. 'Do I look like I can't handle a bit of wind chill?'

'No, you don't. Shall I keep you posted?'

'Why? Where exactly do you see this going?'

'I don't know – probably not very far. I just thought you might be interested.'

'I'll get by,' she said. 'I've got through the last however many years without giving it a thought. I don't mean Ethan; the rest of it.'

As he negotiated the shingle drive down to the road, Ihaka could see Stern in his rear-view mirror. She stood like a statue, the cold wind plucking at her pullover, making sure he was going back to where he came from, leaving her to her dogs and vegetables and green, empty acres.

Ihaka hadn't eaten since breakfast. He'd been hoping that Jeanine Stern would offer him some soup, but maybe it had to last her all week. Or maybe she just didn't break bread with carnivores. Or pigs.

He stopped for fish and chips in Tararu, thinking he'd take them down to the beach and eat listening to the sound of the sea and the seagulls screeching their disapproval of his presence and diet. But as he came out of the takeaway joint it started to rain. Hard rain, hammering on the car roof and cascading down the windows. Sitting in his car, Ihaka felt the desolation that settles on tiny coastal communities when winter closes in. He ate quickly, keen to be on his way.

Why was he in a Coromandel hamlet eating takeaways and watching the rain hose down? Because the ache had started again. Years ago it had dwindled to a kind of simmering resentment of the shitty hand life had dealt him, his father dropping dead well short of the Kiwi male's average life expectancy. Ihaka wasn't sure what that was, but he knew Jimmy hadn't got close. Father and son drastically short-changed.

Thirty-odd years of feeling aggrieved, but eventually coming back to that's the way the cookie crumbles. How else could you process it?

Some of that resentment had been directed at his father: the undisciplined lifestyle, the disregard for family history, the tough-guy code that you only went to the doctor when you'd lost the use of a limb or a bodily function had gone completely haywire, stuff coming out the wrong exit or not coming out at all. A man didn't go to the doctor because he had an ache here or a pain there, because he wasn't feeling a hundred.

But what if it wasn't his genes or his lifestyle? What if someone had robbed him of a big chunk of his life? He'd be seventy-eight now, a cantankerous old bugger wanting to know where the fuck his grandkids were. Some of the time, anyway. A while ago Ihaka had asked his mother, 'What would Dad have been like if he'd got old?' She'd closed her eyes, escaping into memories. 'Just the same,' she'd said. 'My darling Jimmy.'

Ihaka shuddered, clamped his eyes shut, gripped the steering wheel to stop his hands shaking. He really hoped there was nothing to this; he really hoped the old man had died of natural causes. If not, there would have to be a settling of accounts. There would have to be utu.

His phone rang. It was Finbar McGrail.

'And where are you on this dismal day, Sergeant?'

'Right now I'm in Tararu.'

'Don't know it.'

'On the Coromandel, just the other side of Thames.'

'I see. And what are you doing there?'

'Getting some food into me for the first time since sparrow fart. You couldn't ring back in a few minutes, could you? My fish and chips are getting cold.'

'Afraid not, I'm just going into a meeting. Can I take it the fish and chips in Tararu are worth driving all the way from Auckland for?'

109

'I wish,' said Ihaka. 'I'm just passing through, on the way back to town.'

'So which particular aspect of the Polly Stenson case took you to Coromandel?'

'No, it's the other thing.'

'The personal matter?'

'Yep.'

When McGrail eventually spoke, his voice had a bite that Ihaka wasn't used to receiving, although he'd often heard it inflicted on others. 'Now I want you to listen very carefully, Sergeant, because I'm only going to say this once. Your current rather enviable circumstance is a direct consequence of my strong interest in the Stenson case which, as you may recall, is an unsolved murder. While I understand you're exercised by the possibility that there was more to your father's death than met the eye, the Stenson investigation must take precedence. If I conclude that, contrary to our agreement, you see it the other way around, you'll be back on the roster in double-quick time, and I'll find someone who won't be distracted. You would of course have the option of reopening negotiations with DI Charlton, but I've never thought of you as someone who believes in fairies at the bottom of the garden.'

'Christ almighty, I've only just started the bloody —' Ihaka stopped talking because he realised McGrail had stopped listening. In fact, he hadn't even started.

Ihaka ate a chip. It was cold, but he wasn't that hungry any more. He plodded through the rain to dump the leftovers in a rubbish bin. When he got back to the car his phone was ringing again. He snatched it up without checking caller ID thinking, yeah, you old prick, two can play that game. Snarling, 'Give me one good reason why I shouldn't hang up in your ear.'

The little voice shook nervously. 'Tito? It's Billy speaking.'

Ihaka swore silently. 'Sorry, Billy, I was expecting some-one else. How are you, mate?'

'OK, I suppose. I miss you, Tito. When am I going to see you again?'

'Is Mum there?'

'No, she's at work.'

'Does she know you were going to ring me?'

'I asked her if I could yesterday. She said not to because you're real busy – that's why you haven't been here. Mum misses you too. She pretends she doesn't, but I can tell. I'm sorry if you're busy, Tito, but I needed to talk to you. We lost on Saturday. It would've been different if you'd been there.'

'Well, I'm sorry to hear that, mate, but remember what we talked about – you focus on doing your job and forget about all the other stuff. You can't drop your bundle because someone isn't there to watch you; that's going to happen sometimes. And the older you get, the more it'll happen.'

'It's not just you watching, it's what you tell us before the game and at half-time. The other kids think the same. Except Jarrod, of course.'

Jarrod's father was the official coach.

'OK, mate, listen, I'll do my very best to be there on Saturday. Text me when and where.'

'That's ages away. Can't you come round before then? Can't you come tonight? Please.'

'Well, that probably wouldn't suit Mum —'

'She won't be home till late,' said Billy. 'Leanne from next door's coming over.'

Ihaka glanced at his watch. It was almost half past four. 'OK, I'll come round. It won't be for a while, though, because I'm miles away, so you get your homework done and get all set for bed. And Billy: let's keep it between us, eh? Mum mightn't be too happy about me coming over when she's not there.'

'Okey-dokey,' said Billy happily.

'See you soon.'

'Can't wait.'

Ihaka started the car thinking, someone's got to tell the poor little bugger what's going on. Looks like it'll have to be me.

Easier said than done with Billy, shiny-eyed and ecstatic, jumping all over him like a puppy.

They watched a replay of a Super 15 game while the babysitter did homework in the kitchen. Billy chirped away, tucked in under Ihaka's heavy arm: why was this guy an All Black when he couldn't tackle? How come that guy was an All Black when he was so slow? A nation of armchair selectors, thought Ihaka, and we start young. Midway through the second half the questions petered out and Billy's head drooped onto Ihaka's chest.

Suddenly Ihaka felt ashamed of himself. He'd dropped out of Billy's life with no explanation, leaving Denise to spin her 'he's busier than Barack Obama' bullshit. He hadn't concerned himself with what the boy made of it or how he was dealing with it beyond thinking, c'est la vie, kid, shit happens. It's not my fault your mum's a flake.

Billy adored him. All he asked in return was Ihaka's presence for a few hours a week. And what had he got? Absence. Silence.

Looking down at the dark curls, the arm flung across his chest, the little balled fist clutching a handful of shirt to stop him getting away, Ihaka felt a flutter inside. Jesus, he thought, twice in one day. Get a fucking grip.

But why walk away? You didn't get that many shots at happiness. What made him think he was going to get a better offer? Sure, Denise could be needy, but most men would give their left plum to have a woman like her clinging onto them. When you boiled it right down, all she wanted was reassurance. Why withhold it if it meant throwing away something that felt so right? So you could look at yourself in the mirror and think, no woman's going to push me around? I might be a sad fuck, but I'm staunch?

Fuck that.

He stood up, cradling the boy in his arms. Billy stirred, slipping an arm around Ihaka's neck and murmuring into his chest.

Ihaka got Billy into bed and pulled the blankets up to his chin. As he leaned down for a hug, Billy whispered, 'Will you be here in the morning?'

'Don't think so, mate,' he said, 'but I'll see you again real soon. I promise.'

He paid the babysitter and sent her home, then stretched out on the sofa to wait for Denise.

He was woken by a prolonged metallic rattle, the sound of someone having difficulty getting a key into a keyhole. He looked at his watch: five to midnight, Jesus. The baby-sitter's parents wouldn't have been too thrilled.

The front door opened and closed. Late-night sounds floated from the kitchen: a murmured exchange; muffled laughter; an exclamation, unmistakably male and alcohol-fuelled; a 'Shhhhhhhhhh!' that went on too long and ended in giggles.

Ihaka went quietly across the room and looked around the doorway. Denise was on tiptoes stretching for a bottle on the top shelf. Her short skirt had ridden to the top of her thighs, but that wasn't high enough for her companion.

As she half-turned to slap his hand away and tug down her hem, she noticed Ihaka.

The guy saw her expression change, followed her gaze, focused blearily on Ihaka. 'Who the fuck are you?'

Ihaka glanced at him just long enough to note that he was several years younger than Denise and not even worth bitch-slapping. 'A friend of the family,' he said. 'I'll see myself out.'

She followed him to the door. 'What are you doing here?' she said, her voice awash with alcohol and indeterminate emotion.

Ihaka looked down at her, studiously expressionless. 'Just popped in to see Billy.' He opened the door and stepped out into hissing rain. 'Oh, by the way,' he said over his shoulder, 'I paid the babysitter.'

9

Tito Ihaka waited for someone to answer the doorbell, wondering, not for the first time, whether he should rethink his attitude to umbrellas.

He had three issues with umbrellas. First, they seemed kind of prissy. So what if you got rained on? It was only water, for Christ's sake. Then there was the question of what to do with them when it wasn't raining, since there was no getting away from the fact that a grown man carrying a furled umbrella was a ridiculous sight. Third, you kept losing the bastards. Ihaka had never actually bought an umbrella. Over the years and without quite knowing how or where from he'd acquired quite a few, but he never hung on to them for long. There was a definite pattern: the mysterious acquisitions and disappearances always occurred when it was pissing down. Maybe nobody bought umbrellas; they just acquired them when the need arose, as he did.

This was a classic example of the umbrella dilemma. If he had one, he would have made it from his car to Johnny Barton's front door without getting soaked. But then if it wasn't raining when he left, he'd forget it and it would be acquired by this rich prick who was taking for fucking ever to answer the door. And, on balance and all things considered, fuck that for a joke.

The door opened. Barton was a strapping six-footer with a fleshy face and receding hair going silver at the temples which accentuated the sportsman's tan. His sleeveless pullover, worn over a polo shirt with the collar turned up, had an Augusta National logo on the left breast. It was hard to believe he'd ever been a toy boy or a dope fiend.

Barton shoved out his right hand. 'Sergeant Ihaka?' He was one of those guys who treat shaking hands as a contact sport. Probably a life lesson from his old man: remember, my boy, first impressions count. Ihaka wasn't bothered: he had a big mitt and had never come across a grip he couldn't handle. He just wondered, as he always did, if people still believed you could tell a man by his handshake.

He followed Barton down the hallway to a study containing a desk too big for the space, an antique sideboard and a bookshelf full of squat hardbacks, mostly biographies of high achievers and war criminals. On the sideboard were several framed photos of Barton with a dead fish, a silver cocktail shaker and two martini glasses.

Barton directed Ihaka to a chair. 'I'm having a martini,' he said, 'and by Christ I've earned it. It's been a long day. I make a bloody good one, if I say so myself. One of the few things I can claim to be exceptionally good at.' This was accompanied by a self-satisfied chuckle signalling that nothing could be further from the truth. 'You're very welcome to join me, but they are something of an acquired taste.'

'No thanks.'

'Decisive. I like that in a guest. Can I get you something else? I'm sure there's a beer in the fridge.'

'I'm fine.'

Barton sat down behind the desk, raising his glass. 'Good health. The highlight of the day: the first martini. Mind you, the second one's not too shabby either, just

116

quietly. So after all these years you're still trying to find out who killed Polly?'

'There's been a development,' said Ihaka. 'We know why Polly was upstairs.' Barton swigged his martini. His expression didn't support the claims he'd made on its behalf. 'Just as a matter of interest, how's your conscience?'

Barton shrugged indifferently. 'Do I look like a troubled soul?'

'No, you look pretty relaxed for a guy who withheld critical information relating to a murder.'

'Easy for you to say, Sergeant; you have no idea. So who told you?'

'I'm not at liberty to reveal that.'

Barton didn't have to think about it for very long. 'That unctuous bloody hypocrite Andy Maddocks. Had to be.'

'I can neither confirm nor deny.'

'You've certainly got the jargon down pat, Sergeant. I bet you know the police manual off by heart.'

'You lose. Why didn't you speak up?'

Barton sighed, drained his martini, moved on to number two. 'My father told me, in no uncertain terms, to keep my trap shut. Presumably you know what went on with Tina Best?' Ihaka nodded. 'Well, Tim – my father – was working on a big business deal with Tina's husband, Roger. If the affair had come to light, it would've stuffed up their deal, and quite a lot more besides.'

'So it was all about money?'

'And friendship and avoiding a scandal that would've ruined several lives. But, yes, there was a lot of money at stake. You can say "So it was all about money?" in that holier-than-thou tone, but my father was a businessman: his job was to make money.'

'I thought Polly was a friend of yours.'

'I know, looking at it from the outside and with the benefit of hindsight, it seems indefensible,' said Barton in a tone that indicated he had every intention of defending himself, 'but to begin with anyway, I just assumed they'd catch whoever did it, so it wouldn't matter. Put yourself in my shoes: I was twenty-one years old, I'd screwed up big time and my father was rubbing my nose in the fact that I'd jeopardised one of the biggest deals of his career. You didn't know my father. He was a dominating, some would say domineering, individual. At his funeral, one of his oldest business associates told me the key to their relationship was he made damn sure he never got between Tim Barton and a pile of money. That's what I did: I got between Tim Barton and a pile of money. He spelt it out very bluntly that my path to redemption began with not breathing a word about Tina. It was a pretty stark choice: either do what I was told or be disowned.'

'How did he find out about you and Tina?'

Barton snorted, shaking his head. 'Murphy's Law. Roger was out of town so I paid Tina a visit. Roger had some documents for my father but didn't trust the fax, so he'd left them at their place for Tim to pick up. Only problem was, he forgot to mention it to Tina, so when Tim turned up, there was my car in the driveway. Well, he knew I wasn't there to see James, their son, because he'd gone flatting. Tina had a reputation for being what my father used to call "a handful", so I guess he just put two and two together.'

'That's quite a leap: your car in their driveway means you're riding the town bike.' Barton looked pained. 'Pardon me; I forgot I was in Remuera.'

'I don't know exactly what the process was,' said Barton coldly. 'My father didn't volunteer that information and

I wasn't in a position to demand it. Maybe he sneaked around peering in windows. Who gives a damn? He knew, he had me by the balls, and he proceeded to squeeze.'

'So what did your parents – and you for that matter – think happened to Polly?' said Ihaka. 'You must've talked about it, even if it was just to bitch about the inconvenience of it all.'

Barton was taking his second martini slowly. He held the glass under his nose, eyeing Ihaka. 'That's two snide remarks in quick succession. I really don't see why I should put up with it.'

'Don't you?' said Ihaka, sounding genuinely surprised. 'I would've thought it was pretty fucking obvious. Shall we continue?'

Barton washed down his pride with gin and vermouth. 'I don't expect you to believe this, but we didn't really talk about it. My sister and I were just numb; our parents acted not like it hadn't happened but like it had happened somewhere else. They kind of distanced themselves from it.'

'Even though she was murdered under their roof and the killer was probably a friend of theirs?'

'My parents didn't entertain the thought that the murderer was someone they knew,' said Barton, visibly exercising restraint. 'That was simply out of the question. As far as they were concerned, it must've been a gatecrasher who no one noticed or remembered. Bear in mind that even if they hadn't been plastered, very few of the guests wouldn't have known everyone there, so how would they know who was a gatecrasher and who wasn't? My father might've, but he had a lot on his mind.'

'Being the host and trying to make sure you didn't screw Tina and his business deal?'

'What else?'

'I don't know. I'm just wondering if there was other stuff going on that night.'

'Not that I'm aware of,' said Barton. 'As you said, he was the host and there were some high-powered people there, ministers and what not. Tim wasn't one to pass up an opportunity to network, especially when he was footing the bill. But at the end of the day, it was a big party and people did what they usually do at parties – including the host, who was no slouch in that respect. Actually, come to think of it, there was one aspect of it my parents did talk about: they had zero confidence in the officer in charge.'

'Why was that?'

'Well, he'd just arrived in the country, for one thing. Tim called him the Ten Pound Pom and used to imitate his accent. He was a pretty good mimic, but he didn't quite nail it because you could actually understand some of what he was saying, whereas Inspector O'Goober was damn near incomprehensible.'

'He had a foreign accent,' said Ihaka, 'so therefore he didn't know his arse from a hole in the ground? That's the sort of mindset you'd expect from some fuckwitted old pisspot down the RSA.'

'You really can be quite offensive when you put your mind to it, can't you?' said Barton. 'Or does it come naturally?'

'Bit of both. Feel free to complain to my boss.'

'I might just do that,' said Barton, reaching for a pen and notepad. 'Who is it?'

'Inspector O'Goober.' Barton peered at Ihaka, seeking confirmation that he was playing games. 'These days O'Goober, otherwise known as Superintendent Finbar McGrail, is the Auckland District Commander. He's been brooding about this case ever since; you might say he's a bit obsessed. This investigation is his baby, so if you're not taking it seriously on the assumption we're just ticking a box or going through some sort of glorified PR exercise, you better think again. As you say, back then McGrail was the Ten Pound Pom who'd just got off the plane and didn't have anyone in his corner. The guy with the power and influence and friends in high places was your old man. Well, this time around the boot's on the other foot: McGrail's got the clout and you, well, let's just say you ain't your old man.'

'Thanks for pointing that out. I don't know where you're coming from with this: I've never had any desire to follow in my father's footsteps and I've certainly got nothing to hide. By all means, turn Auckland upside down; it's no skin off my nose.' Barton stood up. 'Having said that, I don't think I've got anything further to contribute and I'm meeting someone for dinner so…'

Ihaka leaned back, stretching his legs. 'Why is Maddocks a hypocrite?'

Barton sat down, rolling his eyes. 'So it was him?' Ihaka shrugged. 'Maddocks was hopeless with girls: put them on a pedestal; treated them as if they were a superior species. You could say he made a virtue of necessity: he claimed he wasn't interested in going out with girls just for the sake of it – i.e. for recreational sex – because he was looking for a soulmate, someone with whom he could have serious conversations about all the things wrong with the world. But even girls who were that way inclined didn't want to go out with him because he was timid and boring and, at the end of the day and in one respect at least, bright girls are no different from airheads: they're only young once. He was a hypocrite because for someone so high-minded, he was very keen on hearing the grubby details of other people's sex lives, always on the lookout for a vicarious thrill. My other abiding memory of that party was Andy following around this model – she was some big shot's trophy girlfriend – like a lost puppy. It would've been hilarious if it wasn't so pathetic. I don't think he even talked to her. Just for a laugh I egged him on – you know, "No guts, no glory" – but he didn't have the nerve. To be fair, he would've had to fight his way through the throng.'

As he showed Ihaka out, Barton said, 'You might find this hard to believe, but Polly's death did knock me. I'm sure it had a lot to do with me going off the rails.'

'By going off the rails you mean becoming a junkie?'

Barton wasn't bothered by Ihaka calling a spade a spade. There might even have been a trace of mockery in his half-smile. 'Correct. These days my chequered past gives me a certain cachet.'

'Well, you look better on it than most ex-junkies I've come across.'

'I was lucky,' said Barton. 'I had a father who made it his mission in life to save me from myself and had the resources to do it. If it hadn't been for him, I would've come home in a box. So you can sneer at him and his money-making as much as you like: it goes in one ear and out the other.'

'Fair enough.'

Barton frowned, as if reluctant to take 'I get it' for an answer. 'So what now?'

'I'll go and see your mother.'

A grin of pure delight spread across Barton's soft mahogany face. 'Well, good luck with that. God, I'd love to be a fly on the wall.'

Ihaka sat in his car looking at Barton's house. It was a nice house all right, in a nice street in a nice suburb. Probably worth a couple of million dollars or, for all he knew, twice that. He sometimes felt he was the only homeowner in Auckland who wasn't fixated with the property market. Even so, you couldn't help but be aware that prices were going through the roof and there were a hell of a lot of million-dollar-plus houses around. The key seemed to be owning one in an area where white folks were prepared to live.

He checked his messages. There was a voicemail message from Denise Hadlow, who had decided that attack was the best form of defence: 'Hey. Sorry about that but, you know, really, you shouldn't just turn up unannounced. And, to be honest, I don't know where you get off sending the babysitter home. By the way, whatever you thought was going on, it wasn't what it might've looked like. Just a guy I work with who'd had a few too many.'

Her follow-up texts were more conciliatory: 'Wasn't suggesting u can't be trusted to look after Billy. Thanks for paying the sitter. How much do I owe u? Give me a call. We need to talk.' And: 'Billy's really looking forward to Saturday. We can catch up then or ring me whenever. X'

He texted back: 'I came cos Billy asked me. If he asks again I'll have to explain why its not a good idea. Maybe if u had that chat the situation wont arise. I'll be at rugby on Sat but not sure theres much to talk about.'

He found Andy Maddocks' number in the file McGrail had put together for him. Maddocks answered straight away.

'This is Detective Sergeant Ihaka from Auckland Central. Superintendent McGrail's got me looking into the Polly Stenson case.'

'I was wondering if anything would come of that conversation.'

'I just spoke to Johnny Barton. You should know it took him all of twenty seconds to work out who told us why Polly was upstairs. I wouldn't count on him buying you a beer next time you cross paths.'

'That's OK, I assumed he'd work it out. Besides, I'm fairly choosy who I drink with.'

'You two are a real mutual admiration society, aren't you? He was telling me about a model who was at the party, said you might know who she was.'

'What's she got to do with it?'

'Just a punt,' said Ihaka. 'By the sound of it most people were pretty pissed that night; her being a model, she might've had to take it easy on the grog. If so, she'd probably be worth talking to.'

'Her name was Ashley St John. Not a name – or face – you'd forget in a hurry.'

'What happened to her?'

'Who knows?' said Maddocks. 'What happens to models? Their look goes out of fashion, they get pregnant, they can't stay young and thin forever. One month she was on billboards, next month she wasn't.'

'Who was she with?'

'Benjamin Strick.'

'Have I heard of him?'

'Do you read the business pages?'

'No.'

'Then probably not. He was one of those young hot-shot entrepreneurs who made a ton of money in the eighties. The difference in his case was that he managed to hang on to most of it.'

'Is he still around?'

'Oh, very much so. He's a pillar of the establishment now.'

'Meaning he used to be dodgy?'

'I wouldn't go quite that far, but he was a young man in a hurry and they always ruffle feathers. And in business terms he was a wheeler-dealer and a money shuffler, as opposed to someone who made things.'

'I don't suppose he and Ashley are still an item.'

Maddocks laughed. 'I'd be astonished if they were. Strick was renowned for surrounding himself with an ever-changing cast of eye candy. '

When Ihaka got off the phone, he went through the list of attendees compiled by McGrail's team at the time. It didn't really matter whether Ashley St John was stone-cold sober or utterly wrecked on the night of Tim Barton's party: according to the list, she wasn't there. Nor was her date.

10

Johan Van Roon's ex-colleague finally came through: the car in which Eddie Brightside, or someone very much like him, had fled the winery was registered to a Ms Ann Smellie of Cape Cottages, East Clive, Hawke's Bay. Van Roon googled: Ms Smellie was the proprietor of three holiday cottages 'nestled in park-like grounds' on the road heading out of Clive towards Cape Kidnappers.

Van Roon didn't have fond memories of driving over the Rimutaka hill, those nights like fever dreams when he had swapped cars in Lower Hutt and roamed the Wairarapa secreting the fruits of his corruption, wondering how it had come to this, half-expecting a police road block around the next bend.

So he went the other way, retracing the route that had taken him to the beachfront shack where time stood still and the retired journalist Barry McCormick slept long and deep, his demons tranquillised by the rhythm of the waves.

Before reaching the sea, he had to negotiate an obstacle course of road works whose scale and desultoriness lent them an air of permanence. After hugging the coast for a few kilometres, the road veered inland, becoming a grid-locked strip of garish retail, the growth engine for Kapiti's mushrooming beach communities.

Then it was across the green flats of Horowhenua and Manawatu, flitting through a succession of small towns. Names like Dannevirke and Norsewood told a story (clumsily illustrated with a billboard Viking). Others, seemingly chosen for their blandness (Shannon, Linton, Woodville), slipped the memory as the outskirts disappeared from the rear-view mirror. Names aside, the places themselves left a uniform impression of small-town New Zealand: folksiness, insularity, low expectations.

It was mid-afternoon and, notwithstanding Hawke's Bay's reputation for good weather, as bleak as it had been in Wellington when Van Roon spotted the Cape Cottages sign. He assumed from the numberplate of the Honda Civic in the car port that Ms Smellie lived in the house nearest the road, rather than one of the cottages further down the drive.

The doorbell was answered by a tall, slim woman with high cheekbones and a jagged streak of grey in her artfully mussed dark hair. Her vivid blue eyes were impossible not to notice, like lights flashing in the night. Van Roon guessed she was ten years older than she looked, which was fortyish. Once he would have tried to imagine her twenty-five years ago, but following the sudden onset of middle age and disgrace he'd lost interest in both the past and the future. So this is what made Brightside break cover, he thought. It made sense.

She was used to being scrutinised, standing there with an unfocused half-smile, waiting for him to explain himself.

'You're Ann Smellie?'

'So they say.'

'My name's Johan Van Roon. I've come up from Wellington to see you.'

127

Her eyes widened in mock-surprise. 'At the risk of sounding rather pleased with myself, that hardly makes you unique.'

'I don't suppose it does. I'm a private investigator.'

Without changing her expression, she folded her arms and leaned against the door frame, letting him know that, whatever transpired, he wasn't going to be invited in. 'Well, that does give you a certain... would you call it distinction? What brings you up here, Mr Private Dick?'

'I'm looking for Eddie Brightside.'

She frowned, her gaze tilting upwards. 'Eddie Brightside?' She shook her head. 'Doesn't ring a bell. I'm pretty sure that if I'd ever come across him, I would've remembered the name, even if the man himself hadn't lingered in the memory.'

'A few days ago Brightside was seen at a winery somewhere around here,' he said. 'When the person who recognised him tried to speak to him, he shot through – in the passenger seat of your car.'

'You say you're a private investigator?' Van Roon nodded. 'So this... whatever it is has no official or legal status? Like I'd be perfectly within my rights to bid you adieu and gently but firmly close the door on you?'

'You would,' said Van Roon. 'But I'd have thought most people in your situation would be kind of curious that a private investigator has driven up from Wellington to ask them about someone they've supposedly never heard of.'

She reached back to pull the door shut. 'Let's go feed the ducks.'

Van Roon followed her around to the rear of the house, where a plush, tennis court-sized lawn bordered by flowerbeds rolled gently down to a pond. Without breaking loose-limbed stride, Smellie scooped up a basket containing pieces of bread off an outdoor table. When she summoned the ducks – 'Come on, duck-a-lucks, tea time' – an imposing figure in khaki overalls emerged from the shrubbery on the other side of the pond.

'Oh, there you are, Tip,' she said. She glanced at Van Roon. 'I really don't know what I'd do without Tip; he does all the work around here. Tip, say hello to – sorry, what was your name again?'

'Johan Van Roon.'

'Voilà.'

They eyed each other across the pond. Tip, a Maori, had a thick beard, a barrel chest and what Van Roon knew were dreadlocks tucked into a Rastafarian beanie. The last time they had come face to face was across a desk in an interrogation room at Auckland Central police station. Smellie's unsubtle message – that if Van Roon didn't clear off under his own steam, she'd have her loyal retainer put him out like the rubbish – was pertinent insofar as Tipene Farrell was an experienced practitioner of physical violence with the convictions to prove it.

Farrell gave Van Roon an almost imperceptible nod, then turned away and melted back into the shrubbery.

'A man of few words,' said Van Roon.

Smellie was tossing bits of bread to a flotilla of half a dozen ducks that darted like remote-controlled boats as they manoeuvred for prime position. 'Yes,' she said, without turning her head. 'The strong, silent type who believes actions speak louder than words. Look, I don't know how or why you've got it into your head that I know this Brightside character but, frankly, that process doesn't particularly intrigue me. I can't help you, and if I don't get a move on I'm going to be late for an appointment, so if you don't mind...'

'Fair enough,' he said. 'Sorry to bother you.'

Van Roon drove back towards the main road. About a kilometre from Cape Cottages there was an unoccupied roadside picnic area with a wooden table and benches. He swung off the road, reversed in among the trees and turned off the engine.

A few minutes later Ann Smellie zipped past in her Honda Civic. He followed her into Havelock North, the long straights and light traffic enabling him to hang back at a safe distance. She parked outside a café in one of the streets spoking off the central roundabout and went inside. Double-parked across the street, Van Roon observed her join a couple of women, taking part – a little reluctantly, it seemed to him – in the noisy, tactile, greetings ritual.

He headed back to Cape Cottages at ten kph above the speed limit. Tipene Farrell was sitting at the outdoor table smoking a roll-your-own.

'When the cat's away, the mouse has smoko, eh?' said Van Roon.

Farrell gave him a dead-eye stare. 'This is private property and you're not a cop any more, so that makes you a trespasser. Fuck off, or I'll kick your white-bitch arse.'

'That wouldn't be very smart, Tip. I mightn't be a cop any more, but I've got mates who are. A couple of them are just up the road in Napier, as a matter of fact. Now would I be right in thinking Ms Smellie isn't fully acquainted with your colourful past?'

Farrell didn't reply. He didn't have to.

'I'll take that as a no. But listen, I can keep a secret, as I'm sure you can. I'm going to have a quick nosy. You look the other way and don't mention it to Ms Smellie, and I won't tell her about your scrapes with the law. Deal?'

Farrell stubbed out his cigarette on the sole of his work boot. 'Are you going inside?'

Van Roon nodded.

'That's B and E.'

'Well, Tip, if we're going to be law-abiding, socially responsible citizens, that cuts both ways. You look like you've got a nice gig here, but how's Ms Smellie going to feel about having you around when she hears what you used to get up to?' Farrell had his head down, staring at the tabletop. 'I seem to remember there was some sex stuff in among all the other bad shit. I'll be ten minutes max, then I'll be on my way and what Ms Smellie doesn't know won't hurt her. And don't worry about her: it's not like she's in any sort of trouble, she's just holding out on me.'

As he went up the steps to the veranda Van Roon glanced over his shoulder. Farrell hadn't moved, sitting there forearms on the table, head bowed, as if absorbed in a book.

The house wasn't locked. Van Roon went room to room. There were no men's toiletries in either bathroom; no men's clothes in the wardrobes or drawers in the main or spare bedrooms; no photos of anyone resembling Brightside in the framed collection on the sideboard in the living room or among the montage on the study noticeboard. The laptop computer couldn't be accessed without a password. Everything in the filing cabinet seemed business-related.

Van Roon felt a ripple of queasiness. This wasn't how it was meant to be: breaking into someone's home; bullying an ex-con trying to make a go of it in the straight world into betraying his benefactor. He was supposed to be making himself a better person.

He headed for the exit. As he went though the kitchen, he noticed a postcard on the fridge door, a generic tropical-paradise beach scene which turned out to be Hawaii. He turned it over. It was undated, but the handwriting was easy to decipher:

Well, sweet thing, fancy running into that old prick McCormick, one of the very few people in NZ who'd still recognise me. A pain in the ass end to a delight-ful if all too short visit. Assume you'd have let me know if there'd been repercussions. Stay well. Be in touch soon.

Love, E.

He replaced the postcard and went outside. Farrell was nowhere to be seen. Van Roon drove into Havelock North and checked into a motel. He thought of ringing Caspar Quedley, but decided against it. There'd be more to report tomorrow.

Before going to see Nicky Barton, Tito Ihaka rang Beth Greendale, a former cop who did occasional off-the-books research projects for McGrail. She didn't think it would be too difficult to find out the current status and whereabouts of the former model Ashley St John.

Mrs Barton had an apartment in the Viaduct Basin but obviously wasn't in the habit of entertaining strange men, even if they were police officers. She was prepared to meet Ihaka in the lobby of the Hilton hotel at the end of Princes Wharf at 4.30 pm, and if that didn't suit him, then that was just too bad.

She was already there, a stick figure with her hair permed into an orange-grey helmet who looked as if she no longer derived any pleasure from eating, drinking or being merry, assuming she ever had. The glint in her bright eyes reminded Ihaka of an angry bird, the sort that dive-bombs picnicking children.

He pretended to listen to a monologue in which peevish queries buzzed like trapped flies. Why was he raking over these coals? Why couldn't he leave that poor girl – and her for that matter – in peace? What possessed him to believe she had anything to contribute to what was, in any case, a futile exercise?

'Have you heard from your son?'

'Yes. For some reason he seemed to think you and I would get on like a house on fire.' Her exasperated glare demanded an explanation.

'I think that's his idea of a joke,' said Ihaka.

Mrs Barton sniffed. 'My son has several shortcomings, one of which is a tendency to be amused by things that are no laughing matter.'

'This is a list,' he said, passing it over, 'drawn up by the investigating team with your husband's assistance, of every-one who was at your house that night. Well, that's what it was meant to be, but we now know it's incomplete. I'd appreci-ate it if you could have a look and tell me who's missing.'

Mrs Barton handed the list straight back to him. 'I'll do no such thing.' She said it without heat or particular emphasis, as if no reasonable person would expect any other response.

'Why not?'

'For obvious reasons several of our guests, people of stature, asked my husband to keep their names out of it. For equally obvious reasons he obliged. To give you those names now would amount to breaking my husband's word. I'm simply not prepared to do that.'

'Your husband did the wrong thing, Mrs Barton. He obstructed a murder investigation. This is your chance to put that right.' She responded to this invitation by sipping her tea and consulting her mobile. 'But you're not going to do that, are you? You're going to be as unhelpful as he was.'

'If you wish to put it like that, yes.'

'There are plenty of other ways I could put it. That's as polite as they get.'

'I tend not to respond well to bullying, Sergeant.'

'That makes two of us.'

Mrs Barton put down her teacup with a long-suffering sigh. 'While I think this is a complete waste of time, I'm not setting out to be unhelpful. But you've asked me to do something that I cannot in all conscience do. Respecting one's late husband's wishes is probably a very old-fashioned, fuddy-duddy concept, but I dare say plenty of people would tell you I'm an old-fashioned fuddy-dud.'

'You talked about "obvious reasons". They're not obvious to me, so why don't you spell them out?'

'These were prominent people – leading businessmen, politicians and so forth. I would have thought it was obvious why they wouldn't want to get dragged into that dreadful business. And seeing they clearly had nothing to do with it, my husband saw no harm in obliging them.'

'And the reason they clearly had nothing to do with it was that they were prominent people, correct?'

'Of course. Again, character and substance and social position might be old-fashioned notions, but —'

'You're an old-fashioned person?'

Mrs Barton smiled microscopically. 'There we are. That wasn't so hard, was it?'

'OK, how about this: why don't you put me on to some-one who could do what it's unfair to ask you to do – look at the list and fill in the gaps?'

She sat back, dropping her hands onto her lap and plucking at her skirt, giving Ihaka a glimpse of what lay behind the façade of implacable self-assurance. 'Goodness, that's tricky. The young ones wouldn't be much help: they didn't really know who was who and most of them would have rather hazy memories of the party. A lot of what happened that night could be put down to too much alcohol. That was one subject on which my husband and I didn't see eye to eye. As for my generation, well, it's a question of who's still with us and still has all their marbles. There's Tina Best, of course, but it's a moot point whether she had all her marbles to begin with. Besides, she had other things on her mind.'

'Until you and your husband headed her off at the pass.'

'I beg your pardon.'

'She and Johnny were off upstairs for a romantic inter-lude when you cut in. You took her off to look at your new curtains, and your husband roped Johnny into a conversa-tion with some judge. Isn't that what happened?'

'I don't follow you. Yes, I showed Tina our new cur-tains, but I didn't cut her off at the pass or whatever you called it.'

'Hang on, you're telling me you and your husband didn't stop Tina and Johnny sneaking off for a quickie?'

'You mean a tryst?'

'If that involves sex, then yes, that is what I mean.'

'We didn't do anything of the sort. We didn't find out what was going on between those two until the next day or the day after. I can't remember exactly when Tim told me, but it definitely wasn't until after the party.'

'Is it possible he'd known about it for a while but hadn't told you?'

Mrs Barton rolled her eyes. 'Don't be ridiculous.'

Ihaka sat back, frowning. 'So how did he find out?'

'He told me Johnny had confessed all,' she said, 'and I took his word for it.'

'That sounds like you weren't entirely convinced.'

'I wasn't. Owning up when he wasn't even under suspicion would've been entirely out of character.'

'So why —?'

'Did my husband tell me he'd confessed? Tim would have calculated that, under those circumstances, I'd be less inclined to cast the boy out on his ear.'

'And you went along with it because it gave you an excuse not to practise what you'd preached?'

Mrs Barton thought about taking offence. 'I don't think that's —'

'I don't blame you. So how long did you and Tina look at the curtains?'

She shrugged. 'Five minutes; possibly ten. They were lovely curtains, but they were still just curtains.'

'Then what?'

'It was a party, for goodness' sake. I may be old-fashioned, but there were rather more interesting options than discussing household furnishings with Tina Best. No doubt she felt the same way. One thing you most certainly couldn't accuse Tina of being was old-fashioned.'

Ihaka had a family dinner at his mother's place. When he got home there was an email from Beth Greendale in his inbox.

Well, as we probably should have worked out for ourselves, Ashley St John is a nom de catwalk. You'll see why shortly. She went over to Australia in 1988 and got into the commercial, mainstream, yummy mummy end of the market, doing David Jones catalogues etc. In 1992 she married a stockbroker and quit modelling – as you would. When the marriage broke up in 2007, she reverted to her maiden name Ann Smellie (see what I mean?) and bought a holiday home business in Hawke's Bay. Link to the Cape Cottages website attached.

Beth

11

Ann Smellie had disliked Johan Van Roon at first sight. Since then she'd revised her opinion downwards.

When he reappeared at her place the following morning, she eyed him as if he'd slithered out of her pond with a twitching duck in his jaws. 'Well, this is serendipitous. I was just about to ring the police to lay a complaint against you. Now I can tell them exactly where you are.'

'Farrell told you, did he?'

She nodded. 'When he was explaining why he can't look after my property any more. You must be very proud of yourself.'

'Not particularly,' said Van Roon. 'But if his background doesn't bother you, why should he quit?'

'I tried to talk him out of it, but he'd made up his mind. A matter of principle, he said. Not a concept you'd be familiar with.'

A phone rang inside. Van Roon asked her if she wanted to answer it.

'If it's important they'll leave a message,' she said. 'Anyway, we're done here.'

'You're taking a pretty lofty tone for someone who lied through their teeth,' said Van Roon. 'If you'd told the truth, it wouldn't have happened.'

Smellie's face tightened. 'First off, I had no obligation, legal or otherwise, to tell you a damn thing,' she said, biting off the words. 'Secondly, that's based on information you got by breaking into my house. I'm ringing the police right now, so feel free to make a run.' The mobile she was holding blared into life. 'Hello? You're from the police, you say? Well, there's another coincidence: I was just about to ring you to report a crime. Unlawful trespass – is that what it's called?… I do, as a matter of fact: a private investigator who says his name is Van Roon, unlikely as that sounds… Yes, you heard right: Van Roon. What's more, I can give you his exact current location because he's right here in front of me… What?' She held the phone at arm's length, frowning at it as if it had gone haywire, then handed it to Van Roon. 'He wants to speak to you.'

'Who does?'

'Some policeman. I didn't catch his name.'

He put the phone to his ear. 'Van Roon.'

Tito Ihaka said, 'What the fuck are you doing there?'

Van Roon aped Smellie's expression. 'Tito? I'm on a job. One you helped me get, as a matter of fact.'

'Through Quedley?'

'Yep.'

'What's the job?'

'I'm trying to find this guy who disappeared back in August 1987.'

'Did you say August '87?'

'Yeah, why?'

'Go on.'

'Well, my enquiries led me to this address, as they say.' Van Roon glanced at Smellie, who had brought her sulky model face out of retirement.

'Tell me about this guy.'

Van Roon was warming to the subject of Eddie Brightside when Ihaka cut in: 'Put her back on.'

Van Roon gave Smellie the phone, shrugging to let her know he was as much in the dark as she was.

'Ms Smellie,' said Ihaka, 'you attended a party at Tim Barton's house in Auckland on election night 1987, correct?'

'Yes I did. What's that got to do with —?'

'Was this Brightside character there?' When she didn't respond, Ihaka added, 'I'm sure you remember what happened that night, so be careful how you answer.'

'Yes, he was.'

'OK, I'm getting the first flight down and coming straight to your place, so stay put, all right? Let me speak to Van Roon again.'

She returned the phone to Van Roon.

'I'm coming down,' said Ihaka. 'You've got some explaining to do too.'

'You want me to pick you up?'

'I can think of a couple of reasons why that's a fuckwitted suggestion. Seeing you obviously give that woman the shits, I suggest you bugger off. I'll ring you when I'm on the ground.'

Van Roon returned the phone to Smellie. 'Looks like we're in the same boat.'

'What a horrible thought. Which boat would that be?'

'The boat that's about to get rocked.'

Van Roon got out of his car as Ihaka's taxi pulled up outside Cape Cottages. They exchanged nods. 'How's life?' asked Ihaka.

'Marginal,' said Van Roon.

Ihaka raised his eyebrows, as if he'd expected as much. 'After you.'

140

Maybe Ann Smellie had heeded Van Roon's warning, because she'd gone the extra mile: made a pot of plunger coffee, laid out an array of home baking, put on full make-up and slipped into something less comfortable than the tracksuit pants and baggy sweater she'd had on earlier. It seemed to have the desired effect. While there was nothing pretty about the way Ihaka piled into the food – he claimed he'd skipped lunch in the rush to get down there – he was uncharacteristically mannerly as he outlined his cold-case assignment before inviting Smellie to explain how she came to be at Barton's party.

She was twenty-three then, kind of a hot property on the modelling scene. Being Wellington-based, it was inevitable that she came to the attention of the boy wonder, Benny Strick. These days, so she'd heard, he didn't answer to Benny; it was Benjamin or, if you insisted on being familiar and had something he wanted, Ben. But back when he was the youngest and speediest of the high rollers in the recently opened casino economy, he was Benny. It went with the image of rock-and-roll tycoon, the guerrilla of the stockmarket who made a fortune overnight and had spent half of it by close of trading the following day.

In fact, Strick wasn't all that different from the others. He lived in a mansion overlooking the Heretaunga – Royal Wellington to you – Golf Club, which he'd filled with art deco treasures. He had a ridiculous number of cars. He played a lot of golf. He jetted around the world to watch horse races and Grand Prix. And he exploited his wealth and fame to sleep with a lot of women who wouldn't have looked twice at him if he'd been Benny Strick, plumber, or Benny Strick, chartered accountant, or even Benny Strick, penniless artist with a beautiful mind.

She went into it with her eyes open, aware of Strick's reputation as a scalp collector and understanding her trophy status, but thinking it would be fun while it lasted. Even so, she was surprised at how quickly the thrill wore off. Where's the fun in being extravagant when you can afford to be? She had a reputation for cynicism, but it surprised and disappointed her how many celebrities were either charmless or just another grey drone from the suburbs.

Given that it wouldn't be for long, she thought she could put up with being treated as a possession, an acquisition that Strick could show off to his cronies, like the white Bakelite telephone which had once sat in the office above the Banque Rothschild on Avenue George V from which Madame Claude ran her legendary call-girl operation. But it's hard to maintain your self-respect when you're a prize, put on display, assessed, handled, passed around, just to bolster a rich man's reputation for having the best of everything and always getting what he wants. The problem was that modelling had prepared her for being an actor in someone else's fantasy, and modelling's little everyday humiliations had made her passive. But if she couldn't walk away, she could at least subvert the arrangement by denying Strick the monopoly he took for granted. At least that was how she thought of it at the time. Years later a shrink explained that it was a subconscious exit strategy: she wanted to get caught so the decision would be taken out of her hands.

Eddie Brightside was on the fringe of Strick's circle. He lacked the others' money and status, but he had something none of them had and some of them envied: a whiff of notoriety, a hint of mystery, an association with a world they read about in airport novels. They talked about him when he wasn't there, stuff she barely understood and soon forgot, but she liked that their money couldn't buy his worldliness. And, like her, he was in a relationship he wanted out of, but couldn't summon the will to end.

'So at the time of the party,' said Ihaka, 'how long had you been carrying on with Brightside?'

Smellie arched an eyebrow. '"Carrying on"? How quaint.'

'If I put my mind to it,' said Ihaka, 'I could probably come up with something a bit more down-to-earth.'

Smellie was unprepared for Ihaka's unblinking comeback. She'd expected a better return on the trouble she'd gone to. 'Not long. Maybe a month.'

'And Strick had no idea?'

'Not that I knew. He certainly gave no indication.'

'What about the party itself?'

'I remember thinking no expense had been spared and no one seemed very interested in the election. At some point Benny trotted out his signature line – 'Money never sleeps' – and disappeared. I went looking for Eddie, but it turned out he was at the same meeting.'

'Where did that take place?' asked Ihaka.

'Upstairs, apparently.'

'Seeing you were on intimate terms with two of the participants, you'd obviously know who else was there and what it was in aid of.'

'Really? Benny didn't choose his female companions for their ability to discuss high finance or world affairs, and the job description certainly didn't include being a confidante. If anything, Eddie was even less prone to pillow talk. All I gathered was it was about what effect the election would have.'

'Was Strick into politics?' asked Van Roon, his intervention drawing irritated glances from the others.

'Well, seeing the subject came up,' said Ihaka impatiently, 'was he?'

Smellie examined her fingernails. 'They were all the same, the rich boys: they loved Labour's economic policies but didn't like the anti-nuke stuff.'

'Glad we got that sorted,' said Ihaka. 'Who else was at the meeting?'

'Look, I'm sorry, Sergeant,' said Smellie, 'but I'm not the fund of knowledge you were obviously expecting. I'm sure names were mentioned, but the only one I remember is Gerry Waitz.'

'Super-rich American who's got a place in the Wairarapa,' said Van Roon. 'Friend of Brightside's; thought the nuclear-ships policy was a commie plot.'

Smellie looked at Van Roon as if he had performed a nifty card trick, knowing it involved sleight of hand but still slightly impressed.

'You get that from Quedley?' said Ihaka.

Van Roon nodded. 'Partly.'

'Who's his client?'

'Don't know,' said Van Roon. 'He didn't share that with me.'

Ihaka turned back to Smellie. 'Carry on.'

'Time passed. I drank a lot of champagne and pretended to be interested in what various people were saying to me. Then Benny reappeared with Waitz and a couple of others I didn't know and said, we're out of here.'

'Why?'

'I did ask, and was told to shut the fuck up and do what I was told. Or words to that effect.'

'So Strick was a bit worked up?'

'It would be fair to say there was precious little sign of the bonhomie of earlier in the evening. There was a lot of urgent muttering going on.'

'Was Brightside there?'

'No.'

'Where was he?'

'How would I know? Under the circumstances I thought it best not to show too much interest in Eddie.'

'Then what?'

'Then we left.'

'Waitz and co as well?'

'Yes, we all trooped out together. People were looking at us like, what the fuck? It's not even midnight.'

'You're sure of the time?' said Ihaka.

'Quite sure,' she said. 'I remember thinking, wow, party of the year and we're not even staying till tomorrow. I was pissed off we were leaving so early and Benny was pissed off about whatever, so it was a bummer all round. And the worst was yet to come: Benny dumped me at the hotel; said he was staying on for a couple of days so I'd have to make my own way back to Wellington.'

'When did you find out about the murder?'

'After I got back. I was talking about my weekend and someone said, "Were you at the party where that girl got murdered?" It was the first I'd heard of it.'

'What did you think?'

'Well, being philosophically opposed to murder, I took a pretty dim view of it.'

'Then you were in the minority,' said Ihaka. 'Because, as far as I can tell, most people there didn't give a shit.'

Smellie was finding out that if you sparred with Ihaka, you had to be able to take a counterpunch. 'It was freaky,' she said hurriedly. 'I probably walked right past her and a couple of hours later she was murdered, right there in that swanky house with all those people around.'

'You and Strick must've talked about it.'

145

'Well, it came up, but only in the context of "Can you believe it?"'

'That's it?'

'Yes, that's it. And don't look at me as if I'm a heartless bitch. The fact is Benny and I didn't talk about anything very much from that point on. I only saw him another two or three times.'

'What happened?'

'The phone stopped ringing. And when I ran into him at some do, he looked straight through me. Call me a glass half-empty person, but I took that to mean I was past tense.'

'Because he'd found out about you and Brightside?' asked Van Roon.

Smellie looked to Ihaka, wanting him to tell Van Roon to butt out. He returned her pointed look, waiting for an answer.

Her mouth turned down. 'Well, I don't know that because we weren't speaking, were we?' she said. 'But that's what I was told.'

'How would he have found out?' asked Van Roon.

'I guess someone saw us,' she said. 'As a friend of mine says, Wellington would be perfect if it wasn't for the weather, the earthquake risk and the fact that it's too small to get away with anything.'

Ihaka said, 'How did you find Sydney in that respect?'

She gave him a drop-dead stare. 'It's umpteen times bigger than Wellington. Go figure.'

Van Roon asked, 'How was Brightside when you saw him next?'

'Not himself,' she said. 'Distracted.'

'What did you put that down to?'

'I assumed he was psyching himself up to dump his girlfriend.'

'Were you putting the pressure on?'

'He was putting it on himself,' she said icily. 'I've never put pressure on a man to ditch the other woman. She's his problem, not mine.'

'So you were happy to go on being the bit on the side?'

'You need to get past the Rotary Club clichés, Mr Dick. In those days men were like buses at rush hour; it was just a matter of which one you caught.'

Ihaka cleared his throat. To Van Roon: 'You can brief me on Brightside's disappearance on the way to the airport.' To Smellie: 'What was your take on it?'

'Eddie told me Benny had found out about us and was threatening to do everything in his power to put him out of business, so he was off overseas to check things out work-wise.'

'Did that ring true?'

Smellie shrugged. 'Benny was a rich guy with a big ego: I didn't find it too hard to believe. And as I said, next time I saw him I got the big freeze.'

'When did you next hear from Brightside?' asked Van Roon.

'This is where it gets complicated,' she said. 'I got work in Hong Kong at very short notice. When the gig finished, I went to London planning to do a quick jaunt round Europe but I met someone and, before I knew it, a year had gone by. Eddie eventually tracked me down, but by then I was married and living in Sydney. He actually came to Sydney just to gaze upon me from afar. Well, that's what he told me, anyway.'

'So when did you two reconnect?'

'When I moved back here after my marriage broke up.'

'OK,' said Ihaka. 'Where is he?'

She shrugged again, evasively this time. 'Not here, I can tell you that much. He's overseas. He travels a lot. No fixed abode, you might say.'

Ihaka leaned towards her. 'I need to talk to him. ASAP.'

She nodded. 'I'll tell him.'

Ihaka stayed in close, peering into her face. 'He doesn't go by the name Eddie Brightside these days, does he?'

Smellie shook her head fractionally.

'What does he call himself?'

'I need to talk to him,' she said. 'It's only fair.'

'You do that,' said Ihaka. 'Today. And when I ring you tomorrow morning, all my questions will be answered.'

They were driving to Napier Airport, Ihaka on the phone organising a flight-risk alert on Ann Smellie. When that was done, Van Roon said, 'You went pretty easy on her.'

'No point doing otherwise,' said Ihaka. 'She's going to pass on everything I said, so why spell out that Brightside's the prime suspect in the Stenson murder? Not that it matters: he's going to figure it out for himself.'

'There's no way he's coming back.'

'No,' said Ihaka. 'But one way or another, she's going to give up his alias. Life's about to get more complicated for Eddie fucking Brightside.'

'You're convinced he did it?'

'What do you think?'

'Well, yeah,' said Van Roon, 'the disappearance sort of speaks for itself.'

When he dropped Ihaka off outside the terminal, Van Roon said, 'Just like old times.'

Ihaka looked over Van Roon's shoulder into the middle distance. 'No, it's not,' he said. 'It's nothing like old times.'

* * *

148

As he waited for his plane, Ihaka rang the PR man Caspar Quedley to ask if Benjamin Strick was the client on whose behalf he'd hired Van Roon. When Quedley went into the client-confidentiality routine, Ihaka interrupted to say he'd take that as a yes. That being the case, Quedley should be aware that his client was now up to his eyeballs in a murder investigation. Keeping his name out of the original investigation had probably seemed like a good idea at the time, but now it had come back to bite him on the arse.

Quedley took a while to digest this. 'You obviously want me to do something about it, but I'm having trouble working out what that would be.'

'How about you get hold of the prick and tell him I'm looking forward to getting the cooperation he refused to provide at the time. To get the ball rolling, I'd like answers to the following questions: did he run Brightside out of town for porking his girlfriend? Why is he after Brightside now? And who else was at the meeting that took place at Barton's party?'

Quedley rang back as Ihaka was walking to his car. 'I spoke to the client,' he said. 'He asked me to convey his assurance that you'll have his full cooperation. As we speak, he's racking his brains to remember who was at the meeting. As for your former colleague's assignment, the short answer is that my client's doing it for fun and because he can. He says he most certainly didn't run Brightside out of town for porking, as you put it, his girlfriend. In fact, he only found out about that the day Brightside disappeared. And the reason he found out about it was that Brightside left a message on his answerphone saying, I just thought you'd be interested to know I've been fucking your girlfriend for the past two months.'

12

Finbar McGrail's secretary no longer bothered to protest when Tito Ihaka showed up with that bulldog glower which meant he was going to barge into her boss's office without an appointment, explanation, excuse or, needless to say, an apology.

She'd learned from bitter experience that it was a waste of breath, like telling her Labrador not to belly-flop in muddy puddles when she let him off the lead at the local park. Bitter experience had also taught her that, while her boss encouraged her to err on the side of obduracy in the role of gatekeeper, Ihaka was the exception to the rule, as he was to most rules.

McGrail justified this indulgence on the grounds that Ihaka rarely, if ever, barged into his office just for the sake of it, unlike certain officers who seemed to regard face-time with the Auckland District Commander as an achievement in and of itself. It was a source of constant irritation and occasional despair for McGrail that these officers were at their most creative and proactive when applying themselves to the challenge of getting past his secretary and into his office in order to lobby, undermine colleagues or simply brown-nose.

The secretary didn't buy McGrail's explanation. Over time and with great reluctance she'd come to the conclusion that McGrail didn't put up with Ihaka's unannounced visits; he enjoyed them.

She still found it hard to believe. Yes, she was aware that opposites can attract, but this was ridiculous. If it was a case of Ihaka marching to the beat of a different drum, or thinking outside the square, or even being a bit of a maverick, then fine, she could understand that. She'd read somewhere that organisations need that sort of person, and leaders need to have their thinking tested by them from time to time. But no one in their right mind would describe Ihaka in those terms. Different labels were called for: liability; loose cannon; rogue element; affront to everything McGrail stood for.

However, she couldn't deny the evidence of her own ears. Whenever she put her ear to the door – not that she made a habit of it – she was shocked by what she heard. Oh, she knew Ihaka had a foul mouth – you couldn't work in the same building as him without finding that out the hard way – but she'd taken it for granted that he minded his Ps and Qs around McGrail, who was renowned for being proper, as her mother used to say, or stitched-up, as quite a few people she worked with did say. Not a bit of it. Ihaka was his usual rude, crude and unattractive self, and McGrail didn't seem in the least bothered by it.

So while it went against the grain, the secretary had revised her approach to dealing with Ihaka. Rather than bristle at his high-handedness, she now bent over backwards to be civil. She couldn't bear the man, couldn't for the life of her understand why McGrail had a soft spot for him and, from what she'd observed, so little time for certain other officers. Officers she liked; officers who went out of their way to be pleasant, to ask after her family, swap

151

gossip, have a wee giggle about this or that. Unlike Ihaka, whose idea of a pleasantry was a Neanderthal grunt.

But he was McGrail's favourite, and that was that. She just had to wear it. She couldn't afford to show her true feelings in case he had some sort of hold over McGrail. Because one thing was for certain: if Ihaka knew what she really thought of him, he'd be whispering poisonously in McGrail's ear. That's just the sort of nasty piece of work he was. Luckily she was a pretty good actress, even if she said so herself.

Ihaka entered McGrail's office, firmly closing the door behind him. 'When are you going to give that old dragon the arse?' he asked.

McGrail peeled off his spectacles, taking his time, as if wanting to be sure there wasn't a nugget of idiot-savant wisdom buried in the bluster.

'Marcia? Now why would I want to do that? She's loyal, highly efficient, very well-organised. Can't fault her, really.'

Ihaka dropped heavily into one of the chairs in front of McGrail's desk. 'She hates my guts, the bitch.'

'How can you tell? Doesn't she respond to your friendly overtures?'

'What friendly overtures?'

'Precisely. Therein lies the problem. It actually doesn't take much to get Marcia on side: a friendly word here and there; an occasional dollop of that charm you're so miserly with. The golden rule doesn't play much of a role in your interactions with the rest of the human race, does it, Sergeant?'

'The golden rule would be fine if everybody followed it,' said Ihaka. 'But they don't.'

'So you've decided not to take any chances?'

'Exactly.'

'In fact, you go further than that: you get your retaliation in first.'

'It works for me.'

'Well, I suppose that depends how you define "works". I can't help but notice that no one else seems to have a problem with Marcia.'

'Yeah, right,' scoffed Ihaka. 'As if any of those bumsuckers are going to bad-mouth your secretary. You want to know what really gives me the shits?' He put on a grotesquely smarmy voice. '"Now you have a really nice day, Sergeant, and be sure to pass on a kind wish to your dear old Mum next time you're talking to her." What the fuck's that about? She's never met my mother.'

McGrail shook his head, bemused by Ihaka's overreaction to everyday unctuousness. 'She has, in the past, been a little exercised by your tendency to bypass her and the appointment system in general. I've made the point that you only do it when you have something important to discuss. I hope that's still the case.'

'What do you want first, the good news or the bad news?'

'You know the answer: let's get the bad news out of the way. Then I'll be in a position to judge how good the good news is.'

'Actually, that doesn't work. You've got to have the good news first.'

'Then why offer the choice?'

'It's just a saying: I've got good news and I've got bad news.'

'I'm approaching the point at which no news would be good news.'

Ihaka smiled, appreciating McGrail's tart rejoinder. 'OK, we've got a suspect for the Stenson killing.'

'Now, that's excellent news – on the face of it, and bearing in mind the imminent disclosure of bad news.'

'You know how you got stuffed around during the investigation? It was worse than you thought: some of Barton's mates got him to keep their names out of it. And a bunch of them whose names weren't on your list had a meeting – upstairs. So far I've got three names: Benny Strick —'

'I know who he is.'

'Gerry Waitz, a mega-rich Yank, and a political fixer called Eddie Brightside.'

McGrail shook his head. 'Those names certainly didn't come up.'

'Couple of interesting things about Brightside: one, he was rooting Strick's girlfriend.' Ihaka paused, waiting for McGrail's reaction. There wasn't one. McGrail's blank expression gave no indication whether he was choosing to ignore Ihaka's salaciousness or lacked a frame of reference and perhaps the vocabulary to do justice to it.

Ihaka continued: 'Well, I thought it was interesting. Two, less than a fortnight after the murder, Brightside disappeared. As in vanished off the face of the earth; as in never been seen, heard from or heard of since. Until last week, when he popped up in Hawke's Bay.'

McGrail had been swinging his spectacles by the arm. Now he put the tip of the arm between his lips, dangling the spectacles from his mouth. Ihaka had never seen him do that, or anything remotely like it. If he'd thought about it, he would have classified it as one of those things, like the Great Wall of China and the Siberian tiger, that, realistically, he would probably never set eyes on.

Noticing Ihaka's incredulity, McGrail put the glasses aside, out of easy reach. 'Now that is interesting, Sergeant. Fascinating, even. So where is Brightside as we speak?'

154

'Which brings us to the bad news,' said Ihaka flatly. 'He's skipped the country. When the bloke who recognised him tried to talk to him, he took off. Ann Smellie, the woman he was with, Strick's two-timing trophy girlfriend back in 1987, the one you weren't interested in when I mentioned her just now, she knows where Brightside is. And as soon as we're done here, I'm going to get her to tell me.'

'She'll either refuse, or she'll lie.'

Ihaka nodded. 'Then I'll put the squeeze on her to give up Brightside's alias. We've just got to hope the bastard hasn't got more than one fake passport.'

'So what's your theory, Sergeant?'

'Well, we were working on the premise that Polly saw or heard something she shouldn't have, right? This is the timing: about 11.30 Johnny Barton sent her upstairs; just before midnight Strick and co came back downstairs without Brightside. Something happened up there. According to Smellie, they were jumpy. Strick said "We've got to go", but wouldn't say why. She's absolutely sure they left Barton's place just before midnight; time of death was between twelve and one. I'm thinking Polly walked in on them discussing something pretty bloody shady, so they got the fuck out of there, leaving the fixer to fix it. Which he did.'

McGrail nodded. 'It's plausible.'

'It would explain why Strick was so keen to keep their names out of it, and why Brightside disappeared and has stayed off the radar ever since. And it would kind of explain why Strick hired none other than Johan Van Roon to check out the Brightside sighting.'

'Are you telling me Van Roon's involved?'

'He sure is. I ran into him in Hawke's Bay yesterday.'

'Is he going to be a problem?'

Ihaka laughed mirthlessly. 'Come on, the guy's trouble waiting to happen. You know that.'

'Indeed I do,' said McGrail a little testily. 'But it's one thing to have him down in Wellington ticking away like a time bomb; it's another thing altogether for him to be involved in an investigation.'

'Don't worry about it,' said Ihaka. 'I'll keep him in his box.'

McGrail came out from behind his desk to sit next to Ihaka. He leaned forward, elbows on knees. 'Sergeant, you know I've got great faith in you. You also know I've backed you if not quite through thick and thin then more often than not, and sometimes when it wasn't in my best interests to do so.'

'Yeah, I know.'

'So when you tell me not to worry, that you've got it under control, I'm reassured – up to a point. You don't need me to spell out the scale of the PR disaster we'd have on our hands if the media were to discover the precise circumstances behind Van Roon's resignation, and that we'd subsequently used him in an unofficial capacity in a murder investigation. I need an iron-clad guarantee that won't happen.'

'He's got a pretty good handle on Brightside.'

'Get him to share that knowledge, by all means,' said McGrail. 'But he's not one of us, Sergeant. Treat him as you would any other civilian with known criminal, if not sociopathic, tendencies. Is that clear?'

'Yep.'

'Why do you think Strick hired him?'

'I'm guessing for the same reason he would've been fucking ecstatic when Brightside shot through. He's worried that if we get our hands on Brightside, he'll give it the old "I was only following orders".'

'You really think Strick would've instructed Brightside to kill Polly? She overheard something extraordinarily damaging?'

'Maybe wires got crossed in the panic. Maybe the message was "whatever it takes", and Brightside ran out of ideas when Polly told him to stick the all-expenses-paid trip to Disneyland up his shitpipe. Who knows? The point is, the last fucking thing Strick would want is Brightside in custody saying, yeah, OK, it was me, but I just did what the big shots told me to do.'

'I see what you mean,' said McGrail. 'Which raises the question: if Van Roon had tracked Brightside down, what was Strick planning to do then?'

When Ann Smellie answered the phone, she got, 'This is Ihaka. Where is he?'

'Good morning to you too, Sergeant.'

'We did that stuff yesterday,' said Ihaka. 'Now it's for real. So I'll ask you again: where is he?'

'Look, it's not that straightforward —'

'Can I be blunt, Ms Smellie?'

'Something tells me you're not really seeking my permission.'

'Don't fuck with me, all right? Because if you do, I promise you, you'll regret it. You could fill your cottages for a year with people who wish to Christ they'd never even thought about crossing me.'

'You say that with some pride.'

'Not proud of it, not ashamed of it; it's just the way it is. See, what I'm doing here is trying to find out who murdered a seventeen-year-old girl who probably didn't do a bad thing in her life. A nice, bright kid who loved her parents and just wanted to make them proud. When she went, she took a big piece of them with her, and they hadn't done anything to deserve it either.' Ihaka's voice dropped and his tone softened, as if he was sharing a confidence. 'I don't have time to be the friendly neighbourhood policeman. If people are going to make this thing more difficult than it already is, if they're going to lie and fuck me around to protect the killer, they need to understand there'll be consequences. They need to know I'll smash their fucking little world to pieces.'

'I get the message,' said Smellie shakily. 'This isn't easy for me. I'm in a very awkward position.'

'Just tell me where he is and what name or names he's using. He can't expect you to put yourself in the shit so he can walk away without a scratch. Well, maybe he does, but what sort of arsehole would that make him?'

'You think he killed her, don't you?'

'I think he could help us solve this case.'

'That's cop-speak. It's obvious you think he did it. More to the point, he thinks you think he did it.'

'Ms Smellie, don't waste my time. If you're not going to cooperate, just say so and I'll go to Plan B.'

'He swears he didn't do it.'

'They always do. You'll be hearing from us.'

'Just hold your horses, all right? Eddie's prepared to talk to you, face to face. Well, not to you per se.'

'Who's he got in mind, Oprah?'

Smellie laughed nervously. 'Not quite. He'll talk to your friend Van Roon.'

'Van Roon's not a friend of mine and he's not a cop. The fact that he used to be doesn't count for shit.'

'Oh, Eddie knows all about Van Roon. Does the name Tipene Farrell mean anything to you, Sergeant?'

'Maybe.'

'Until the day before yesterday Tipene looked after my property. Very well too, I might add. Then Van Roon turned up. Apparently they go way back. Van Roon guessed, correctly, that Tip hadn't been entirely forthcoming with me about his chequered past and tried to blackmail him into looking the other way while he – Van Roon, that is – broke into my house. Tip told me all this in his resignation speech. He also said word on the street has it that Van Roon left the police force under a cloud. Not to put too fine a point on it, he was a corrupt cop.'

'I'm not going to discuss internal police matters.'

'You don't have to. It doesn't matter. What matters is that Eddie's intrigued by Van Roon – the compromised individual, the rise-and-fall narrative. I can assure you I didn't encourage it. In fact I was quite damning in my assessment of Van Roon, which was probably a mistake because it was all just grist to Eddie's mill. You should know that he has a perverse sense of humour – and a highly developed sense of mischief.'

'Jesus Christ,' muttered Ihaka. 'Just what I fucking need. So what's the deal?'

'The meeting will take place overseas. Eddie's getting in touch today to tell me when and where; I'll pass that on to Van Roon. Then it's a matter of Van Roon getting himself to the rendezvous point. Assuming you want to take up the offer, of course.'

'Who's supposed to pay for it?'

Smellie laughed. 'Sergeant, if you think Eddie gives a flying fuck about that, you really have no idea who you're dealing with.'

Ihaka left a message telling Van Roon he'd be hearing from Ann Smellie and to ring as soon as he'd spoken to her.

159

The call back came late that afternoon, Van Roon saying, 'Well, shit, I didn't see that coming,' and Ihaka replying, 'Join the fucking club. What's the story?'

'I fly to Nadi, go to the Fiji Airways transfer lounge and await further instructions. That's it.'

'So you might have to jump on another plane?'

'That was the implication.'

'Fuck.'

'Your call, Tito: do I do this?'

'We don't have a choice.'

'Of course you do. It's a twenty-seven-year-old cold case: no one's expecting it to be wrapped up all nice and neat. You've got your suspect; now you can write a report saying "This is where I got to, over to you".'

'I don't operate like that,' said Ihaka.

'I know you don't, but that's exercising a choice, as opposed to not having one.'

'Let's not split fucking hairs. Brightside fits, but we need to look him in the eye. When you've done that and questioned him, you'll know if he did it. And if the answer's what we expect it to be, I can go to McGrail and say here's your killer; over to you.'

Van Roon said, 'You reckon you can get this past McGrail? I wouldn't have thought he'd want a bar of me.'

'McGrail's not going to know. Nor is anyone else. This is strictly off the books, OK?'

'I know you keep saying it's not like old times, but it certainly feels that way.'

'I wouldn't read too much into it if I was you,' said Ihaka. 'I'm just playing the hand I've been dealt. Ring me when you're ready to go and I'll talk you through it.'

'I haven't forgotten how to interrogate a suspect,' said Van Roon stiffly.

'I find it helps to know the full facts of the case.'

'Why not just send me a copy of the file?'

'Well for a start,' said Ihaka, 'I can't be fucked doing all that photocopying. I could probably come up with some other reasons if I put my mind to it.'

'There is one other thing.'

'What?'

'Who's paying?'

'Yeah, I've been thinking about that. You know that dirty money you've got salted away? Well, here's a chance to put some of it to good use.'

13

As usual, Tito Ihaka woke up on Saturday morning with a hangover. As usual, he half-heartedly blamed it on whoever invented those screw-cap tops they put on wine bottles these days.

This was how he rationalised it: you have a few beers and knock off a bottle of red; so far, so run of the mill. But this is one of those times when quite a lot isn't quite enough. You feel like one more glass. It's a Friday night and you've got the weekend off, so why the fuck not? And the thing with these screw-caps, you can open another bottle, have a glass or two, then put the cap back on and it's like you never opened it in the first place. The wine's not going to go off; in fact, it'll be just as good if not better tomorrow night. Or the night after if, through some extraordinary set of circumstances, it lasts that long.

The problem wasn't that the preservative properties of the screw-cap encouraged you to open a second bottle, or even that the second bottle went the way of the first. Let's face it, when you talked yourself into 'just one more glass', you didn't literally mean a single glass and not a drop more. No, the problem was that the lure and logic of the screw-cap was just as strong after two bottles as it had been after one. And so on. Which was how you came to wake up with someone pelting your skull with ball bearings and your tongue feeling like a small furry animal buried alive in a sandpit.

And as usual, it was raining.

He lay there, listening to the rain on the roof and the commotion in his head. All week abrupt downpours had alternated with patches of tentative sunshine, or squally showers had swept across the city from the Waitakeres to the Waitemata. This rain sounded different. It sounded like it wasn't going anywhere.

Keeping his promise to go and watch Billy play rugby meant getting out of bed, which would kick his hangover into the red zone, and getting drenched. Fuck. That. The obvious solution was to can the game. The people who ran kids' footy weren't complete deadshits. They understood that people who'd done a hard week's work didn't want to stand in the rain for over an hour watching a bunch of cold, wet, miserable kids mud-wrestling. It was a no-brainer.

Pleased he'd sorted that out, Ihaka rolled over, pulled the blankets up to his chin and closed his eyes. A few minutes went by. He could feel himself sinking into sleep, his mind suspending all activity, shutting down until further notice. His mobile pinged, announcing an incoming text. That'll be Denise, he thought, to say the game's been cancelled. He groped for the phone to make sure he was off the hook. It was Denise saying 'Same time, different place. Game transferred to Cox's Bay Reserve. See you there.'

The teams were going through their warm-up routines. Ihaka was rugged up in wet-weather gear and a hoodie, so it took Billy a couple of minutes to register his presence. Billy smiled and waved, but his body language said something was amiss. All was revealed when the backs and forwards came together for team drills: Billy, who normally played first five eighth, was on the wing; the coach's son Jarrod, who normally played on the wing, was at first five.

Denise was in a huddle with some other parents under a canopy of umbrellas. Deciding he'd rather get wet than socialise, Ihaka went out onto the field to give Clayton the coach a hand, as he'd been doing for most of the season. Seeing him coming, Clayton blew the whistle on a passing drill and sent the boys jogging off to the far end of the reserve.

Clayton was a thirty-five-year-old vet with a head of glossy black hair. In Ihaka's opinion it was the most impressive thing about him. Ihaka hadn't sought a coaching role; the other parents had encouraged him to get involved because Clayton, being a fount of theoretical knowledge who took himself way too seriously, tended to complicate things and take the fun out of it. The pair of them hadn't discussed Ihaka's role, and the arrangement had never been formalised. Ihaka was vaguely aware that Clayton didn't always welcome his off-the-cuff interventions but, as was his way, he didn't dwell on it. He was making a contribution, Clayton had the tracksuit top with 'Coach' in big, bright, yellow letters across the front and the arrangement seemed to be working. And, at the end of the day, it was the Ponsonby under-elevens, so who gave a shit?

'He's back,' said Clayton, not sounding ecstatic about it.

'I've been flat stick,' said Ihaka. 'I hear we had a bit of a mare last week.'

'It wasn't good. I've been working on a few new things at practice, so it might be better if you just take a watching brief this week.'

'Fine by me.'

'You might've noticed I've rejigged the backline,' said Clayton, reading too much into Ihaka's amenability. 'It

164

just wasn't gelling. Billy's a talented kid, but I'm not sure he's got the head to play ten. He was taking too much on himself, getting a bit greedy. Jarrod really understands the game plan: he'll steer us around the park and give us more direction.'

'Pretty big call,' said Ihaka. 'Lose one game so you change what's worked all season and shift your best player out of the position where he can make the most impact.'

'You missed the last two games, right? Billy was poor last week and not that flash the week before. And I've been picking up a vibe from the other kids that they're getting frustrated with his tendency to go away from the game plan. Right from day one I've hammered the message "There's no i in team". I thought everybody involved, players and supporters, had bought into that. This outfit we're playing is unbeaten, so we need to get it right and play as a team, rather than a bunch of individuals. That's why I made the call, and I'd appreciate you getting behind it.'

Ihaka nodded. 'I'll observe with interest.'

Clayton had just enough sense not to react to Ihaka's scepticism. He walked back out onto the field. Ihaka went over to Denise, who was looking good despite the shapeless puffer jacket and a beanie pulled down to her eyebrows.

'So, did El Maestro bring you up to date?'

'Yeah.'

'Billy's really pissed off.'

'He's got every right to be.'

'I freely acknowledge I don't know shit about rugby,' she said. 'And every night I ask God to strike me down with a bolt of lightning if I turn into one of those parents who think their little Johnny is the second coming of Dan Carter and the rest of the team are just there to make up the numbers. But even I can see that swapping Jarrod and Billy around is idiotic. Can't you talk him out of it?'

Ihaka shook his head. 'He pretty much told me to butt out.'

'So it's all about precious little Jarrod? Jesus, it makes me sick.'

'I wouldn't say that,' said Ihaka. 'Some of it's about Jarrod, but it's mostly about Clayton. This is where he gets to prove he's a coaching genius: he pulls a rabbit out of the hat and, hey presto, the boys get their mojo back and knock off the top team. He's been dreaming of this situation all season. It probably gives him a half-mongrel.'

'A what?'

'An in-betweener; mid-way between slack and full stalk.'

'What language is this?'

'A semi-erect penis,' said Ihaka loud enough to attract the attention of the nearest cluster of spectators. 'You should be familiar with the concept: you were up close and personal with one the other night.'

Denise hunched against a gust of wet wind. 'Oh, we're still there, are we? I was daring to hope we'd moved on.'

'Where to?'

The teams were in position for the kick-off. 'Back to where we used to be,' said Denise. 'Before we started finding whole new ways to screw it up.'

The referee blew his whistle to get the game under way.

With time almost up in the first half, Ponsonby were down 20–0. Ihaka was reminded of the old gag about getting such a hiding you were lucky to score nil. Billy had hardly touched the ball. Jarrod had touched the ball a lot, but not with the Midas touch. Having had Clayton in his ear all week telling him to be a playmaker rather than a glory hunter, Jarrod had simply shovelled the slippery ball on. The problem with making his intentions so clear was that the opposition also got the message and eagerly zeroed in on whoever was on the receiving end of Jarrod's hospital passes.

Prompted by Clayton's frantic semaphore, Jarrod had gone to Plan B: field position, otherwise known as hoofing the ball aimlessly downfield. The opposition had returned his kicks with interest in the reasonable – and, as it turned out, well-founded – expectation that Ponsonby would be as flaky under the high ball as they were in most other aspects of the game.

Ihaka joined Clayton, who was pacing up and down the touchline under his umbrella. 'What do you think?' he asked in a studiously neutral tone.

Clayton kept his eyes on the action. 'It's going to be your classic game of two halves,' he said with the rasp of someone having to explain the bleeding obvious. 'We've got the wind in the second half.'

That was debatable. Ihaka would've said the way the wind was gusting and swirling it didn't particularly favour either side. 'Thinking of making some changes?'

Clayton sighed theatrically. 'If you mean am I thinking of putting Billy back to ten, then no way. Jarrod's finding his feet. You can't expect him to be perfect from the get-go, especially against class opposition.'

'Oh, I wasn't expecting perfection,' said Ihaka. 'Billy's not getting much of a go.'

'Yeah, well, he's got to go looking for work, doesn't he, instead of waiting for the ball to come to him.'

'Last week he was greedy, this week he's lazy. The kid's got issues.'

The half-time whistle blew. Ihaka fell in beside Clayton as he marched onto the field. 'I won't speak to the boys,' he said. 'I'll just have a quiet word with Billy, tell him to get more involved.'

Clayton shrugged indifferently.

Ihaka's mobile rang: no caller ID. 'Yep?'

It was an anxious adult male. 'Is that Detective Sergeant Ihaka?'

'Yep.'

'This is Barry Shanklin, Miriam Lovell's partner. She told me to contact you if anything untoward happened.'

Ihaka came to a halt. 'Has it?'

'Yes. Miriam was attacked last night. She's in a coma.' Shanklin struggled on through ragged sobs. 'There's no guarantee she'll come out of it.'

'Oh, Jesus. Where is she?'

'Auckland Hospital. That's where I'm calling from.'

'I'm on my way.'

Denise intercepted him, getting that look on her face. 'Where are you going?'

'Auckland Hospital. Serious assault case.'

'There's always something, isn't there?' she said.

'Yeah, I'm sorry, but —'

'That's the way it is?'

'Yeah.'

He set off towards his car at a slow jog.

Detective Constable Joel Pringle was waiting for Ihaka at Intensive Care. An anonymous caller had rung 111 just before midnight to say there was a body on the eighteenth fairway of the Akarana Golf Course in Mt Roskill. It looked as though Miriam Lovell had been beaten up somewhere else and dumped there. Her backpack, satchel-cum-handbag and contents, including her iPad, were missing presumed stolen. The doctors weren't saying much, but she was clearly in a bad way.

'How did you ID her?' asked Ihaka.

'We found her driver's licence at the scene. They must've dropped it.'

Ihaka grunted. 'Careless of them.'

'Fucking animals,' said Pringle. 'I bet she told them "Take whatever you want" but they kicked the shit out of her anyway.'

'Where's the guy who rang me?'

'In the waiting room,' said Pringle, pointing the way. 'He's been here all night.'

'What'd he have to say?'

Pringle consulted a notepad. 'She works from home, but was out most of the day. She texted him late afternoon to say she'd probably be late so he should go ahead and have dinner rather than wait for her. When he hadn't heard from her by about 9.30, he started trying to get hold of her. No joy. He was just about to ring us when we rang him.'

Shanklin had the waiting room to himself. He looked up as they came in, his expectant expression disappearing into itself when he realised they weren't doctors.

If Ihaka had had to guess what sort of bloke Miriam would hook up with, he wouldn't have been far off the mark. Shanklin was in his mid-forties, slim with longish hair and an earring, wearing cargo pants and a T-shirt demanding that something be done about global warming. Gentle, thought Ihaka; sensitive; arty. Probably plays the guitar and writes songs about how hard it is being gentle, sensitive and arty in this fucked-up world.

Ihaka introduced himself. 'The fact that Miriam told

you to call me if anything untoward happened suggests she was worried.'

Shanklin nodded wearily. 'That's exactly what I said. She said she was probably over-dramatising, but once or twice she'd had the feeling she was being followed.'

'Who by?'

'She had no idea.'

'Did you believe her?'

'I'm not with you.'

'I don't know Miriam very well,' said Ihaka, 'so I might be reading her wrong, but is it possible she actually did have some idea but didn't tell you because you would've put pressure on her to drop it, whatever it was?'

Shanklin shrugged. 'I guess that's possible. That's what I would've done.'

'Had she mentioned anything, you know like this guy gave her the creeps, that guy warned her to back off?'

'No, but I suppose it's the same issue: my reaction would've been, "Let it go, it's not worth it." Doing what she does – freelance investigative journalism – she's bound to stand on people's toes from time to time, but this isn't Russia, for Christ's sake.'

'What was she working on?'

'Well, she's always got a few story ideas on the go, but lately she's been pretty much focused on finishing her doctorate.'

'So you've been here since just after midnight?' Shanklin nodded. 'Is there anyone who lives handy who's got a key to your place?'

'Well, my sister's only five minutes away. Why?'

'Why don't you ask her to pop round and check the place out?' said Ihaka. 'Whoever did this has got your address and Miriam's keys.'

'Shit, I hadn't thought of that.' Shanklin dug his mobile out of one of his many pockets. 'If she can't do it, I will.'

Ihaka and Pringle went looking for a doctor. 'You really think they'd hit their place, Sarge?' said Pringle. 'That's pretty fucking cheeky.'

'It's happened before. I just wonder about the licence. If they bashed her somewhere else, you'd think they would've gone through her stuff there, rather than on the golf course. And besides, who the fuck goes wandering around a golf course in the middle of the night? Maybe we were played: they dump her, leave her licence there for our benefit and call 111. We get onto Shanklin; he rushes over here. Net result: no one home all night. One thing's for sure, if that's what happened, we won't get any prints off the licence.'

They found a registrar, a redhead who looked too tired to be at work and too young for her responsibilities. She told them Miriam had suffered major head trauma and was in a critical but stable condition.

Ihaka said, 'What are the chances of her remembering what happened?'

The registrar had just enough energy to signal, via raised eyebrows, that Ihaka was getting ahead of himself. 'Well, that would mean our best-case scenario had eventu- ated. Frankly, as things stand, we'd settle for her coming out of it.'

'Does it seem like overkill just to get your hands on some credit cards and an iPad?'

'It all seems like overkill to me, Sergeant. But you know what alcohol and drugs can do.'

'And you know what some of these bastards are like, Sarge,' said Pringle. 'Once they start, the red mist rolls in. They'll half-kill some poor prick because he brushed against them in a bar.'

171

'You know what's even worse?' said Ihaka. 'When there's no red mist. When some poor prick ends up half-dead – or dead – because someone planned it that way.'

They met Shanklin on the way back to the waiting room. He was in even more of a daze. 'We did have a break-in last night.'

'What did they take?'

'Not that much by the sound of it. Both our laptops are gone, though.'

Ihaka nodded. 'You'll probably find they also took files, information storage devices, that sort of stuff.'

'Why? What the hell is going on here?'

'I don't think it was a random mugging,' said Ihaka. 'I think Miriam was on to something; someone realised where she was heading with it and freaked out. They started beating her to find out what she knew. And when she told them, they went on with it to stop her going any further.'

Shanklin stared at Ihaka. 'When Miriam told me to contact you if anything untoward happened, I asked, "Why him?" She said, "Because he'll take it personally." I didn't particularly like the sound of that, but she said I was taking it the wrong way: it wasn't about her, it was about you. What did she mean?'

'I can't tell you. All I can tell you is Miriam was right. I am taking this very fucking personally.'

14

Johan Van Roon sat in the Fiji Airways transfer lounge in Suva Airport making hard work of the novel he'd bought for just this eventuality: hanging around airports; getting the run-around; waiting for Eddie Brightside. It ran to 800 pages, roughly twice as long as the longest book Van Roon had ever finished. He'd gone for bulk in the expectation that this would be a drawn-out exercise, but the mazy narrative and ornate scene-setting – how many times a day could the sky possibly change colour? – made him regret his ambition. He should've just got some magazines or a fuckwit-friendly self-help book.

A soldier came into the lounge, turning heads and halting murmured conversations. He was tall and loose-limbed with a pantomime villain moustache, sub-machine gun, uniform ironed to a cutting edge, boots polished to a new-car sheen. He scanned the room, his stony gaze settling on Van Roon. 'What's your name?'

'Van Roon.'

'What are you doing here?'

'Waiting for someone.'

The dozen or so other transients watched intently, anticipating drama.

'Who?'

'I don't think he'd appreciate me mentioning his name.'

It was either the right thing or the wrong thing to say. The soldier summoned Van Roon with a jerk of his head. Van Roon slung his bag over his shoulder and led the way out of the lounge.

The soldier unlocked a door marked 'Airport Security Staff Only' and herded Van Roon down a long corridor past a succession of numbered doors. They stopped at door six. The soldier tapped on it with his sub-machine gun, got the go-ahead from within and stepped aside. Van Roon entered a small, windowless interrogation room containing a desk, two chairs and Eddie Brightside. The door closed behind him.

Van Roon had wondered what Brightside would look like. At first he'd thought in terms of dramatic change: reduced to a haunted shadow of a man by two and a half decades underground, or gone to seed through over-medicating with alcohol and narcotics, or transformed by cosmetic surgery. But then his rekindled affair with Ann Smellie and the fact that he'd been recognised at a glance by the old journo McCormick suggested Brightside still bore a strong resemblance to the man he used to be.

As proved to be the case. Brightside didn't look like a casualty or a refugee. He wasn't shrunken or wasted. He hadn't been remodelled. He still smiled like the only person in the room who got the joke. He just looked older: the yellow hair had gone grey and the round face had started to deflate.

Van Roon sat down. 'Mr Brightside, I presume?'

'Now there's a blast from the past.' Brightside had a golden-oldies radio voice, mellow but potentially cloying. 'No one calls me that any more.'

'What do they call you?'

'That's for me to know and you to find out.'

'It shouldn't be too hard,' said Van Roon. 'Now that we know where you've been.'

'We? So you're back on the payroll?'

Van Roon shook his head. 'No, I'm still a private operator.'

Brightside's thin smile stretched. 'Not on this gig. You're working for the man, my friend – not that he'll ever acknowledge it. You do realise that, if this goes bad, you're on your own?'

'Why should it go bad?'

'No particular reason. Then again, shit happens. If it didn't, we wouldn't be here. And by the way, knowing I've been in Fiji won't get you anywhere: the people I work with here know I like to stay low. Besides which, these days the Fijians are very selective about what they share with the land of the long white cloud. Any request for that information would come back stamped Go Fuck Yourself.'

Van Roon shrugged. 'No skin off my nose. So what do you do here?'

'I'm a consultant,' said Brightside blandly. 'My clients are ultra security-conscious; I advise them how to be ultra security-efficient.'

'Your clients being politicians in uniform?'

Brightside chuckled. 'Military dictators are people too, you know.'

'How do you sleep?'

Brightside leaned forward, putting his elbows on the desk, resting his chin on clasped hands, staring at Van Roon. 'Like a baby. How about you, Johan? You look tired. Is that because you work too hard or don't sleep too well?'

'I couldn't honestly say I'm run off my feet.'

'A little late in the day to develop a conscience, isn't it?'

175

'Oh, it's not my conscience that keeps me awake,' said Van Roon. 'It's the noisy pricks who live above me.'

Brightside's smile returned. 'So complain to the landlord.'

'They are the landlord.'

'So relocate. A man needs eight hours stacking Zs.' Brightside said it the American way: 'Zees'.

'I keep having to tell people this,' said Van Roon. 'I didn't come here to talk about me.'

'Well, as a matter of fact, you did. The only reason you're here is because I'm intrigued by your chequered past. I know quite a bit about you, Johan: there mightn't be much information-sharing between your ex-colleagues and their Fijian counterparts, but they still exchange tittle-tattle. I assume this Ihaka guy's not bothered by it?'

'My chequered past?' Brightside nodded. 'If only. Ihaka and I used to be mates. You could say he was my mentor, although he'd pretend he didn't understand the word. He was also the one who worked out what I'd been up to in my spare time. How's this for irony? If it wasn't for Ihaka, I wouldn't have made detective inspector, but if it wasn't for him I'd still be one. A minute ago you said if this goes bad, I'll be on my own. In actual fact, if this goes bad, Ihaka will put his hand up and say it was his idea, even though he'd be out on his arse. He wouldn't disown me, but on the other hand he'll never forgive me.'

'Sounds like an interesting guy.'

'Put it this way: he's not like any other cop you've ever come across.'

'I've come across a few bent cops in my time. I'd have to say you don't remind me of them.'

'I'll take that as a compliment,' said Van Roon.

'I'm not sure it was meant as one. Those other guys

were predictable; you felt like you knew which way they'd jump in any given situation. I don't have that feeling with you, Johan, and that worries me a little.'

'You don't need to worry about me, Mr Brightside.'

'Call me Eddie.'

Van Roon nodded. 'As I said, you don't need to worry about me. You tell me what happened that night, I go home, I tell Ihaka what you said, word for word, and that'll be that. Literally: it'll probably be the last conversation he and I ever have.'

'And when he asks you whether you believe me?'

'I'll give him an honest answer – unless you make it worth my while to do otherwise.' Brightside cocked his head questioningly. Van Roon said, 'That was a joke. Apart from anything else, Ihaka's a hard guy to lie to.'

'If I wasn't such a busy man, I'd take that as a challenge,' said Brightside. 'So now that you're just another civilian, are you worried that someone you fucked over, either in the course of enforcing the law or breaking it, might come looking for you?'

Van Roon shrugged. 'I've got more pressing stuff to worry about. Hopefully, as far as the pros are concerned, it was all just part of the game. Hopefully the psychos are behind bars.'

'Or dead?'

'Even better.'

'You can't beat the old pre-emptive strike.'

'I'm not sure what you're driving at, Eddie.'

'Oh yes you are.'

'If you mean who I think you mean, a certain self-styled master criminal whose unsolved murder has been the subject of lurid speculation, he was never going to come after me. That wasn't his style.'

'So why did you blow him away?'

Van Roon's smile was a mirror image of Brightside's. 'Assuming I did, that would be for me to know and you to find out.'

It was all because of David Lange and his fucking anti-nuke crusade, said Brightside. And Gerry Waitz and his fucking paranoia.

Waitz's parents were Russian Jews who'd fled to the west at the end of World War Two. His extended family wasn't so lucky: aunts and uncles and cousins transported like livestock to the Gulag Archipelago, never to return. Waitz had little patience with anyone, including fellow Jews, who as he saw it were obsessed with a threat that no longer existed. He called them 'Ghostbusters', telling them, 'Stop fixating on the fucking Nazis – they're history.' Waitz wanted people to focus on the Soviets: they were just as bad as the Nazis; more to the point, they were right here, right now and getting stronger by the day. If those fuckers got their way, which was world domination, there'd be death factories from Inverness to Invercargill, working around the clock.

While he had the tycoon's tendency to assume that what he wanted to happen would happen, Waitz had heeded Brightside's warnings that Labour was going to be re-elected and would stick to its anti-nuke policy. Plan B included putting together a mini-network of strategically placed people who shared his view that New Zealand effectively opting out of ANZUS would be the crack in the dyke holding back the red tide.

Brightside was an agnostic, a card-carrying Cold Warrior who believed the Soviet Union had to be contained but couldn't quite see why New Zealand not allowing the US

Navy into its ports would undermine the western alliance. As usual, he managed to have a foot in both camps, enthusing about the political benefits of the no-nuclear-ships policy when advising the Government and nodding along while Waitz and his cronies catastrophised.

Waitz arranged for his little group to gather at Barton's party for a post-election stocktake. About eleven o'clock, when the threat to everything they held dear had been confirmed and their mood had soured accordingly, a meeting convened upstairs in what Tim Barton somewhat grandiosely called 'the library'. As well as Waitz and Brightside, there were MPs from both the major parties; a guy from the US Embassy in Wellington; a couple of spooks, one from the SIS, the other from ASIO, the Australian equivalent; and stock-market pin-up boy Benny Strick, whose recent conversion from apolitical dilettante to fire-breathing anti-communist was a by-product of his man-crush on Waitz.

Being aware, courtesy of his ASIO contacts, that the Australian government and defence/security apparatus were freaking out over New Zealand's nuclear ships stance, Brightside had put Waitz in touch with like-minded people in Canberra. Kiwis tended not to fret over national security on the basis that isolation and insignificance were the best forms of defence. Scarred by their World War Two experiences – Japanese bombers over Darwin, Japanese submarines in Sydney harbour – Australians saw their place in the world in very different terms: a vast, empty, mineral-rich expanse of desirable real estate eyed covetously by the inscrutable, over-populated Orient. Defence wasn't an issue across the Tasman: it was an article of faith for both major parties that the lucky country's freedom, prosperity and security depended on the alliance with America.

179

The political dimension came in the form of Australian Prime Minister Bob Hawke's fury at the awkward position he found himself in as a result of what he regarded as Lange's naiveté and crowd-pleasing theatrics. Naturally ego was involved – the Labour leader from down under who happened to be the darling of the international left-wing intelligentsia wasn't the bloke in Canberra – but Hawke also resented the way in which Lange had exposed him to pressure and invidious comparisons from his party's left wing and the extra-parliamentary left. In a vernacular nutshell: what's stopping us being an independent, principled nation with a Prime Minister who doesn't have his nose permanently planted in Uncle Sam's clacker?

Waitz opened the meeting with an epic rant about how he wouldn't stand idly by while that grandstanding tub of shit (Lange) undermined freedom and democracy. He even channelled Henry II – 'Will no one rid me of this turbulent fat fuck?' – but the man from the US Embassy shut that thread down very smartly.

The ASIO guy waited till everyone else had had their say – invariably long on doom and gloom but short on constructive suggestions – before delivering his glad tidings. ASIO had electronically eavesdropped on Lange at some international gathering. While they hadn't overheard him touching base with the Kremlin, they had learned that he'd embarked on an adulterous affair with his speechwriter. The suggestion was that they should leak the story to a friendly journalist then stand back and enjoy the fun. At the very least, Lange's saintly image would be tarnished; in the best-case scenario he'd choose – or be forced – to step down as Prime Minister. Even if he toughed it out, it would give the pro-ANZUS faction in Cabinet an opportunity to rein him in and relitigate the anti-nuke stance.

It was as if a genie had popped out of Barton's antique inkwell offering to grant them their most heartfelt wish. There was much yahooing and backslapping – these were the days before high fives – and, as sometimes happens, everyone stopped yahooing at exactly the same moment. And into that sudden silence floated the unmistakable sound of female laughter.

Cue pop-eyed consternation. The man from ASIO was the first to react, lunging for the door and yanking it open. Standing there looking embarrassed yet at the same time not quite able to keep a straight face was a teenage girl.

Of course Waitz started bellowing, but the others hushed him up. The spooks fired questions. She told them she was a friend of Barton's daughter; she'd got bored downstairs and decided to explore; she'd heard voices coming from the library and couldn't resist being nosy.

Waitz declared that he was getting the fuck out of there and advised the others to do likewise. He paused at the doorway, jabbing a finger at Brightside: 'Deal with it.' There was an exodus, leaving Brightside and the girl looking at each other wondering, 'What now?'

Having got over the shock of being caught with her ear to the keyhole and roared at by Waitz, Polly was remarkably unfazed. Brightside's opening gambit 'You've got nothing to worry about' met with 'Neither have you'. She found it all pretty hard to believe: that the roly-poly Prime Minister was a bit of a Romeo; that Brightside and his friends were planning to name and shame him; that they were so worked up because she'd overheard.

Brightside tried pomposity: they were very important people discussing very sensitive subjects; if the nature of their discussions became public, it would cause considerable embarrassment.

Polly got that, but why would she tell anyone? Besides, who would she tell? And even if she did tell, they could just deny it. Who was going to take her say-so over the word of a bunch of important men?

That was all very well, said Brightside, but the reality was she would tell someone. That was just human nature. And whoever she told would pass it on to someone who'd pass it on to someone else. And so on and so forth until the tramps who lived under Grafton Bridge were the only people in Auckland who weren't in the know.

Polly thought that was over the top. Even if she blabbed to everyone she came across, most of them would dismiss it as just another of those far-fetched rumours about famous people that do the rounds from time to time, like the one about the TV personality turning up at A and E with a Marmite jar up his bum. And anyway, what was he planning to do: keep her locked up in his basement for the next five years?

Well, when she put it like that... Brightside had done some questionable things in his time, but he drew the line at heavying a teenage girl to protect Gerry Waitz. And protect him from what? Polly didn't have a clue who Waitz or any of the others were. All very well for her to claim she'd stumbled across a conspiracy to bring down the Prime Minister, but if she couldn't name names, the media wouldn't take her seriously. And if she spread the word that Lange was screwing his speechwriter, well, so fucking what? Wasn't that their plan? Where, exactly, was the downside? He told her to forget everything she'd heard, just put it out of her mind. If she chose not to do that, she'd run the risk of bringing unwelcome attention on herself and her family. That wouldn't be a pleasant experience.

Polly got the message. Drawing attention to herself and her family was absolutely the last thing she wanted to do.

Brightside believed her.

He told her to hang around upstairs – somewhere other than the library in case one of the others came back to see what was going on – while he went downstairs to check out the state of play. He wanted to make sure the others had left so there wouldn't be any drama and he could put off explaining how he'd handled it until Waitz had got his paranoia under control. If he hadn't come back in ten minutes, that would mean everything was OK and she could rejoin the party.

She left him in the library, saying she was going to do some more exploring. He waited a few minutes before going downstairs in case someone or something had delayed the exodus.

And what had troubled him, haunted him even, ever since was this: if he hadn't told her to stay upstairs, maybe she wouldn't have been murdered.

Brightside leaned back, hands behind his head. 'That's it.'

'Is that right?' said Van Roon. 'Unless my ears deceived me, you seemed to be saying you didn't kill her.'

'I didn't,' said Brightside placidly. 'Nor did anyone else who was at that meeting. When I got downstairs they'd all left.'

Van Roon nodded. 'OK. I'll report back to Ihaka, then it's up to him. My guess is he won't buy it. He'll say you – the collective you – had motive and opportunity and conspired to obstruct the course of justice. That's the basis of a pretty solid case right there. And at the risk of repeating myself, don't assume Ihaka's like other cops: if you think he's going to go away, you're kidding yourself.'

183

'You obviously don't believe me.'

'It doesn't matter what I believe. I'm just telling you how Ihaka – or any experienced detective, for that matter – is going to look at it. The bottom line is that what you're saying now carries a lot less weight than what you actually did then.'

'So you think I killed her?' Brightside could have been asking if Van Roon took milk and sugar.

'Not you necessarily. Maybe one of the others suspected you'd baulk and went back to do what had to be done.'

Brightside waggled his head. 'You're barking up the wrong tree. Tell Ihaka he'd be better off trying to find out who else was upstairs.'

'What do you mean?'

'We weren't the only ones. There was a couple up there.'

'How do you know?'

'I heard them. As I was heading downstairs, I heard a guy mumble something and a woman… I don't know what you'd call it, it was halfway between a laugh and a moan.' Brightside produced a wolfish grin. 'The low, throaty, lascivious sound of a woman not being a lady.'

'That's a finely tuned ear you've got there.'

'You'd better believe it.'

'Well, I'll be sure to pass it on.'

'You do that. And be sure to tell Ihaka he'll be wasting his time trying to find the phantom formerly known as Eddie Brightside. I've had twenty-seven years of being the invisible man; I'm really fucking good at it.'

'Speaking of which, I take it you disappeared because you thought you'd be the prime suspect?'

'Well yeah, but not in the sense you mean. I wasn't worried about the cops; I knew Gerry would cover our tracks. I took off because I figured Waitz would assume I'd killed the girl. As I said, Waitz is paranoid. He would've thought, yeah, Eddie shut her up all right, but if the cops get hold of him, he'll say it wasn't his idea, he just did what he was told to do. You see what I'm saying? He would've decided that I represented a threat to him. And when Gerry Waitz feels threatened, he takes steps to nullify the threat.'

'Like what?'

'Put it this way,' said Brightside. 'I wasn't going to overlook the obvious.'

'You thought Waite would have you whacked? Now who's paranoid?'

Brightside tilted his head like a boxer slipping a punch. 'You're being naïve, Johan. Waitz was – is – very rich and very well connected. When you've got that combination going for you, you can make pretty much anything happen just by picking up the phone. And while we're on that subject, I hope you appreciate the risk I'm taking here, given who you're working for.'

'Strick?'

Brightside snorted. 'Are you shitting me? Benny's an empty vessel, bobbing around in his little private pond. No, the guy who wants to get his hands on me now is the same guy who wanted to get his hands on me back then – and for exactly the same reason. Big Gerry.'

'So what happens now?'

Brightside stood up. 'We say goodbye and catch a plane. You go one way, I go another.'

'What about Ann?'

'Yeah well, you've fucked that up for me, haven't you?' said Brightside. 'Thanks a million, pal.' He stuck out a hand, his round face creasing into an uncharacteristically sunny smile. 'But I'm the forgiving kind, unlike some others we know. Take care of yourself, Johan. I hope things work out for you.'

They shook hands. 'You too, Eddie.'

Brightside pulled a mock frown. 'You sure about that? I wouldn't have picked you as the sort of guy who'd wish me well if you really thought I killed the girl.'

'That's one way of looking at it,' said Van Roon. 'On the other hand, I'm a complicated guy.'

'That makes two of us, brother.'

15

Johan Van Roon flew home via Auckland, rendezvousing with Tito Ihaka in the international terminal arrivals area. Ihaka greeted him with an interrogative hitch of the eyebrows. 'Well?'

Van Roon, thinking two can play that game: 'He didn't do it.'

Ihaka turned and headed for the exit, throwing a 'fuck' over his shoulder.

Van Roon delivered his report on the twelve-minute walk to the domestic terminal, Ihaka saying nothing, not even looking at him. Outside domestic Ihaka rounded on Van Roon. 'Sounds like you swallowed every fucking word this prick said.'

'I wouldn't go that far,' said Van Roon.

'So which bit don't you believe?'

'I don't believe he'll ditch Ann Smellie.'

'Why not?'

'Would you?'

Ihaka said, 'That's an interesting question. While I'm thinking about it, I might put a tap on her phone.'

'You're probably too late,' said Van Roon. 'I'd be amazed if Brightside hasn't set up some sort of tricky back-channel by now. In fact, I'd put money on it.'

Ihaka flared up. 'You know what you sound like? You

sound like a teenage girl who just presented her hymen to a guy in the next tent at Rhythm and Vines. She's all starry-eyed now, but in a few days she'll realise she's been played. It's not a summer romance; it wasn't even a music festival hook-up. All that happened was she got rooted by some jerk-off she'd known for all of two hours and will never see again, and who right now is having a laugh with his mates telling them how he popped this dumb-as-fuck little bitch's cherry by telling her she looks just like Miley Cyrus.'

Van Roon nodded thoughtfully. 'Well, when you put it like that… And here was me thinking I'd done you a favour.'

'I didn't send you up there to bend over.'

'As a matter of fact,' said Van Roon with slow emphasis, 'you didn't send me up there. I chose to go.'

'Oh, that's right,' said Ihaka. 'You're a private citizen these days. I keep forgetting.'

'You could've fooled me.'

Van Roon picked up his bag and walked into the terminal.

Ihaka drove back into town cursing himself, the weather – it was raining – and the driver of any car that got within five metres. The catalyst for his dark mood was the thought of Miriam Lovell, brain shut down, suspended between life and death. He was pissed off with her for withholding information so she could play amateur Sherlock. While it looked as though the bashing was connected to her PhD research and possibly his father's death, he was starting from a long way behind. Whoever bashed her had made sure there wasn't much of a trail to follow.

And he was pissed off with himself: for being pissed off with Miriam; for allowing her to withhold whatever she'd blacked out on that page from Ethan Stern's diary; for making a pig's ear of the meeting with Van Roon.

The bottom line was that he didn't really know what to make of Van Roon, or how to deal with him. Just seeing the guy was unsettling. Sometimes he saw the vulnerable young man – shy, pale, awkward, not remotely streetwise – he'd taken under his wing all those years ago. The one he'd put an arm around when murder victims, children with their throats cut, started appearing in Van Roon's dreams; the one he'd trained and toughened up; the one who became a top detective and his best friend in the cops. Other times he saw a guy he barely knew and maybe had been wrong about right from the start: a corrupt cop who used the instincts and street craft he'd learned from Ihaka to make dirty money; who killed a man in cold blood, admittedly a lowlife piece of shit.

Look at him that way, it should be black and white: never forgive, never forget, don't have a bar of him. The trouble was Van Roon's loyalty – even devotion – to Ihaka had contributed to him going off the rails. When Ihaka had his card marked for being too gung-ho (but, as it turned out, right) in a case involving a suspect with friends in high places and was subsequently overlooked for promotion and exiled to the provinces, Van Roon felt betrayed by the organisation he'd idealised since childhood. The first casualty of disillusion was his sense of duty. With nothing to guide him, no faith, no lodestar, he got lost in the underworld.

Even the hit came back to Ihaka. Van Roon swore he did it because the lowlife piece of shit was talking of having Ihaka taken out. In other words, he became a killer to save Ihaka's life. Finbar McGrail, resolutely unsentimental and as sceptical as the polar day is long, thought it was more a case of Van Roon fearing the lowlife piece of shit would sell him out: get himself off the hook by telling the cops who their rotten apple was. In other words, Van Roon became a killer to save his own skin.

Finally, he was pissed off that Van Roon had cleared the prime suspect. Whether Van Roon was a fallen angel or bad to the bone, he was good at this stuff. If he was pretty damn sure Eddie Brightside was telling the truth, that was good enough for Ihaka. So instead of being able to tell McGrail he'd identified Polly Stenson's killer, Ihaka would have to admit he had nothing to show for his efforts beyond closing down the most promising line of enquiry. Not the ideal prelude to informing McGrail that the Stenson investigation was going on the back burner while he focused on finding whoever had beaten Miriam into oblivion.

It being a Sunday evening, the meeting took place at McGrail's house, a gracious villa on a leafy section on the slopes of Mt Eden. Ihaka had got into the habit of dropping in there when he had something on his mind, usually turning up around nightcap time.

These visits had become something of a ritual: McGrail calling Ihaka's appearance 'an unexpected pleasure' or 'a welcome surprise'; Ihaka saying he happened to be in the neighbourhood and hoped he wasn't interrupting anything; McGrail not bothering to address Ihaka's concern, instead ushering his visitor into the study and wondering if he could 'interest him in' or 'tempt him to' a drop of something; Ihaka being open to persuasion, but 'only if you're having one'; McGrail handing him a glass of vintage port with the recommendation that it be lingered over or savoured; Ihaka asking, 'As opposed to swilled?' – originally a McGrail line; Ihaka taking a sip, giving it the furrowed brow, saying, 'I'm thinking ninety-four'; McGrail revealing the actual vintage – it was never 1994 – and venturing a little wine-snob parody, 'An elusive wine, but not without its rewards.' They were like an old comedy duo, thought Ihaka, reduced to amusing each other because their audience has died off or drifted away.

He updated McGrail. Van Roon didn't feature at all, Ihaka making out that Ann Smellie had facilitated a telephone exchange with Brightside.

'Where is Brightside?' said McGrail.

'He was in Fiji. Christ knows where he is now.'

'That makes sense. We have precious little leverage in that neck of the woods. So you tend to believe him?'

'Afraid so.'

'Where does that leave us?'

'Pretty much back at square one.'

'What's the next step?'

'I'll think of something.'

McGrail was sitting behind his desk, an old farmhouse table. He tilted his chair back. 'Sergeant, if you think this is a wild-goose chase, you should say so.'

'Shit, it's way too early for that. We had a lead; we checked it out; it didn't stand up. That happens in pretty much every investigation which isn't a slam dunk.'

McGrail sighed. 'That may be so, Sergeant, but it was a very promising lead. And when the crime in question took place twenty-seven years ago, promising leads are few and far between.'

McGrail was renowned for his inscrutability, but he was looking as morose as Ihaka had seen him, sipping his port as if it was canteen tea. This wasn't the time to talk about putting the investigation on the back burner. In fact, now that I've buggered up his evening, thought Ihaka, maybe I should leave him to it. He finished his drink and stood up. 'Listen, sorry to be the bearer of bad news —'

McGrail snapped out of it. He leaned over his desk, offering Ihaka the bottle. 'Actually, there's something else I wanted to talk to you about.' Ihaka took the bottle and sat back down. 'You're aware my appointment expires next year?' Ihaka nodded. 'A few weeks ago, I was sounded out on the possibility of an extension – another year or eighteen months. I agreed to think about it. Well, I've obviously managed to get on the wrong side of the wrong people, because late last week I was unofficially but authoritatively advised that I can stop thinking about it. That proposal is no longer on the table. Indeed, I got the distinct impression that when my time is up, a delegation will fly up from Wellington to help me clear out my office.'

'Yeah, well, we're a pretty tolerant outfit, but one thing we can't hack is competence.'

McGrail smiled his ghost smile. 'The same source, who resides not a million miles from the Minister's office, also let it be known that my successor will be your friend and mine, Detective Inspector Charlton. It's too soon for him on a number of grounds, which I assume is why the extension option was canvassed. It seems they've decided that the risks inherent in Charlton's premature elevation are outweighed by the ghastly prospect of having to put up with me for any longer than they absolutely have to. I'm giving you what I believe is known as a heads-up so that you can start thinking about your future. You have to face the reality that, once I'm gone and Charlton's in the chair, your life is going to be very different.'

'As in turn to shit?'

'Well, you certainly won't have anything like the same leeway. If he gives you any rope at all, it'll be just enough to hang yourself.'

Ihaka shrugged. 'I appreciate you putting me in the picture, but the reality I really have to face is there's fuck all I can do about it.'

'You could apply for a transfer.'

'Where to?'

'Up north, perhaps. Your family's got a beach house up there, haven't they? I imagine life in the winterless north would be rather agreeable.'

'Weed World?' Ihaka shook his head. 'Too much turning a blind eye for my liking.'

'Yes, I suppose that could be vexatious for a man of your temperament. Does a return to the Wairarapa have any appeal?'

'Been there, done that.'

'Very well, how about something completely different? Apparently there's a lot to be said for embarking on a new career path in mid-life. I've even heard it likened to drinking from the fountain of youth.'

Ihaka examined McGrail with frank curiosity. 'That's pretty out there, don't you think? I mean, did you ever consider it?'

'I did, as a matter of fact. I came to New Zealand instead.'

'You thought about it because you were on an IRA hit-list. Charlton's just another arsewipe with more ambition than ability; they're fucking everywhere. The fact is I've never done anything else and never thought about doing anything else. And anyway, what else am I qualified for: being a bouncer at some club, having fucking drug dealers slip me fifty notes to let their underage hotties in the door? When you brought me back from the Wairarapa I realised, for better or worse, Auckland's home. I'll be fucked if I let that little weasel run me out of here again.'

'Well, that's fine,' said McGrail. 'But I make no apology for raising the subject. And while there's an element of do as I say, not as I did, you never know what your options are until you start thinking beyond your current circumstances. As a fellow once said to me, the most secure prison on earth is a closed mind.' He allowed Ihaka to mull over that for a few seconds. 'But then, he was an IRA gunman who shot two people in the head because they made a joke about the Pope.'

Denise Hadlow had texted, asking when would be a good time to talk.

Ihaka got home just before 9.30 pm. He had a sandwich and channel-surfed without finding anything that wouldn't make him fall asleep on the sofa. When he figured he'd given Denise enough time to go to bed, he texted saying he'd just finished work. She rang thirty seconds later.

'Busy weekend?'

'Yeah, I've been flat out. How did the game finish up?'

'You could've asked Billy that.'

'Give me a break, Denise.'

'What, another one? That's all Billy and I seem to do these days. Have a guess how it finished up.'

'Well, Clayton seemed to think it'd be a game of two halves. It didn't look that way to me.'

Denise snorted. 'Jesus, that guy is such a dickhead. The final score was forty-five to five. Billy got the try which, I have to say, was a stunner. The try of the season, someone said.'

'Good on him. At least he had something to show for it.'

'Get this, though. After the game, El Maestro marched over to tell the parents that we couldn't choose a man of the match. Some shit about the boys failing as a team and having to deal with it as a team. Then he got them in a huddle and gave them a ten-minute speech. Andrew's dad was hovering at the back and heard most of it. Do you know what that wanker said?'

'Let me guess: the boys need to focus on their roles in the team instead of trying to be the big star; there's no point in individual brilliance if it's at the expense of teamwork; the rest of them could take a leaf from Jarrod's book, the way he stuck to the task and never gave up.'

Denise said, 'You've talked to Andrew's dad, right?' It sounded like a genuine question.

'I wouldn't know Andrew's dad if I tripped over him.'

'Who then?'

'I haven't talked to anyone. I told you: I've been head down, arse up. Remember I've had a bit to do with Clayton; he's not exactly complicated. What you see is what you get – over and over again.'

'Well, seeing as you can read him like a book,' said Denise, 'tell me this: is he going to put Billy back to first five?'

'And admit he fucked up? No chance.'

'Can you talk to him, then? Why don't you go to practice this week? God knows they need you.'

'The heat's on at the moment, so I'll have to see how it goes. But I suspect it's got to the stage that if I go into bat for Billy, Clayton will just dig his heels in. Maybe the best bet is to let him work it out for himself. If they lose again next Saturday – which is on the cards because he's got them playing like headless chooks – then self-interest will kick in. Getting back to being a winning coach will become a higher priority than being right about Billy and Jarrod. And by then he'll have come up with some rationale for the chopping and changing that doesn't make him look like a complete fuckwit.'

'That's pretty self-serving, isn't it?'

'Well, we are talking about Clayton.'

'You might be,' said Denise. 'I'm not. I'm talking about you. You say you shouldn't get involved because that would be counter-productive, but this whole Billy/Jarrod fiasco only happened because you went AWOL. I know it's all about Clayton, but he wouldn't have had the nerve to swap them if you'd been there. If you really wanted to, you could talk Clayton into back-tracking and get these kids enjoying playing rugby again. But you obviously don't want to.'

'By going AWOL, you mean missing some under-elevens footy because I was investigating a murder?'

'We're all busy people. The way it works is we make time for the things we value and the people we care about. It's pretty clear Billy and I don't make the cut. So what I really rang to tell you is that I'm done covering up and sugar-coating. Next time the subject comes up I'm telling Billy that he's going to have to get by without you. And not just when it comes to rugby.'

'Go for it. I seem to remember I suggested being straight with him a while ago. But before you go, you remember what started all this?'

'All what?'

'Us at each other's throats all the time. Us falling apart.'

'How could I forget? It started with you bailing on going to Devonport with us so you could hook up with your old girlfriend.'

'Well, she wasn't my old girlfriend and we didn't hook up, but that's your story and you're sticking to it. Do you remember her name?'

'Of course. Miriam.'

'So I assume you also remember our conversation at Depot, when I told you what Miriam had wanted to talk to me about. You laughed your head off, reckoned it was the biggest load of bullshit you'd ever heard.'

'And your point is?'

'That serious assault case I was called to – it's Miriam. She's in a coma she mightn't come out of. I'm pretty sure the reason she got her head smashed in was because she went poking around in the biggest load of bullshit you've ever heard and found out it actually wasn't bullshit. Not by a fucking long shot. You should hear yourself sometimes, Denise.'

'Don't call me again.'

Before Ihaka could point out that she'd called him, the line went dead.

16

Miriam Lovell's partner provided the name of the 'old union guy' who'd put her on to Ethan Stern's diaries.

Stu Boyle was into his seventies, a bald, bright-eyed, freckle-splattered bantam cock whose barrel chest had gone south. Inside and out, his Birkenhead villa was a testimony to house-proud retirement or keeping up with the Joneses. 'I knew an Ihaka,' he said. 'You wouldn't by any chance be —'

'I'm Jimmy's son.'

Boyle lit up. 'Is that right? He was a good bloke, Jimmy, but Jesus, talk about always swimming against the tide. My mother had a term for those sort of people: "contrary blighters" she used to call them. Well, your old man was the most contrary blighter I ever came across. You like boxing?'

Ihaka shrugged. 'I don't mind it.'

'Boxing's my thing,' said Boyle, wriggling back into his La-Z-Boy with the contented air of a man about to hold forth on his favourite subject. 'I did heaps of it as a young bloke. Amateur stuff, of course. You know the Rumble in the Jungle – Muhammad Ali against George Foreman, Kinshasa, Zaire, 1974? Every man and his dog reckoned Foreman was going to give Ali a real dusting, shut that big mouth once and for all. Sure, some of it was wishful thinking, people who'd been waiting a long time to see Ali taken down a peg or two. But to be fair, he was a lot older than Foreman, he'd been beaten by Joe Frazier and Ken Norton, who Foreman had absolutely murdered, and it was seven years since they took the title off him. "No Vietcong ever called me nigger." When you think how much hot air was expelled saying why we shouldn't be in Vietnam, Ali nailed it in six words. I was a big fan so I was talking up his chances – I could give you more reasons why he was going to win than you could shake a stick at – but, deep down, I was scared for him.

'Then I came across an interview with a fellow by the name of Bill Faversham, who was part of a group of white businessmen who managed Ali before he joined the Black Muslims. Faversham still called him Cassius – his "slave name" – but obviously had a soft spot for him. Before the Foreman fight he said, "I can see Cassius isn't hitting with his left any more and doesn't dance after a couple of rounds, but nothing overwhelms Cass. Not even if he met God."' Boyle shook his head, smiling like Punch. 'Isn't that great – "Not even if he met God"?'

Ihaka smiled back, humouring the old guy.

Boyle leaned forward to tap Ihaka on the knee. 'I can see you're sitting there thinking you didn't come here to get a history lesson from this old coot, but there's a point to the story. Jimmy was like that: he wouldn't have been overwhelmed if he met God.'

'I don't know about that,' said Ihaka. 'He was a pretty staunch atheist, so I reckon meeting God would've pissed him off no end.'

Boyle chuckled. 'I hadn't thought of it that way.' He settled back in his chair, his little mouth flattening to a grim dash. 'You think this dreadful bloody business had something to do with Miriam's research?'

'It's unlikely,' lied Ihaka. 'These things are usually crimes of opportunity – the victim's in the wrong place at the wrong time. We're just trying to put together a picture of where she'd been and what she was doing.'

'Well, from what she said to me, she was interested in how much trade union militancy in the seventies and early eighties was about politics as opposed to industrial relations. See, you had union leaders who were staunch communists, so when they were shit-stirring the question was – and the likes of me and your old man used to raise this all the time – was it to put a few more bucks in their members' pockets or strike a blow against capitalism? There was this outfit called the Workers' Vanguard Party, Moscow-aligned commies. It had bugger-all members, a few hundred at most, but they included a fair number of union officials and jokers who had a lot to say in the workplace. There were plenty of times when these blokes pushed hard for strike action even though it obviously wouldn't achieve very much and their members were going to end up out of pocket.'

'So why did they do it?'

'Because they were dyed-in-the-wool reds. They believed capitalism was an assault on the working class and had to be resisted and sabotaged. When push came to shove, that was more important than their members' welfare. As your old man always said – and, by Christ, didn't the WVP hate him for it – they used the rank and file as cannon fodder in a war it hadn't volunteered for.'

'Who called the shots?'

'Willie Smaile ran the WVP, with an iron fist. One thing Miriam was trying to get a handle on was whether Smaile steered his own course or took his lead from the Soviet embassy.'

'The guy's name was Smaile?'

'Yeah, Willie Smaile. Why?'

'Ethan Stern's widow told me that, after his death, she was rung up by some union guy called Small wanting to get his hands on the diaries.'

Boyle shook his head. 'I don't remember any Small.'

'So it could've been Smaile?'

'I suppose so, although Willie preferred to operate behind the scenes. He was a puppet master, see. Other blokes would front the stoush – they'd be on TV and in the paper, copping flak from the media and the Tories – but Willie was pulling the strings. He wasn't a union heavy-weight – assistant deputy something or other in one of the little unions no one took too much notice of – but he was General Secretary of the WVP, so if you were a party member, even if you ran a big union, you bloody well did as you were told.'

'Or what?'

'Well, we weren't in the Soviet Union so you got sent to Coventry, not Siberia. But if all else failed, the WVP had a few bruisers on its books and wasn't shy of using them.'

'You mean muscle?'

'I mean big buggers with small brains who'd put the slipper into their granny if the boss told them to. You must know the type, Sergeant. Never been a shortage of them in your mob.'

'Can't think of any off the top of my head.'

Boyle had his full-face smile back. 'There's none so blind as those who will not see.'

'Whatever you say, Mr Boyle. How did Miriam get on with Smaile?'

'She got nowhere. He wouldn't give her the time of day. What's more, he put the word out to the old comrades, so

Miriam just kept running into a brick wall. Willie might be getting on – he'd be ten years older than me – and the WVP might've folded the best part of twenty years ago, but what he says still goes.'

'So when she got stonewalled by Smaile and co, you suggested she should look for Stern's diaries?'

'That's right. She didn't find them, but she did come across a reference to Tom Murray in amongst Stern's stuff. It's funny: it hadn't occurred to me to mention that name. I see him on TV from time to time, but he's a very different kettle of fish to the young fellow I knew.'

'I'm not with you,' said Ihaka. 'Should I know this guy?'

'Don't you follow politics?'

'Why the fuck would I do that?'

'I just thought being Jimmy's son.'

'Maybe that's why not.'

'You're not interested in Maori issues, the Waitangi process and that?'

'I wouldn't mind if some of the dough they chuck around came my way, if that's what you mean,' said Ihaka. 'I'm Maori, I belong to an iwi, so what? Everyone comes from somewhere. Not saying I'm not proud of it, but just because I'm Maori doesn't mean I act and think a certain way. Opinions aren't like steak knives: you don't get a set when you're born. I'm just me; I don't belong to anyone.'

Boyle looked sceptical. 'Not even the cops?'

'Not even the cops. They get first call, but that's as far as it goes.'

'Well, Jimmy got accused of all sorts of things, but being apolitical certainly wasn't one of them. Apart from that, you strike me as a chip off the old block. I bet you create merry hell.'

'I move in pretty straight lines – it shouldn't be that hard to stay out of my way. Tell me about Murray.'

'He's Scottish,' said Boyle. 'Well, he was Scottish. These days he sells himself as a true-blue Kiwi, not the easiest thing to do with that accent. He's been here thirty years now, so I suppose he's earned the right to call himself a New Zealander and wrap himself in the flag. After all, patriotism is the last refuge of a scoundrel. He pitched up here in the early eighties, worked at a grog outlet at the bottom of Khyber Pass and became very active in the Storemen and Packers' Union, which is how he came to Smaile's attention. Smaile recruited him into the WVP and for a while there he was the golden boy. It looked for all money like Willie was grooming him as his successor. But Murray blotted his copybook and Willie turfed him out on his ear. It was your classic purge: one day he sat at Smaile's right hand; next day he was a non-person.'

'What did Murray do wrong?'

'Jesus, who knows? You didn't have to do much to fail the purity test. The comrades took ideology very bloody seriously. If you deviated from the party line or were luke-warm when you should've been red-hot, you were in the gun. Mind you, if you look at what's become of Murray, you'd have to say it was a good call. Smaile obviously saw the signs.'

'What do you mean?'

'Are you serious? You mean to say you've never heard of the Muffin Man?'

'That's him?' said Ihaka incredulously. 'The Scotch prick in that fucking TV ad?'

Boyle did a passable impersonation: '"Hello New Zealand, I'm the Muffin Man and I'm here to tell you a Murray muffin will make your day." That's our boy. He's made a fortune out of muffins; now he wants to run the country.'

'Which party is he?'

'Ah well, when you're Tom Murray, you can afford your own party – the Prosperity Party. You could say it picks up where Rogernomics left off – flat tax rate, slash red tape, let big business do whatever the hell it wants so the rich get even richer. He's got this slogan, "The role of government is to eliminate the role of government". Absolute textbook case of the zeal of the convert. You'd think we'd be once bitten, twice shy, but the pundits seem to think he could pick up enough votes to get himself and maybe one or two others into Parliament, which would give him a seat at the negotiating table. He might even end up being the kingmaker, God help us. That's obviously what he's got in mind, which I suppose is why he wouldn't talk to Miriam either. If you're making yourself out to be the saviour of the free-enterprise system, you probably don't want people to know you were once the teacher's pet in a hard-line communist party.'

The Muffin Man ran his muffin empire from a plush suite of offices in Ellerslie. There are times, thought Ihaka, when it's good to be me. You show up at the office of someone who thinks they're important. Self-important people tend to have gatekeepers, secretaries or receptionists whose mission in life is to ensure that the Special One isn't bothered by little people. The gatekeepers glance up from their magazines or Sudokus, register the large, unkempt Maori shambling through the reception area and think it's high time we got some proper security around here. But being professional hypocrites, among other things, the gatekeepers pretend they haven't pigeon-holed Ihaka on the basis of his jeans, hoodie and sneakers, all of which have seen better days. They greet him with the same smiley mask and honeyed tones they bestow on desirables: gelled, shaved, plucked, exfoliated, fragrant, glossy people in clean underpants (you can just tell) and proper shoes; go-getters with the latest accessories who belong in the marbled foyers where money is made. And they ask him the most insincere question in the English language: 'Can I help you?'

'I'm here to see Tom Murray.'

'Hmm. And your name is?'

'Tito Ihaka.'

'Bear with me for two ticks.' The receptionist tapped her keyboard to access the Special One's diary and confirm what she already knew: Mr Murray hadn't taken leave of his senses. 'Did you have an appointment?' It wasn't a sentence as such, more like five stand-alone words. The laborious emphasis conveyed a message: 'It's not too late. If you walk away now, you can avoid humiliation.'

'No.'

Still looking down at the screen with a tight, fake smile, the receptionist permitted herself a fractional shake of the head. The only thing missing was a thought bubble: what planet is this simpleton on? 'Well, I'm afraid, Mr... Sorry, what was the name again?'

All good things must come to an end. 'Ihaka. Detective Sergeant, Auckland Central. I'm not here to beg for a job picking rat shit out of the muffin mixture, I'm investigating an assault that left a woman in a coma. So why don't you pick up the phone and tell the Muffin Man I'm coming, ready or not?'

Two minutes later, the Muffin Man was escorting Ihaka into his office. Murray was shorter, greyer and rougher around the edges than he looked on TV. His body shape suggested a weakness for his product, unlikely as that seemed. His accent was as intact as Finbar McGrail's. He indicated the newspaper on the coffee table. 'I couldn't believe my eyes when I saw it. A few days ago she was sitting right where you are, full of vim and vigour.' After a decent interval – three seconds – solemnity gave way to resolution. 'I'll tell you this, Sergeant, if there's one thing I intend to achieve in politics, it's giving the police the resources they need to stamp out this epidemic of violent crime.'

Ihaka glanced at his watch. 'What did Miriam want?'

Murray smiled crookedly. 'You'd prefer I didn't practice my stump speech on you, eh Sergeant? Can't say I blame you. She wanted chapter and verse on my union firebrand phase, particularly my involvement with the WVP. You know what I'm referring to? Because I have zero interest in revisiting that period of my life, I wasn't able to oblige and we didn't part bosom buddies. In case you think I was being precious, let me give you some context. Three years ago a reporter from the *Herald* phoned up wanting to do a feature on me. She pitched it as a feel-good, rags-to-riches story: Glaswegian tearaway leaves school at fourteen, arrives here with five quid in his pocket, builds a multi-million-dollar business from scratch. I thought it'd be good publicity, free advertising if you like. And I'm not going to lie: my ego was all for it. I felt I was overdue some recognition. You pick up the paper week after week and see people you know for a fact are thieves and charlatans written up like they're Warren Buffett, and you think, what the hell am I doing here? Running a greasy spoon? So I agreed to do it.

'My youthful dalliance with communism came up, almost by the by. I said I didn't want to go there, I was a different person back then, the product of socio-economic circumstances most Kiwis simply couldn't imagine, and it wasn't relevant to the theme of creating something from nothing. The reporter gave every appearance of seeing where I was coming from, then went away and wrote a piece basically saying, isn't it ironic that the poster boy for self-made capitalist pigs used to be a card-carrying commie? They even managed to dredge up a photo of me giving the clenched-fist salute at some rally. That article caused me no end of grief. I had customers cancelling orders; guys I played golf with suddenly deciding they'd really rather not be seen on the same fairway; even people I thought were mates carrying on like I'd conned them, as if having me round for a barbecue entitled them to full disclosure. In my book a fool is someone who doesn't learn from bitter experience. Well, that experience taught me there's absolutely no percentage in raking over those coals, and that goes double now I'm in politics.'

'Why were you kicked out of the WVP?'

Murray sighed. 'Really? It's ancient history.'

'Just as a matter of interest.'

'All right, but it's not much of a story. Like most hard-left groups, the WVP – i.e. Willie Smaile – expected its members to tick all the boxes, ideologically speaking. I struggled with the unquestioning acceptance of dogma; the lack of meaningful discussion, let alone debate; the insistence that, when it came to having a view on world affairs, I had to follow the lead of a bunch of old men in Moscow. With the benefit of hindsight, I'd already set out on the journey that brought me here. I didn't mind a drink in those days and got plastered the night before the Day of International Solidarity with the Working Class – May Day to you and me. It was a big day in the WVP calendar, standing shoulder to shoulder with comrades around the world and all that bollocks. Anyway, I forgot to set the alarm and woke up around lunchtime to the sound of Smaile's goons hammering on the door. I was carpeted, denounced and warned as to my future conduct.

'A couple of weeks later, I was well and truly in vino and overdid the veritas. I thought I was in safe company but Smaile had eyes and ears everywhere. There were these ghost party members – only Smaile knew they belonged to the WVP – whose job was to keep tabs on what the rest of us were saying and doing behind the great leader's back. I got another tongue-lashing. Smaile accused me of being a counter-revolutionary snake in the grass and cast me into the outer darkness, although not before the goons gave me the worst working over of my life. That tinpot tyrant did me a huge favour, and I've never thanked him for it.'

As he showed Ihaka out, Murray said, 'I knew an Ihaka in those days.'

'So did I,' said Ihaka.

As he walked to his car, Ihaka got a call from Detective Constable Joel Pringle. 'Sarge, I just talked to that registrar we saw up at the hospital. Ms Lovell's condition has deteriorated. They're getting worried that she's not going to make it.'

17

For someone who didn't believe in private property, Willie Smaile occupied an enviable chunk of real estate: a secluded, architect-designed two-storey house in Browns Bay with sweeping views of the Hauraki Gulf.

A variable wind ruffled the screen of trees and skimmed the sea; rain flurries alternated with pale yellow sunbursts. Within this swirl of colour and energy, Smaile was a still life in grey – hair, eyes, skin, clothes, shoes. He observed Ihaka with blank detachment, like a morgue attendant checking in the latest John Doe.

Smaile's wife, a tiny Vietnamese, brought green tea, then departed without acknowledging their visitor or, indeed, appearing to notice they had one.

When he'd rung Smaile beforehand, Ihaka had mentioned the family connection in the hope it would speed things up a bit. Now, in a voice so breathy it was almost a hiss, Smaile said, 'So you're his son?'

'That's right.'

'I seem to remember he saddled you with an odd name.'

'Tito.'

Smaile bared surprisingly white, well-maintained teeth. 'Tito. How could I forget? Tell me, how does it feel to be named after a Croatian pimp?'

'I can't say I've ever thought of it that way.'

'I pointed out to him that he'd named you after a degenerate class traitor who loved nothing more than hosting Hollywood movie stars on his private island.'

'I'm sure he was crushed.'

'Actually, he reminded me that Brezhnev's daughter was a corrupt drunk. Do you know who I'm referring to?'

'Brezhnev was the Russian leader, wasn't he?'

'Except it wasn't Russia then, but geopolitics clearly isn't your strong suit. Your father might've been a dilettante, but at least he was a self-educated one. Probably the only thing we had in common was an abhorrence of wilful ignorance.'

'Go fuck yourself.'

'That was uncalled for: I took it for granted you'd inherited his vulgarity, if nothing else. Now if you're expecting sentimentality, you're going to be disappointed. Not speaking ill of the dead is a bourgeois concept.'

'A bit like this place?'

'Come on, Sergeant, you can do better than that. If we weren't living under a system that creates and institutionalises economic inequality, I'd be more than happy in a house that was no better or worse than anyone else's. As I was saying: your father called himself an anarcho-syndicalist, although he hadn't read Proudhon or Bakunin. In practice, his half-baked ideas amounted to nothing more than obstructionism and mischief-making. To put it bluntly: he was an enemy of the people.'

'Listen, I could spend all day talking about anarcho whatever the fuck, but duty calls and all that. What contact did you have with Miriam Lovell?'

'I spoke to her just long enough to tell her I wouldn't speak to her. It was a two-minute conversation, if that.'

'Why wouldn't you speak to her?'

Smaile held Ihaka's stare. 'Reframe the question: why wouldn't I validate her falsifications? Because I'm not a fool.'

'So how come you put out the welcome mat for Ethan Stern?'

'That's a reasonable question,' said Smaile, nodding slowly. 'First of all, Stern's credentials, while not impeccable, were sound. He'd been active in Marxist and student radical circles in the US. It didn't take me long to realise that, notwithstanding his background, Stern wasn't and never would be one of us but, as you'd expect of an academic, he was strong on the theoretical side. He also had an insight into the American political system and power structure which I lacked and was keen to acquire. I couldn't fault my comrades' commitment and resolve, but they were working people in the main, which of course meant they'd been denied a decent education. They were unworldly, if you like, and dialectical materialism was, frankly, over their heads.' He paused. 'You don't have any idea what I'm talking about, do you?' Ihaka gave no indication he'd heard the question. 'Ask a silly question, eh? Anyway, the long and short of it was that Stern was one of the few people I could have those discussions with. It was as close as I got to self-indulgence.'

'But then he was killed?'

'Indeed he was. While jogging – another bourgeois concept.'

'And before his corpse was cold you were trying to get your hands on his diaries.'

'What's the basis for that statement?'

'His widow.'

Smaile's superiority complex went on the blink. 'You've spoken to her?' Ihaka nodded. 'Well, well, you are casting the net wide.'

Ihaka shrugged. 'Just retracing Ms Lovell's steps. Standard procedure.'

'Stern was granted unique access on the basis of his political pedigree and involvement with like-minded groups elsewhere, but I wouldn't have contemplated it for one second if I'd thought there was any chance of his notes falling into the hands of our adversaries or the state. I was determined not to let that happen.'

'So when the widow wouldn't play ball, you sent one of your boys around pretending to be a post-grad student?'

Smaile leaned back, closing his eyes. 'Did I?'

'That didn't work either. Someone got hold of the diaries, though. Miriam found the cartons they were in, but someone had got there before her. Does that worry you?'

Smaile's shoulders shook with silent laughter. 'Oh, we got there before her all right – twenty-seven years before her.' He bared his teeth again as he watched Ihaka work it out.

'A colleague of Stern's, some woman, I forget her name, volunteered to take his stuff into the department. It was her, right?'

'Julia Prince. She was a sympathiser. We sought her assistance and she obliged.'

'So what happened to the diaries?'

Smaile raised a thin, fluttering hand. 'Gone. Vanished into the ether. I burned them.'

Ihaka stood up. 'We'll leave it there for now. I don't want to overtax you, Willie – you're looking a bit grey around the gills.'

'The expression is "green around the gills". And if I was you, Sergeant, I'd look out for myself. Who knows? Given your genes, it's not beyond the bounds of possibility that I'll outlive you.'

* * *

It was dark when Ihaka, without prior warning, rang Johnny Barton's doorbell. Barton said he had company, so if Ihaka wouldn't mind coming back some other time...

Ihaka grunted derisively. 'What do you think I am, a fucking Mormon? It'll only take a few minutes.'

'But we're right in the middle of dinner.'

'You can always bung it in the microwave. Works for me.'

Barton stood his ground. 'This is completely unacceptable. You turn up unannounced at this time of night and expect me to drop everything —'

'I thought I'd made myself pretty clear,' said Ihaka. 'This time around we're not playing by Barton rules, we're playing by my rules. You either talk to me here and now or you're going downtown. Your call.'

Barton was still grumbling as he led Ihaka into his study. 'Put a fucking sock in it,' snapped Ihaka. 'If you'd told the truth last time, I wouldn't be here.'

'What on earth are you talking about?'

'You told me your parents knew before the party that you were poking Tina Best and put the kibosh on the upstairs rendezvous, right?'

'Yes.'

'Your mother says that's bullshit. She says she only spent a few minutes discussing her new curtains with Tina. She says she and your old man didn't find out about you and Tina till the next day.'

Barton's face froze. 'My mother told you that?'

'What the fuck did I just say?'

'I don't believe that woman. What the hell's that all about?'

'Are you saying she's the liar?'

Barton dropped his gaze. 'No, I'm not saying that.'

'Well, maybe she just thought it was about time someone in the family developed a conscience.'

'That'll be the day,' said Barton darkly. 'This is more about dropping me in the shit than cooperating with you, I can assure you of that.'

'I don't give a fuck either way. We've also got a witness who heard a couple fooling around upstairs. That was you and Tina, wasn't it? You got together up there just as you'd planned.'

'Yes.'

'Did you see Polly?'

'No. Once I got to grips with Tina – or she got to grips with me would be a better way of putting it – I forgot all about Polly. We did the deed then went back downstairs – not together, obviously; me first. I went back outside and got sozzled with my mates. Next thing I remember is waking up to find Tim screaming at me to be in his study in two minutes or he'd be back with a bucket of cold water.

'When I got up there, he went completely apeshit. What had happened was he'd been woken up, with a horrendous hangover which didn't help matters, by a call from Roger Best who basically told him to stick their business deal up his arse. I got the whole nine yards: my sick relationship with a woman old enough to be my mother had ruined friendships and cost him hundreds of thousands of dollars; he'd tolerated my indiscretions in the past, but this was unforgivable. I assumed it was all leading up to me being cut off without a brass razoo – never darken our door again – but in mid-rant he got this pained expression and said that his head was about to burst, he had to have a sauna. And off he went to almost literally stumble over Polly's body. Suddenly there was more to worry about than shattered friendships and business deals going south. He made me swear not to tell the police or anyone else I'd been upstairs and I'm pretty sure he got Roger to drum that message into Tina. From then on it was a taboo subject. Sorry I misled you, but old habits die hard.'

'Yeah, but you told Maddocks.'

Barton nodded. 'Which was bloody stupid of me, but I had to tell someone – keeping a real secret is a lot harder than you think. And by then the Bests had left town, so it wasn't like I was dropping Tina in the shit.'

'How soon after did they shoot through?'

'Can't have been much more than a month. Roger and Tina went to Sydney, James went farming down south and that was that. I've had nothing to do with them since.'

'I need their contact details.'

'I don't have them.'

'But you can get them, can't you?' said Ihaka. 'The sooner you do that, the sooner you can get back to your macaroni cheese.'

'I suppose my mother might know someone who's got them.'

'Well, let's find out.'

Ihaka made three phone calls when he got home. The first was to ask a *Herald* police reporter to search their electronic archive for the Muffin Man feature and email him the photo of Tom Murray in his power-to-the-people phase. The reporter kept her curiosity in check. She knew from experience that if Ihaka wanted to enlighten her, he would; if he didn't, there was no point in asking. She also knew Ihaka never forgot a favour.

Next he rang his former colleague and unofficial research assistant Beth Greendale to ask her to find out if Willie Smaile owned his Browns Bays residence and, if so, how much he'd paid for it.

Then he rang Roger Best in Sydney.

Best was predictably underwhelmed. Why? Why now? What could it possibly achieve?

'We might catch the murderer,' said Ihaka. 'That wouldn't be all bad.'

'With respect, Sergeant Ihaka, that doesn't seem very likely. As I recall, the original investigation went precisely nowhere. Now here we are, what, twenty-seven years later? What makes you think you can do any better now than your predecessors did then?'

'We already have. We've identified people who were at the party but went to some trouble to hide the fact. We know why Polly went upstairs. We've identified individuals who were upstairs around the time of the murder. We call them suspects. They include your former wife. You don't need me to tell you what she was doing up there, do you?'

Best's 'No' was a long time coming.

'I don't really blame you for not wanting that to come out,' said Ihaka, 'but, as you said, it's twenty-seven years on. You've had plenty of time to get over it. So let's hear it, from the beginning.'

Roger and Tina's circle regarded them as Exhibit A for the proposition that opposites attract. He was low-key, stitched-up, not exactly anti-social but definitely unspontaneous. She, as she never tired of saying, was a 'people person', which covered a multitude of things, some of them sins. The view from inside their marriage was less sanguine: for the first fifteen or so years what they had in common outweighed their differences. Then the equation evened up. Then it tilted the other way: what little common ground that remained an island in a sea of divergence. She liked

216

to stay up late; he liked to go to bed early with a book. At dinner parties his eyelids would droop before the cheese board appeared, and he'd slip off to bed when the ladies were washing up. When they went to someone else's place, he'd go armed with a reason for bailing out early and would drive home – unlike her, he hardly drank – leaving her to get a cab or flop in the hosts' spare bedroom.

He assumed there was the odd fling. (Sometimes he even wondered if his own behaviour amounted to what these days they call 'enabling'.) Confirmation came in the form of cryptic comments from male friends trying to walk the line between covering up for her and forcing him to face a potentially life-changing reality. A spike in their female friends' solicitousness was another straw in the wind.

He knew some of his friends thought he was a wimp for putting up with it; others thought he was a sap for not seeing what was going on under his nose. He rationalised it this way: he didn't want to be alone and didn't want to be with anyone else, therefore turning a blind eye was the most sensible, if not the only, strategy. As long as it was ships passing in the night; as long as she didn't formalise it by becoming someone's mistress, or get emotionally involved. In hindsight, it was uncharacteristically optimistic of him to think this precarious arrangement would hold up indefinitely.

Until mid-1987 Tina's behaviour was no guide to whether she was straying or thinking of straying: she didn't disengage or alter her routine. So the sudden change was like violent chest pains: an ominous development that couldn't be ignored or explained away or put in reassuring perspective. She'd always been demonstratively tactile and teased him for his sense of decorum but, almost overnight it seemed, she mothballed her repertoire of physical affection – the hugs and squeezes, the lingering touches and nuzzling embraces. When he went to kiss her hello or goodbye, she'd tilt her face, offering cheek rather than mouth. If he was away on business, his calls home went unanswered as often as not. If he asked, she'd invariably been to a film by herself, although she wasn't a big movie fan and had never liked doing things on her own.

He spiralled down to a place where the worst-case scenario (so he thought) was the obvious explanation. On the basis of flimsy circumstantial evidence, he decided her lover was someone who worked for him. That elevated it to an intolerable breach of trust and propriety which undermined him professionally and repaid his excellence as a provider with gross betrayal. For the first time he gave in to self-pity and the urge to repay humiliation in kind. He constructed a revenge fantasy: him as the ice-cold prosecutor letting her dig herself into a black hole, then burying her alive beneath a barrow-load of irrefutable evidence. He hired a private investigator.

The investigator reported that the signs pointed to Johnny Barton, the twenty-one-year-old son of his friend and business partner-to-be, and a pal of his son James. Best thought it was preposterous, but was persuaded to hear the man out. There were no incriminating photos or tape recordings, just an awkward reality. During the surveillance period, Best had spent two nights away from home; on both occasions Johnny had turned up at their place and stayed till well after midnight. Given that James was flatting, Johnny was obviously there to see Tina. What for? Why else would he be spending hours on end with Tina when her husband was out of town?

Tim Barton's election-night party was an opportunity for first-hand scrutiny. He positioned himself where he could watch Tina without her being aware of it. He observed her constant eye contact with Johnny. He saw them surreptitiously brush hands as they passed. He saw them in a corner, hiding in plain sight (so they thought), Tina with hooded eyes and parted lips, her face sagging with desire. He saw her check her watch – he checked his; it was 11.55 – back out of a four-way conversation, slip up the stairs unobserved (so she thought). He saw Johnny do likewise a couple of minutes later. He rushed outside and threw up in a rose garden, then drove home to a sleepless night in the spare room.

He confronted her the next morning. She erupted in furious denial, trying to make his lack of trust and low opinion the issue. How could he believe she'd do such a thing? So this was what he really thought of her? But she cracked when he threw in the private investigator and announced that he was off to share the evidence – and that of his own eyes – with Tim Barton. A cooler head might have demanded to see the evidence, pointed out it wasn't definitive and improvised an explanation that, while hard to believe, was also hard to disprove. But not being calculating by nature and slightly unhinged at the prospect of being abandoned by both husband and lover, Tina wasn't up to that.

Roger rang the Bartons and got Nicky in grande-dame mode: she wouldn't wake Tim because he'd be like a bear with a sore head, but it was nice of Roger to call and she'd pass the message on. He told her he wasn't ringing to compliment them on their ability to throw a party; something had come up that Tim needed to know about immediately.

Tim Barton's really bad day began with him being woken up at least two hours too soon and with a hangover that exceeded his worst fears. He didn't even try to talk

219

Best out of junking their deal. A bit later he rang back to say there was a dead body in his sauna – yes, you heard right – and urge Best to give Tina the same instruction he'd given Johnny: keep your fucking mouth shut.

For months Roger and Tina had been toying with the idea of shifting to Sydney, where they had friends and he had business interests and opportunities. For much of that time James had been trying to break down their resistance to the idea of him dropping out of law school to work on his uncle's South Island sheep station. Under the circumstances, both moves had a lot to recommend them.

But the notion that they could rescue their marriage by making a fresh start in new surroundings was a delusion. Tina bordered on schizophrenic, half the time unable to forgive herself, the other half resenting him for not being able to move on. That proved impossible. When you can't trust your wife with your son's friends, there is no respite: no able-bodied male who enters your orbit can be disregarded. And when it gets to that, there's simply not enough solid ground left on which to rebuild.

Within eighteen months of settling in Sydney, it was over. Tina remarried on the rebound, a disaster that triggered her mental decline. She convinced herself that it was all Sydney's fault and returned to Auckland. Two years ago, after various alarms and embarrassments, she accepted that she wasn't making a very good fist of looking after herself and went into a retirement home. Thankfully things hadn't deteriorated to the point where she needed to be in the secure unit. He spoke to her every couple of weeks, although it was increasingly depressing. Sometimes he got the feeling that she didn't really know who she was talking to and didn't really care.

18

Next morning Ihaka's inbox contained a portrait of the Muffin Man as a young militant, Tom Murray front and centre at a No Nukes demo. Before forwarding it to Jeanine Stern, Ihaka mulled over the wording of the accompanying message. Eventually he settled for, 'Recognise anyone here?'

The retirement home was in Kohimarama, not nearly close enough to the sea to justify the promise of 'harbourside location' in its marketing material. Ihaka watched the comings and goings as he waited for a supervisor. The staff, mainly Filipino he guessed, seemed pleased to be there; the residents were either still making up their minds or past caring.

The supervisor was a large, middle-aged Samoan woman, Beatrice according to her name tag, whose air of no-nonsense efficiency bordered on impatience. She and Ihaka eyed one another warily, each sensing the other might require careful handling.

'I need to talk to Tina Best, if that's what she still calls herself.'

An unforced smile spread across Beatrice's face. 'Tina? Oh, she's a sweetheart.'

'What sort of shape is she in?'

'Health-wise, good as gold – but I guess you mean her state of mind?' Ihaka nodded. 'Well, that depends on who you ask. Some of the staff would tell you she's lost it; some would say she comes and goes; and some have a sneaky suspicion she likes to give people the impression she's lost it when she hasn't.'

'OK, so she's either pretty much a vegetable, taking the piss, or somewhere in between?'

'That's not a term we use,' said Beatrice, 'or like to hear.'

'Understood. Which camp are you in?'

'I'd say she comes and goes. Like a lot of the residents, she has good days and not so good days and the occasional shocker. No question her short-term memory is failing, and longer-term isn't the best either. But it's that classic thing: she'll tell you about something that happened fifty years ago, in detail – what she was wearing, who said what to who. Then next day she'll tell you again, practically word for word. So her recollection of whatever it was fifty years ago is crystal-clear, but she can't remember the conversation she had yesterday. Where it gets a bit tricky is if you ask her about, say, living in Sydney. She'll go all vague, but it's hard to tell if that's because she doesn't remember or doesn't want to talk about it. Older folks can be ultra-sensitive and craftier than you'd think. We get it a lot with hearing issues: they'll make out they're quite deaf – "Sorry, dear, you'll have to speak up, I can't hear a word you say" – then out of the blue they'll go, "I heard that Mrs Bloggs down the hall talking about me behind my back." Sometimes it's just their little game; other times they're trying to catch you out saying what you really think of them because you've assumed they can't hear you. A couple of my co-workers think Tina puts on the dementia so people will talk about her like she's not there.'

'Why would she do that?' said Ihaka. 'From what I've heard, she never gave much of a stuff what people thought of her.'

'Yes, but when was that? We see people get old on the outside – the wrinkles, the white hair, impaired mobility.' She tapped the side of her head. 'Something similar's going on in here.'

'Does she have many visitors?'

'A reasonable number, allowing for the fact she hasn't got immediate family in Auckland. Her son farms down in the Waikato; we don't see much of him. He tends to put in an appearance when his dad comes over from Sydney, but that's about it.'

'What's the atmosphere like at the family reunions?'

'Don't know. We don't intrude on family time.'

'But her ex, Roger, rings pretty regularly?'

'Yeah, which is nice.'

'He told me it sometimes feels like she doesn't really know who she's talking to.'

Beatrice shrugged. 'There you go. If she says she's had a call from him, I might ask, you know, "What's the weather like in Sydney?" And she'll go, "Oh, they're having a terrible heatwave" or "I forgot to ask" or whatever. So she knew it was him, she has some recollection of the conversation, but she's given him the impression she wasn't really there. Maybe she was just having an off day. Or maybe she didn't particularly feel like talking to him. They did get divorced, after all.'

Beatrice offered to sit in on the conversation as a reassuring presence, but Ihaka pointed out it could work the other way, Tina fearing her dirty laundry might get hung out for everyone at the home to see. He promised to go easy.

Tina Best looked robust enough, but there was a fatalistic undertone to her dreamy lassitude, as if night was falling and she was drawing the curtains on the outside world. She responded to Ihaka's introduction with a brief, polite smile, the sort air travellers give the stranger in the next seat the first time they try to strike up a conversation. If she was surprised that a detective had come to see her, she didn't show it.

'I want to ask you about a party,' he began.

'Oh, there were lots of parties,' she said. 'They all just rolled into one. Same old people, same silly games.'

'What sort of games?'

'Party games. The games people play at parties. I thought everyone knew what they are.'

'You'll remember this party. Tim and Nicky Barton's place, election night 1987. It was quite an occasion.'

'I'm sure it was. There were no half-measures with those two. They had an image to live up to, you see. The best of everything.'

'Their son Johnny was there. You remember Johnny?' She looked away. 'You and Johnny were pretty close, weren't you?' No response. 'When was the last time you saw him?' She took a peek at Ihaka out of the corner of her eye. He couldn't tell if it was anxious or furtive. 'Would you like me to ask Johnny to come and see you?'

That generated a spark. 'I'm perfectly all right, thank you. If people want to visit, that's fine, but I don't want them here under sufferance.'

'What about your son, James? Would you like to see more of him?'

She frowned. 'James? James comes as often as he can. He's very busy on the farm.'

'Do you remember what you and Johnny did that night?'

'Please don't ask me about Johnny,' she said, avoiding Ihaka's eye. 'It upsets me.'

'Why?'

'Why are you asking these questions?'

'Because a girl called Polly Stenson was murdered at that party. She was seventeen years old.' Tina sat perfectly still, eyes tightly shut. 'You must remember that.'

She sighed, like someone giving up on an intractable crossword. 'I wish I didn't. I've forgotten lots of things – it's like parts of my life never happened. Then there are things you wish you could forget, but you can't.'

'Polly was murdered upstairs. You were upstairs around the time it happened. Did you see anyone else up there or hear anything? Anything at all?' Tina tried to blink back the tears, but a few fat droplets slid down her cheeks. Ihaka got tissues from a box on the bedside table and dabbed away the tear trails. 'I'm sorry, Tina, I didn't mean to upset you. I'm just trying to find out what happened to Polly before everyone forgets about her.'

'They said we had to forget her. They said no good would come from dwelling on it.'

'Who did?'

'Tim and Roger. They said we had to put her out of our minds. I never could.'

'You did the only thing you could do for Polly: you remembered her.'

Tina slumped back in her chair.

Ihaka stood up. 'I'll leave you alone now. Thanks for talking to me.'

'It's strange what your mind holds on to,' she said to the ceiling. 'When I was ten and my brother Brian, who's dead now, was twelve, he made a stepladder at woodwork class. A proper stepladder, not some flimsy, rickety thing you wouldn't dare stand on. He was very proud of himself. A couple of days after he brought it home, he came into the kitchen when Mum was getting something out of the top cupboard. We both looked at Brian expecting him to be pleased she was using the stepladder, but he went mad. He yelled at Mum, saying it wasn't her stepladder, she had no right to use it without his permission. I could tell she was hurt, but she got straight down and said she was sorry for using it without asking, she wouldn't do it again.'

Tina sat up, looking steadily at Ihaka now. 'I was furious. I said to Brian how could he be so horrible to Mum after all she'd done for him? That just made him even angrier. He grabbed the stepladder and took it outside. I had to go to the toilet. When I came back, there was this racket coming from outside and my mother was standing at the kitchen window. I went over to see what she was looking at. Brian was out on the driveway taking an axe to the stepladder. Mum wasn't making a sound, but there were tears running down her cheeks. I'd never seen her cry. I didn't think grown-ups ever cried; I thought only children did.'

Tina got up and went to a bookshelf stacked with romance novels and photo albums. She opened one of the albums, took out a photo and handed it to Ihaka. It was a black-and-white print of a teenage girl in an old-fashioned dress blowing a kiss to the camera.

'Weren't you the pretty one?' said Ihaka. 'Not that anything's changed.'

Tina put her hand on his arm, tilting her head coquettishly. 'Why thank you, kind sir.'

'It's a very nice photo; too nice to give away. You should hang on to it.'

'But I want you to have it,' she said forcefully. 'Please.'

* * *

Ihaka went looking for Beatrice.

'How did it go?' she asked.

'Well, she gave me a photo of herself.'

Beatrice laughed. 'Sorry to rain on your parade, Sergeant, but you're not the first male visitor she's sent away with a photo.'

'Should I have taken it?'

'If she comes to me tomorrow morning complaining someone's swiped her favourite photo, I'll sing out. I'd be surprised, though. I'm not qualified in that area, but I've been doing this stuff for a while: I suspect Tina's self-esteem has always been tied up with how men react to her. I hope you were nice.'

Ihaka nodded. 'And the story about her brother's stepladder?'

'Oh, we've all heard that one,' said Beatrice. 'Some of us more than once. I'm not even going to try to guess what's going on there.'

Jeanine Stern emailed back.

OK, provisos:

1. *It was a long time ago. Longer than I care to dwell on.*

2. *I only saw the guy once.*

3. *I don't want to be held to this. If asked to do so in a court of law, I'd almost certainly refuse.*

Bearing all that in mind, I'm reasonably sure the guy in the forefront doing the clenched fist thing is the post-grad student – so he said – who showed up trying to claim the diaries because Ethan had said he should feel free. As if.

Ihaka rang Beth Greendale to see how she was getting on.

'I was just about to ring you,' she said. 'It wasn't straightforward.'

'I had a feeling it wouldn't be.'

'I know it's been a boon for paedophiles and terrorists but, speaking as someone who enjoys having the odd break from being a suburban housewife-mother, I say thank God for the internet.'

'So do millions of masturbators. What have you got?'

'First off,' said Beth, 'Smaile doesn't own the property. He's lived there since 2008 when it was purchased for $1.7 million by Kelvingrove Ltd. Kelvingrove, which is listed as a property investment company, is a wholly owned subsidiary of an outfit called Trongate Ltd. You'll never guess who owns Trongate.'

'You want to bet?'

'Tito, if I've wasted the best part of a day, neglecting my kids in the process, to find out something you already knew, I'm going to be mightily fucked off.'

'Settle down, Elizabeth. I don't know, which is why I got you to find out. But you said I'd never guess who owns Trongate. Well, I'm prepared to take up the challenge.'

'Go for it.'

'The Muffin Man, Tom Murray.'

'You're a prick, you know that? Don't ever call me again.'

'You're the second woman who's said that to me recently. I'm pretty sure the other one actually meant it.'

Ihaka decided dinner could wait. He drove over the Harbour Bridge to see Stu Boyle, picking up a cold six-pack on the way. It turned out that Boyle had given up beer, at least for the time being, because his doctor had told him he needed to lose weight.

'Oh, is that how it works?' said Ihaka. 'Good to know.' He popped the top off a bottle and half-emptied it in one go.

'You might want take it easy, mate,' said Boyle. 'I mean, look what happened to your old man.'

Ihaka gave him a stare. 'You saw that coming, did you?'

Boyle shrugged awkwardly. 'No, shit no, it was a huge shock. Having said that, Jimmy was a big bloke with a big appetite – for food, grog, the works. And he only had one speed: flat-stick. It was a hell of a shock, but I'd be lying if I said it never crossed my mind that maybe he should take his foot off the gas every once in a while.'

'Did you ever suggest that to him?'

'Just the once,' said Boyle with a rueful snort. 'Your old man didn't take kindly to unsolicited advice – on any subject. He told me to pull my fucking head in, or he'd do it for me.'

Ihaka shook his head. 'Un-fucking-believable. You just can't help some people.'

'Whereas you, on the other hand, are always open to advice?'

'Exactly. In fact, that's why I'm here. I've come across something a bit bloody strange and I'd like your take on it. Remember you were telling me about Smaile booting Tom Murray out of the WVP? Well, Murray – reluctantly, I'd have to say – told me the same story in more detail. He was quite specific on the timing. The first time he blotted his copybook was when he slept through the May Day rally – that's the first of May, right? Two weeks later he fucked up again and that was that: goneburger. Ethan Stern was killed on June the twentieth. Smaile made no bones about how he was determined to make sure no one else got hold of the diaries. He admitted ringing Stern's widow and as good as admitted sending one of his boys around to her place pretending to be a post-grad student. Well, the widow's pretty sure the fake post-grad student was none other than Tom Murray. So the question is: how come Murray was doing dodgy stuff for Smaile a couple of months after he'd been expelled from the party?'

'I see what you mean,' said Boyle. 'That doesn't make sense. Smaile didn't muck around. In fact, he was renowned for being a vindictive bastard. If you crossed him, you were history. I never heard of anyone who got the broom from the WVP being allowed back in the fold. But, Christ, talk about never forgetting a face – I wouldn't recognise someone I met once or twice thirty-odd years ago if I tripped over them.'

'All I can tell you is she picked him out of an old group photo, without any help from me. I didn't tell her what it was about or who she should be looking for. And there's something else: have you been to Smaile's place?'

'That'll be the bloody day. I heard he's somewhere up in the Bays.'

'He's on the fucking pig's back, that's where. The house he's in cost $1.7 million in 2008.'

Boyle goggled. 'What? How the hell could he afford that?'

'He didn't have to. The purchaser was a company owned by a company owned by that well-known counter-revolutionary snake in the grass, Tom Murray.'

'You're telling me Smaile's living in a house that belongs to Murray?'

'I am indeed. You might say, OK, water under the bridge, the MVP doesn't exist any more, time heals all wounds – all that shit. Except to hear Murray tell it, there's no way they've buried the hatchet. And given Smaile hasn't changed his views, how likely would he be to kiss and make up now that Murray's not just on the other side of the fence, he's three fucking paddocks away?'

'You know, for someone who was saying just yesterday he didn't think Miriam's research had anything to do with her being beaten up, you're giving a pretty good impression of a bloke who actually believes otherwise.'

Ihaka dead-batted Boyle's probe with a bland half-smile. 'So what do you make of all that?'

'Something's going on, that's for sure,' said Boyle. 'To be honest, I don't have a clue what it could be, but I know somebody who might, this ex-SIS guy I was going to put Miriam in touch with. He spent years keeping an eye on the WVP, probably knows more about them than anyone bar Smaile. He tried to recruit me to basically spy on the red brethren. Well, there was no way I was going to do that. I didn't agree with the WVP on a lot of things and didn't like their methods, but when push came to shove we were on the same side of the argument. Even though I knocked him back, we hit it off in an odd sort of way. We used to get together for a quiet one every now and again. It was a bit of a game really, each trying to pump the other for some inside information. Anyway, we've stayed in touch. He's retired now, lives out at Karekare, near Piha. If you want, I could set up a meeting. He's become a cranky bugger in his old age, so I'd have to sort of smooth the path.'

'Go ahead,' said Ihaka. 'The sooner the better.'

19

Ihaka took what was left of his six-pack home. He boiled water in a saucepan, threw in a fistful of spaghetti and defrosted a slab of Bolognese sauce in the microwave. He made the sauce once a month, doubling the amounts in the recipe on the theory that what would make two meals for a family of four would make four meals for a large single man with a tendency to overeat.

After he'd eaten, he poured himself another glass of the supermarket Shiraz he favoured on the more-bang-for-your-buck principle, opened his notebook and reviewed the timeline of the comings and goings around Polly Stenson's murder.

End of June/beginning of July: Johnny Barton & Tina Best begin affair.

15th August: Tim & Nicky Barton's party.

11 pm: According to Eddie Brightside, Waitz group meets in library upstairs.

11.30 pm: A/c her girlfriends, Polly leaves basement, goes up to ground floor.

11.30 pm: A/c Andy Maddocks, Johnny leaves his mates outside, goes inside.

11.35 pm approx: Johnny sees Polly, tells her to go upstairs.

11.40 pm approx: Polly caught eavesdropping on Waitz group.

11.45 pm approx: Waitz group goes back downstairs.

11.50 pm approx: A/c Ann Smellie, Waitz group departs.

11.53 pm approx: A/c Brightside, Polly leaves the library to go exploring.

11.55 pm: A/c Roger Best, Tina goes upstairs.

11.57 pm approx: A/c Roger, Johnny goes upstairs to join Tina in master bedroom.

Midnight approx: A/c himself, on his way downstairs Brightside hears male & female voices/laughter, presumably JB & Tina.

16th August between midnight & 1 am: estimated time of death.

12.10 am approx: Johnny goes downstairs.

12.15 am approx: Tina goes downstairs.

10.40 am: Mrs Stenson rings Polly's friend's place where she was supposed to be sleeping over.

10.45 am: Mrs Stenson rings the Bartons.

11 am: Roger Best rings the Bartons.

11.05 am: Tim B wakes Johnny.

11.10 am: Tim goes apeshit at Johnny.

11.15 am: Tim finds Polly's body in sauna.

One month later approx: Bests move to Sydney.

Two months later approx: Johnny tells Maddocks about him & Tina.

He went through it again, and a third time, not sure what he was looking for, or even if there was anything there. On the fourth read, he spotted it. It had been staring him in the face all along.

He looked at his watch: 10.33, well before Johnny Barton's bedtime.

The landline wasn't answered so he tried Barton's mobile, getting a pissed-off 'Who is this?' after ten rings. In the back-ground a woman was registering her dissatisfaction.

'Ihaka. Is this a good time?'

Barton strangled a snarl. 'Christ, I should've known. No, it's not a good time. Last night was bad enough, but that was perfect timing by comparison.'

'I think I get the picture,' said Ihaka with a wheeze of amusement, 'but you know what they say about delayed gratification.'

'I have no idea. What do they say?'

'It's a sign of maturity.'

'How do you get away with it?' said Barton, genuinely curious.

'Think of it as Inspector O'Goober's revenge.'

'What the hell does that mean?'

'Work it out for yourself. The reason I'm calling: you told Maddocks about Tina because you just had to tell someone, right?'

'Oh God,' groaned Barton, 'we're not back on that, are we?'

'How about you just answer the fucking question?'

'That is correct, officer.'

'Even though your old man threatened to boot you out without a penny if you blabbed about it?'

'Well, he never said that in so many words —'

'Then at the party, by which stage you'd been knocking Tina off for a month or so, you decided to put on a show for Polly?'

'Well, that was a spur-of-the-moment thing. Don't go all Gestapo on me, Sergeant, but what's your point? We've been through this.'

'The point is, given all that, do you really expect me to believe you hadn't told anyone about Tina before the shit hit the fan?' Barton didn't answer. 'Who did you tell?'

'Even if I did tell someone,' said Barton sourly, 'what's the big deal? I don't see the relevance of it.'

'You're a fucking slow learner, aren't you? Still getting me mixed up with someone who gives a shit what you think. Who was it?'

'My sister.'

'No one else?'

'No,' said Barton. 'And that's the gospel truth.'

'Why her?'

'The simple, honest answer is I wanted to see how she'd react. Lucy had this "I'm more worldly than you" attitude. Still has for that matter. And it still bugs me.'

'I'm assuming you swore her to secrecy,' said Ihaka.

'Of course.'

'But we both know that hardly ever works.'

'Lucy's no fool. She could be dangerous in all sorts of little ways, but she understood why it couldn't go any further.'

'So where do I find Lucy?'

'Ah, well, that depends,' said Barton. 'When she's in the country she divides her time, as they say, between here and Queenstown. But for much of the time she's not in the country. Her current whereabouts might depend on whether the snow is better in Japan or Colorado at this time of year, or whether there's a cutting-edge arts festival in Adelaide or Albuquerque. Then again, maybe she's in Portugal, because there can't be a wine region in France, Italy or Spain she hasn't done by now. You get the idea?'

'You're not exactly on the bones of your arse.'

'I have to get up and go to work five days a week,' said

Barton. 'She gets up and opens the curtains: if it's raining, she rings her dog walker.'

'So did the old man shaft you after all?'

'Not that it's any of your business, but we were treated exactly the same. Mommie Dearest was the big winner when Tim went to his reward. No, the secret of my sister's lifestyle is she married well, so when the time came she divorced well. And to prove she isn't a one-hit wonder, she married even better second time around.'

'It's probably harder than you make it sound.'

'I'll be interested to see if you're as charitably disposed after you've met her. I love my sister like a sister but, as one of her dearest friends once said, she has most of her mother's faults and few of her mother's redeeming features.'

When Ihaka got off the phone, he thought – briefly – about ringing Ron Firkitt. It was after eleven, though, and sunnier-natured people than Firkitt would give the bum's rush to anyone who woke them up to ask a favour. So he left himself a note on the kitchen table and went to bed.

He rang Firkitt first thing.

'Tito Ihaka, eh?' said Firkitt. 'That name rings a bell. I used to know a Tito Ihaka. Fat hori cunt he was.'

'I think you'll find that term's a no-no.'

'Sorry, big-boned hori cunt. So, how's the cold-case bullshit?'

'It's great. No pointless meetings that drag on forever, no having to write reports that nobody reads, no fuckheads to deal with. I recommend it.'

'Make the most of it, mate. Uncle Finbar hasn't got too many more of those gigs up his sleeve.'

'I need a favour,' said Ihaka.

'Big one or a little one?'

'Could be a major. Would that be a problem?'

'Let me ask you something,' said Firkitt. 'Do you know who's going to be the next District Commander?'

'No.'

'You lying prick. Don't fucking pretend McGrail hasn't told you.'

'Come to think of it, he sort of hinted your mate's in the running.'

Firkitt guffawed. 'In the running? They cancelled all bets on that one, mate – it was a fucking one-horse race. It could be announced as early as next week.'

'Well, I'm happy for him,' said Ihaka. 'Getting back to the favour…'

'Oh, we never left that subject,' said Firkitt. 'Follow-up question: who do you think Charlton's got in mind to step into his shoes?'

'Well, I haven't felt a tap on my shoulder, so I'm picking it's you.'

'Well picked. I can think of a couple of things that might make Charlton change his mind. One would be if he got the impression you and I are bum chums. I thought he was coming around, but he's right back to believing you're the anti-Christ.'

'He thinks I went over his head and got McGrail to pull me out of the front line. For what it's worth, I didn't.'

'It's worth fuck-all now, mate,' said Firkitt. 'The other thing would be if I got mixed up in some colossal goatfuck. And when DS Ihaka asks me to do him a major favour, you know what I hear? I hear a little voice saying, watch out Ron, this mad bastard's trying to drag you into what's bound to be a colossal goatfuck. Do you see my dilemma?'

'I see a vague outline.'

'Then again, even if I had a supporting role in a goatfuck starring the anti-Christ, Charlton would think twice before he weaselled on me. The man owes me, big time.'

'And you know where the bodies are buried,' said Ihaka. 'So to speak.'

'So to speak. Charlton terminated a few careers, but no actual people.'

'That's what he's got you for, right?'

'Exactly,' said Firkitt. 'Anyway, I've got to look out for myself now: how am I going to operate as a DI? Who's going to be on my team? And most important of all, who's going to be my Ron Firkitt?'

'I can think of a few blokes at Central who'd fancy themselves in that role.'

'Shit, so can I, but you and I both know they're not up to the job. It's what you did for McGrail all those years, and what I've done for Charlton for longer than I fucking care to remember. How would you feel about being my Ron Firkitt?'

'Ron, I know what I did for McGrail; I'm not entirely sure what you've done for Charlton, although I've heard some, shall we say, colourful stories. What exactly would I be signing up for?'

'Mate, you know what it's like: give a dog a bad name. Besides, it suited me that people thought I was the biggest fucking hard-arse this side of the black stump. What I'm talking about is your go-to man, the bloke you turn to when the heat's on and can rely on to get the job done. I'm talking about loyalty. Say what you like to my face behind closed doors, but outside that room you couldn't get a cigarette paper between us. Likewise, I'll bollock you when it's just us, but I'll back you to the hilt in front of the troops – and when Charlton comes after you wanting your head on a stick.'

'He's not going to like it.'

'Course he won't,' said Firkitt. 'But Charlton's a realist: he knows I'll have to run my own race and be seen to run my own race. No better way of doing that than having you on board. Charlton wants to go all the way; it won't be long before he's got bigger fish to fry. As long as we're getting results, he's not going to give a shit whose cock's in whose pocket. Anyway, think about it.'

'I'll do that. So what about the favour?'

'No worries – unless it's completely fucking crazy.'

'I wouldn't go that far, but it's not your routine op.'

'Christ, I took that for granted. If it was, you wouldn't be asking.'

When Ihaka tracked down Lucy Barton-Frost she was on her way to the airport. In two and a half hours she was flying out to Bali with a few girlfriends for a winter break, then on to Shanghai where her husband had business to attend to. She wouldn't be back in Auckland for three weeks. Until the boarding call, though, she'd be filling in time in the airline lounge.

Ihaka had the siren blaring most of the way to the airport. When Lucy and friends entered the lounge in a gust of jarring laughter and expensive perfume, he was waiting for them.

There was no particular family resemblance, but he could tell which one was Lucy. She wasn't the one who'd put on too much make-up and talked too loud. Or whose jeans were too tight and heels too high, or whose fake blonde hair was too blonde and fake tan too dark. She was the one looking five years younger than she was, rather than aiming for ten and making a hash of it. She was the one who saw the big picture when it came to throwing money at middle age. And, if her brother was to be believed, she was probably the biggest bitch of the lot.

'All right, ladies,' she said, 'why don't you have a glass of fizz while Detective Sergeant Ihaka here gives me a grilling.' Her voice had faint echoes of west London. 'This way, Sergeant. I rang ahead and organised a space for us.'

She led him into a small meeting room, an oval desk and four chairs hemmed in by glass walls. 'You're on holiday,' said Ihaka as they sat down. 'You should feel free to have a drink.'

Lucy dismissed the notion with a lazy flick of the wrist. 'They'll have the real thing on the plane, an endless supply. I've been looking forward to meeting you, Sergeant. My mother and brother have differing perspectives. In fact, you'd swear they were talking about two completely different people. Mother was quite taken with you, which is a surprise on a number of counts, some of which we needn't go into. Johnny, on the other hand, isn't a fan. He feels you were unnecessarily rough on him.'

'That might count as rough in Remuera, not in the real world. And he made it necessary by only telling the truth when all else failed.'

'You must get that all the time.'

'Sure. Doesn't mean I have to like it.'

'Try not to be so hard on him next time,' she said. 'If there is a next time. What you have to remember about Johnny is he's spent most of his life playing a role he detests: that of Tim Barton's son. He grew up craving Father's approval, which of course meant he was resentful when it wasn't forthcoming. Then there was the expectation – his and other people's – that went with being the only son. I can understand that his manner gets people's backs up, but he's not as sure of himself as he makes out. That rather smug exterior is just that: it's to stop people seeing he's actually quite screwed up. And while you may think he was callous about Polly, bear in mind Father put him under awful pressure. I know he felt responsible for what happened. I think he still does.'

'He's got a funny way of showing it. So you reckon it was because of Polly he went off the rails?'

'Oh, you know about the lost years? I don't have the slightest doubt it was because of her. Father came to recognise that, which is partly why he went to such lengths to save Johnny from himself.'

'But you sailed through it all without a scratch?'

'My conscience is clear,' she said with the sparkle-eyed smile of someone whose outlook is all blue sky. 'And I don't have a social conscience, which means I don't lose any sleep over my enviable existence.'

'Do you have kids?'

'Oh, I did my duty, don't you worry: I have two from my first marriage. They're old enough to do without me now, so I have freedom and the means to make the most of it.'

'Just as well I'm not the envious kind.'

'Really?' she said. 'That puts you in a distinct minority.'

'I was already there.'

'So you were. Now I sense this could be a much more interesting conversation than any I'm going to have in the next eight days, but I'm also conscious that time isn't on our side. What can I do for you, Sergeant?'

'How long before the party did Johnny tell you about him and Tina Best?'

Lucy shrugged, not overdoing the mental effort. 'Probably a couple of weeks.'

'What did you think?'

'I thought it was gross – but also hilarious. I've always liked the idea that the sign of a sophisticated mind is the ability to hold contradictory ideas simultaneously.'

'Who did you tell?'

'What makes you think I did?'

'People always do.'

'Hmm, that's disappointing. Still, I was young and irresponsible. I told James Best.'

Ihaka was simultaneously impressed and appalled. He wondered what that said about him. 'Jesus. Why?'

'He dumped me,' she said matter-of-factly. 'I was never going to take it lying down, but what really hacked me off was I wasn't even keen on him. We'd known each other since we were little kids, and I'd been a friend to him in my own way. Like, when he didn't have anyone to take to his school ball and Tina got Mother to lean on me to go with him, I went along with it even though I had better offers. I only went out with him because I was waiting for a guy I liked to get sick of his drip of a girlfriend, and I thought going out with James might speed things up. You know how it works. We had a few forgettable dates, then next thing I know he's telling people, friends of mine, that he'd dumped me.'

'Any particular reason?'

'Well, since you asked: apparently because I wouldn't suck his cock.' Ihaka acknowledged her candour with a fractional raise of the eyebrows. 'I never got this American thing that blowjobs are no big deal, in fact not even real sex, whereas intercourse is terribly significant. I tended to see it the other way round. What are your thoughts?'

'I've never really understood what's in it for the blower,' he said, which made Lucy laugh. 'So when did you tell James?'

'That very night. It would've been getting on for midnight, I suppose. Johnny sidled up to me and said, 'Guess what I'll be doing in a few minutes.' I said I'd rather not, to which he said he'd be screwing Tina in the royal bedchamber – our parents' boudoir. Again, I thought it was gross but could see the funny side of it. A few minutes later I spotted James. Factor in that I'd had quite a lot to drink and still had nothing to show for the hours I'd spent trying to think of a way of getting him back. I thought, OK, buster, payback time. And I waltzed up to him and let him have it.'

'How did he handle it?'

'He was off his face, so I didn't get the reaction I was hoping for. It was pretty standard stuff: "That's bullshit; you're a fucking bitch." So I gave him the second barrel: that, as we speak, your mama's getting a right royal rooting in my parents' bed. Not a bad parting shot, I think you'll agree.'

Ihaka drove to Central. After picking up some equipment and briefing Ron Firkitt, he went upstairs to update Finbar McGrail. As he came out of the lift, Marcia said, 'He's not here.'

Ihaka was used to Marcia greeting him with a hawkish glare, or a burst of canned bonhomie. Now she just looked hangdog.

'Is he back any time soon?'

'He's in Wellington all day.'

Ihaka thought of his conversation with Firkitt. 'Dotting the i's and crossing the t's, are they?'

'He told you then?' Ihaka nodded. 'Did he tell you they want him to bring it forward? Take early retirement, in other words.'

'Since when?'

'He got a call from the Minister's office yesterday. They made it sound like they're doing him a favour. I think he'll take it. I really think he's had enough of all the political crap.'

'What will you do?'

'Probably call it quits,' she said. 'I don't think I could work for anyone else.'

'I know what you mean. But listen, if you're talking to him, give him a message from me. Tell him to take his time. Tell him he might be feeling better about things in a few days. He'll know what it's about.'

'I will,' said Marcia, bucking up. 'I'll make a point of it. Thank you, Sergeant.'

'Us friends of Finbar have to stick together.'

Marcia was almost beaming. Ihaka headed for the lift thinking, Jesus, McGrail was right: it's not that hard.

Ihaka sat at the table in his kitchen/dining room, no closer to deciding what to have for dinner than he'd been half an hour earlier because he'd been thinking about Polly Stenson and Ethan Stern and Miriam Lovell – and his father. He wondered if the killers could hear his footsteps, if they realised he was coming for them.

His mobile rang. Stu Boyle said, 'How are you placed tonight? He's willing to talk.'

'What, right now?'

'You've got to strike while the iron's hot with this guy. No telling what sort of mood he'll be in tomorrow.'

'OK, well, in that case —'

'I'll pick you up,' said Boyle. 'Can you be on the corner of Nelson and Wellesley in half an hour?'

'I'll be there.'

'OK. See you soon.'

Ihaka went into the bedroom to get his leather jacket and car keys. The photo of herself that Tina Best had given him was on the chest of drawers, beside the keys. He studied it for a couple of minutes. Then he put on his jacket and went to meet Boyle, knowing who killed Polly Stenson and why.

20

Stu Boyle drove a five-year-old hatchback with the radio tuned to talkback idiocy. After Ihaka raised the possibility of turning that shit off, Boyle filled the vacuum with tales of old boxers – Tuna Scanlon, Earl Nikora, Lionel Rose, Henry Cooper. Some of the names rang a bell: Ihaka was pretty sure he'd heard his father talk about them. Or maybe driving through the Waitakeres on a wet night with the windscreen wipers flailing and the heating cranked up and hardly any traffic about took him back to his childhood: rolling down an empty, unlit country road to visit relatives up north, half-asleep after a six-hour drive but vaguely aware of the rhythmic slap of the windscreen wipers and his parents' murmured exchanges, floating through the night in a warm, secure bubble.

Realising Ihaka wasn't paying attention, Boyle fell silent. The rain eased to drizzle then to spits, so Boyle put the wipers on low frequency and turned down the heating to reduce the fug. In the sudden hush, Ihaka heard the sigh of the sea. At dawn the wind would come up and the sighs would give way to the thump and boom of heavy waves breaking on black west coast sand.

Boyle drove to the end of Karekare beach and turned into a drive that snaked through thick bush up to a house, an indistinct shape in the night. As he parked behind an SUV, Ihaka said, 'What's this guy got against lights?'

'Turning them on costs money,' said Boyle. 'Don't worry, I know where the switch is.'

He led Ihaka up a few steps to a deck, pulled open a sliding glass door and turned on lights to reveal a large, modern room with polished wooden floors, white walls, a table for six, a huge open fireplace and sofas arranged around a wall-mounted television.

'Not what I was expecting,' said Ihaka.

'You're not the first visitor to say that,' said Boyle. 'Take a seat; I'll go flush him out.'

Ihaka sat on a sofa. He tested his eyesight on the cluster of bottles on the sideboard across the room. If his eyes didn't deceive him there were at least three different brands of single-malt scotch.

Boyle reappeared followed by an overweight middle-aged man with watery eyes, a flattened nose and long, thinning, greasy hair plastered across a boulder head. He brought a .38 revolver out from behind his back and held it up for Ihaka to see, his predator's grin exposing jumbled, discoloured teeth. Bringing up the rear and looking as if he'd rather be anywhere else was Tom Murray.

'Well, I've done my bit,' said Boyle to no one in particular. 'I'll leave you blokes to it.' He retraced his steps, avoiding eye contact with Ihaka.

Ihaka asked Murray, 'What the fuck's going on?' Jerking his head at the other guy: 'And who's this ape?'

Murray carried on looking miserable. 'This isn't my idea.'

'This isn't my idea.' Boulder Head's idea of mimicry was a cry-baby whine. 'But you'll also do your bit, won't you?'

'What's his bit?' asked Ihaka.

'If I was you,' said Boulder Head, 'I'd be in no rush to find out.'

Ihaka took a good look at him. 'You look like the sort of brain-dead scum who'd get a buzz out of kicking a woman's head in. I'm guessing it was you who bashed Miriam Lovell.' Boulder Head's grin stretched. 'I'm also guessing that fat little fuck Boyle pulled the same trick on her, bringing her out here to meet a non-existent ex-SIS guy.'

'Aren't you the smart fart?' said Boulder Head. 'Fat lot of good it'll do you.'

Ihaka nodded thoughtfully. 'So you're going to knock off a cop because Willie Smaile doesn't like people poking around in stuff that happened thirty years ago? That old prick must have some dark secrets.'

'Don't even try to second-guess Mr Smaile,' said Boulder Head. 'He's way ahead of a stooge like you.'

'Shut up, Wayne,' said Murray.

Ihaka switched back to Murray. 'Still, I suppose you might as well be hung for a sheep as a lamb – it looks like Miriam might not make it.'

Murray told Wayne, 'Something's not right here. Why isn't he shitting himself? He's walked into a trap, but he's sitting there like he holds all the cards.' Wayne shrugged blankly, not sure what Murray was on about. 'What's with the blithe unconcern, Sergeant?'

'I've got you to thank for that,' said Ihaka. 'You remember telling me Smaile had these secret party members, guys who pretended to be anti the WVP so they could keep tabs on the other members? Well, Miriam's a smart lady. She wouldn't have put herself in harm's way, so she must've been set up by someone she trusted. I got to thinking: what if Boyle was one of Smaile's spies? What if Miriam took Boyle at face value and confided in him, and he was funnelling everything back to the great leader? If so, he probably set her up. So when Boyle suggested this little jaunt, I thought chances are he's lining me up for the same treatment.'

'Search him, Wayne,' said Murray. 'Give me the gun. I'll keep him covered.'

'No fucking way I'm giving you the gun,' said Wayne, glowering at Ihaka. 'That's exactly what the cunt wants me to do.'

'All right then, I'll search him,' said Murray.

'You'll do as you're fucking told,' said Wayne. 'And I'm telling you to stay right where you are.'

Wayne stood in front of Ihaka, pointing the pistol at his forehead. 'Get up.' Ihaka did so. 'Turn around and spread your arms out.' He jabbed the muzzle into the back of Ihaka's neck. 'If you try anything, I'll blow your fucking head off.'

He patted Ihaka down, starting from the top. Feeling something in the front left pocket of Ihaka's jeans, Wayne thrust a hand in and brought out a black rectangular device about the size of a Zippo lighter.

Showing it to Murray: 'What the fuck is this?'

'I can answer that,' volunteered Ihaka. 'It's a GPS personal tracking device. It tells my partner exactly where I am.'

Ron Firkitt came through the door holding a Glock 17 semi-automatic pistol at eye level in a two-handed grip. 'Police. Drop the gun and move away.'

Wayne wrapped his left arm around Ihaka's neck, planting the muzzle in his right ear. 'I've got a better idea. You drop your gun and I won't put one in this cunt's brain.'

Ihaka said, 'Don't even think about it, Ron.'

Wayne rapped Ihaka on the side of the face with the pistol. 'Shut your fucking hole.'

'Don't worry,' said Firkitt. 'It's not going to happen.'

Murray had his hands out, palms opened upward, like a mediator urging both parties to give peace a chance.

Wayne yelled, 'What the fuck are you doing there, Tom?'

'I'm not doing anything,' said Murray firmly. 'This has gone far enough.'

Firkitt to Wayne: 'Let Ihaka go and beat it out the back door. That's the best offer you're going to get.'

'Now we're getting somewhere,' said Wayne. 'But what's going to happen is, I don't let Ihaka go, me and him beat it out the back door. If you come after us, I'll waste him.' He cracked Ihaka on the side of the face again. 'OK, shithead, let's move. Out through the kitchen.'

Wayne backed across the room, keeping Ihaka between himself and Firkitt. Firkitt stayed in the firing position, waiting for a cue. Ihaka gave him a wink. They shuffled backwards through the kitchen and out the back door onto another deck. As Wayne adjusted his grip, the muzzle came away from Ihaka's ear. Ihaka launched himself backwards, lifting Wayne off his feet. The gun roared, the balustrade gave way under their combined weight and they toppled backwards, crash-landing in a rock garden a metre and a half below the deck. Wayne hit the ground first, cushioning the impact for Ihaka.

Ihaka heaved himself up, ears ringing. Wayne was on his hands and knees, rasping like an asthmatic, scrabbling among the rocks for the pistol. Ihaka steadied himself and slammed his right foot into Wayne's exposed mid-section, sending him over the edge of the rock garden and rolling down a slope into the undergrowth.

Firkitt was on the deck. 'You all right?'

Ihaka tapped his ear to indicate his hearing was on the blink. Firkitt jumped down to the rock garden and put his mouth close to Ihaka's better ear. 'I can hear him in the bush – he's heading for the beach. I'll run the bastard down. You look after the other one. He doesn't look like he's up for a fight, but you never know.'

Firkitt plunged into the bush. Ihaka found the revolver and went inside. Murray, looking much more at ease, was at the sideboard pouring himself a whisky. He glanced up. 'I take it Wayne's exit strategy didn't go quite to plan?'

Ihaka's hearing was coming back. 'You could say that.'

'There's a surprise. Are you a single-malt man, Sergeant? I can offer a choice of Islay, Highlands or Speyside.'

'I'm still on the job,' said Ihaka. 'You own this place, right?' Murray nodded. 'As you said to me a few minutes ago, you're looking pretty relaxed for a man in your position.'

Murray sat down, cupping his drink in both hands. 'What position would that be?'

'Well, let's see,' said Ihaka. 'Potentially there's accessory to murder…'

'You mean Ms Lovell?'

'Let's start with her.'

Murray shook his head. 'Nothing to do with me.'

'I can't see your mate Wayne copping to that on his own.'

'I can,' said Murray. His assurance bordered on complacency. 'First of all, that's the way it happened. Secondly, Wayne has two talents in life, if you can call them that. One is for inflicting brutality on people weaker than himself; the other is for following orders. And his orders include keeping me well out of it if things go sideways, which they clearly have. And a good thing too, I might add.'

'Orders from Smaile?'

'Correct.' Ihaka started to say something, but Murray gave him the stop sign. 'We're going to have to leave it there, Sergeant. Much as I'd like to give you a full and frank account, that's simply not possible. As long as Willie Smaile's alive and twitching, I have nothing further to say. That's just the way it is. He's an old man and not a very well one, so he probably won't be with us a whole lot longer. Let's hope not, anyway. The day he goes to the inferno, I'll tell you everything.'

'Will my old man feature?'

'Yes, he will.'

'Was he murdered?'

Murray looked into his glass for a few seconds. He swallowed what was left of his drink, set the glass down on a side table and, without looking up, slowly raised and lowered his head.

'You sit tight,' said Ihaka, heading for the back door.

Firkitt jogged along the beach under a full moon that threw pale half-light across the beach, wondering if Wayne was too dumb to realise he was leaving a trail of footprints in the sand. There he was, only fifty metres away, lurching like a lame animal. Firkitt slowed down. No need to bust a gut. It was touch and go whether the guy would even make it to the rocks.

He did, but only to sit down, elbows on knees, head bowed, sucking in air. When he lifted his head, Firkitt was right in front of him. 'You're under arrest,' said Firkitt.

Wayne dropped his head again, nodding.

'Let's go.'

Wayne shook his head. 'I'm fucked,' he panted. 'Give us a mo.' After a couple of minutes, he hauled himself upright, clutching his side. 'Feels like I've done some ribs.'

'Tough shit.'

Firkitt cocked an ear, hearing human sounds on the breeze. He stepped away from Wayne, glancing around. Ihaka emerged from the darkness, talking on his mobile. He stopped a few metres away, slipping the phone into his jacket pocket. 'The boys are on their way. I'll take it from here, Ron.' Talking to Firkitt; looking at Wayne.

Firkitt seeing the look, thinking, Jesus Christ. 'Tito, listen, mate —'

'It's OK, Ron. You head back and babysit the Muffin Man. I'm just going to have a quiet word with this piece of shit.'

'A quiet word?'

'Yeah.' Ihaka's ominous stare didn't waver. 'There's not much to say, but it has to be said.'

'I don't think that's such a good idea,' said Firkitt.

'Don't leave me here with this bastard,' said Wayne, his voice rattling with anxiety. 'Look at him.'

'What's the matter, pal?' said Ihaka almost soothingly. 'You're a big boy. Off you go, Ron. Don't look back.'

Firkitt looked from Wayne to Ihaka, then back to Wayne. 'Fuck you – you asked for it.' He turned and walked quickly back up the beach.

A minute went by, Ihaka still staring at Wayne, who kept his eyes down, watching Ihaka's feet. When Ihaka advanced, Wayne took a ragged breath and bounced a weary roundhouse right off Ihaka's cheekbone.

Ihaka didn't seem to notice. 'Much more fun hitting chicks, isn't it?' he said.

He rammed the heel of his right hand into Wayne's chest. Wayne staggered back a couple of steps. Ihaka followed, giving him another explosive shove. Wayne went over backwards, almost hitting his head on the rocks.

Ihaka bent down, clamped his left hand, reverse grip, over Wayne's mouth and dropped a knee onto his ribs. Wayne's eyes bulged and frothed and sweat popped on his forehead.

'It's a horrible place to be,' said Ihaka conversationally. 'In pain, knowing there's more to come but there's not a damn thing you can do about it. Completely at the mercy of someone who doesn't give a fuck.'

Ihaka switched his left hand to Wayne's chest, grabbing a handful of fleecy, and hauled him into a sitting position. He gripped Wayne's face in his right hand and slammed the back of his head down on a rock. Wayne's skull caved in with a mishmash of contrasting sounds: sharp and dull, hard and soft, dry and wet.

Three hours later, around 2 am, Stu Boyle awoke from an interesting dream. He was on a train somewhere in Eastern Europe with his late wife's sister, who was giving every indication of reciprocating the covert desire he'd nursed for almost two decades. It was sometime in the early 1980s, before the Berlin Wall came down and his late wife's sister let herself go – not that the two were connected.

Boyle lay there in the dark resenting the interruption of the rare and promising developments in his resting mind and dormant groin. In the faintly static silence of deep-night wakefulness the culprit revealed itself. Tap, tap, tap. A minute went by, but it could have been two. Tap, tap, tap.

It didn't make sense. He lived alone, without pets. It didn't sound like a dripping tap and, anyway, drips are regular. You can anticipate them to the second; that's what drives you nuts. Maybe a machine or appliance was acting up. Tap, tap, tap.

Boyle swore, got out of bed, put on his dressing gown and went to investigate. As he groped for the light switch in the hallway, he heard from behind him: 'Seconds out. Ding.' He spun around. Next thing he was airborne, feeling as though his face had exploded.

Boyle came down hard on his back, blacking out for a few seconds. When he opened his eyes, the lights were on and Ihaka was looking down at him the way people look at giant cockroaches. Boyle knew from experience that the fiery pain engulfing the middle of his face signified a broken nose. This was his sixth and, by some distance, the messiest.

Six hours later Ihaka sat in a meeting room at Auckland Central. In two minutes he would have been sitting there for fifteen minutes. That was his limit. With thirty seconds to spare, Detective Inspector Tony Charlton and Ron Firkitt walked through the door.

Charlton looked as Photoshopped as ever. Ihaka had often thought he really belonged on TV, either as head of an unfeasibly perky but scrape-prone family in a vomitous sitcom, or in an advert claiming that you too can have it all if you just choose the right brand of breakfast cereal. Charlton dropped a file on the table and sat down. 'You look tired, Sergeant.'

Ihaka nodded. 'You don't.'

'That's probably because I wasn't out at some west coast beach in the middle of the night putting someone's lights out.' Charlton flipped open the file. 'I assume you're aware that Wayne Rex Mowbray was DOA?'

Ihaka glanced at Firkitt, who had his chair tilted back, arms folded, studiously expressionless.

'I didn't know that,' said Ihaka. 'But he didn't look too good.'

'What happened?'

'He whacked me.' Ihaka tapped the bruise on his left cheekbone. 'I gave him a shove. He fell over and hit his head on a rock.'

Charlton nodded, his mouth turning down, the expression of someone who wasn't expecting much and hadn't been pleasantly surprised. He tapped the file. 'Ron and I have just spent a couple of hours on this. It's interesting, but I'm afraid to say it's not going to fly.'

'What are you talking about?'

'I don't think we can get this into court, let alone obtain convictions. There's virtually nothing in the way of hard evidence, for the old stuff or Lovell. Murray and Boyle – what happened to him, by the way?'

'I dropped the cunt,' said Ihaka. 'He set me up for a bullet.'

'For God's sake,' said Charlton, 'he's seventy-one years old and half your size.'

Firkitt lurched forward, causing the legs of his chair to bang on the floor. 'Who gives a fuck?'

Charlton gave Firkitt a long, questioning look, then refocused on Ihaka. 'As I was saying, Murray and Boyle are hanging tough, putting it all on Mowbray, who of course is the ideal fall-guy, having nothing to say for himself. I've spoken to the Crown Prosecutor. To say he's doesn't want any part of it scarcely does justice to his lack of enthusiasm.'

'What about Smaile?' said Ihaka.

'Oh yes, Smaile,' said Charlton. 'I've had his oncologist on the phone. Smaile's terminal: he's got a year, year and a half tops. Putting a terminally ill eighty-two-year-old on trial for this…' Charlton pushed the file towards Ihaka, shaking his head. 'Sorry, but it's a non-starter.'

There was a knock on the door. Detective Constable Joel Pringle poked his head in. 'Excuse me, sir.'

'What is it?' said Charlton.

'I thought DS Ihaka would like to know. We've just heard from the hospital. Ms Lovell's come out of the coma. The signs are all good – they're pretty confident she'll make a full recovery.'

Pringle backed out, closing the door. Ihaka looked at Firkitt, who stared back, hitching his right shoulder in a fatalistic shrug.

'Well, that's great news,' said Charlton with a curious glance at Ihaka. 'Or am I missing something here?'

Ihaka stood up. 'Yeah, fantastic.'

'Hang on,' said Charlton, 'we haven't finished.'

'I'm getting close on McGrail's cold case,' said Ihaka. 'Real close.' He leaned forward to slide the folder back towards Charlton. 'And you can keep this one open, because it's not over.'

21

Is this how it starts? wondered Johan Van Roon: not wanting to get out of bed in the morning. Actually, it wasn't
so much a case of not wanting to get out of bed as having
no particular reason to. And while the bed wasn't all that
cosy or comfortable, it was cosier and more comfortable
than anywhere else in his flat.

He hadn't had any particular reason to get out of bed
since his trip to Fiji. The PR man Caspar Quedley had com-
mended him on his professionalism and paid the balance
of the fee, but there was no bonus because the client had
gone sour on the whole exercise the moment Ihaka stuck
his beak in. Quedley had nothing for him at the moment,
but promised to keep him in mind.

Van Roon had rung around his shrunken circle of
contacts and former clients, an exercise that netted him
some expressions of sympathy but no assignments. He'd
even rung his competitors to see if they had any shit work
they wanted to offload or needed an extra pair of hands
to tide them over. They didn't.

Meanwhile, his ex-wife Yvonne had confirmed that she
and the kids (and the Labrador) were moving back to
Auckland at the end of the school term. He had to admit
it made sense: she had family and a support network
there and the kids were all for it. They were nostalgic

258

for the simple certainties that Auckland represented; Wellington was where it had all gone wrong. It probably made sense for him to move back as well. There had to be more work in Auckland and he was never going to regain the ground he'd lost with his children while he was stuck in this dump. And with Yvonne having less time on her hands and less to complain about, she might wean herself off the urge to sabotage what was left of his relationship with them.

Christ, he envied Eddie Brightside. He envied the way Brightside operated beyond the horizon. He envied the easy, bone-deep amorality that simplified everything, boiling it down to pure self-interest. Most of all he envied Brightside's rootlessness: he'd walked away from everything – job, relationships, commitments, burdens, the whole magnetic suck of networks and circumstances – to an existence that owed nothing to expectations or convention.

His mobile rang.

'Van Roon.'

'Hello there, this is Ann Smellie.'

'I wasn't expecting to hear from you again. Not that I'm complaining.'

'I should hope not. I hear you and our mutual acquaintance got on like a house on fire.'

'I don't know about that but, yeah, he's an interesting guy. You could say charming in his own way.'

'You could and he does,' she said. 'I wish I had a hundred dollars for every time I've heard him say it.'

'I assume you're still in touch?' said Van Roon. 'I only ask because he tried to tell me he'd have to call it off with you because of me. I didn't believe him. In fact, I told Ihaka it was probably the only thing he said I flat-out didn't believe.'

'If I didn't know better,' she said, 'I'd think there was a compliment lurking in there somewhere.'

'I wouldn't have thought you could miss it.'

'It's just as well we're getting along because we need to meet,' she said. 'I have a message from you know who. He insists I deliver it in person.'

'Good for him.'

'How are you placed today?'

'Fine.'

'I'm coming down to stay with some friends in Wairarapa. There's a place in Carterton, on the main drag, called Café Mirabelle. It's on the left if you're heading north. Can you be there at 12.30?'

'Sure.'

'Then we have a date.'

Van Roon lay there staring at the ceiling. If he couldn't get out of bed for Ann Smellie, he never would. He threw off the covers.

Beatrice the supervisor spotted Tito Ihaka crossing the foyer. She caught up with him in the corridor. 'Tina's ex is over from Sydney. As I said the other day, we don't intrude on family time.'

'This is a murder investigation,' said Ihaka. 'They intrude on whatever they like.'

He knocked on Tina Best's door and went in. She was sitting in the armchair by the window. Roger Best had dragged the other chair across the room so they were sitting knee to knee. He had a full head of white hair, none of it out of place, and wore a navy-blue blazer with a red silk tie and matching breast-pocket handkerchief, dark-grey trousers and black brogues. Ihaka's instant impression was that Best didn't mind what he saw in the mirror.

Before Best could complain about the interruption, Tina said almost gaily, 'Well, speak of the devil. We were just talking about you, Sergeant. This is my ex-husband, Roger.'

Ihaka stuck out his hand. 'Detective Sergeant Ihaka. We spoke on the phone.'

'Of course.' Best's handshake was as perfunctory as his eye contact. 'Nice to meet you.'

'Roger's not very good at pretending,' said Tina. 'He's not really pleased to see you.'

'Don't be silly, Tina,' said Best huffily. 'I was just hoping for a little privacy.'

'But you rushed over from Sydney when you heard the police had been to see me,' she said. 'And just now you were telling me I had to be very careful what I said to them.'

'Now you're being a naughty girl,' said Best. The baby talk and pasted-on smile didn't soften the reprimand. 'I said nothing of the sort. I was just trying to remind you, as I've often had to do, that you can be your own worst enemy.' He turned to Ihaka. 'I'm afraid Tina's memory's not too good and she has a tendency to, shall we say, be rather creative when filling in the gaps.'

Tina's face fell. She turned away, staring out of the window at the pruned rose bushes and leaf-strewn lawn.

'Is it Tina you're trying to protect,' said Ihaka, 'or your son?'

'I beg your pardon?' said Best ponderously. He took off his spectacles, applied the handkerchief and put them back on. Going by his expression, the view hadn't improved. 'What on earth is that supposed to mean?'

'It means your son's a suspect in the Polly Stenson case.' Ihaka glanced at Tina. Her eyes were bright, mind beams burning off the dreamy haze.

Best had gone red in the face. 'That's insane.'

'We have reason to believe he was at the scene of the crime around the time the crime took place,' said Ihaka. 'If you tick both those boxes and don't come forward, you're a suspect in anyone's language. I get the feeling you two can shed more light on this than you've done so far. Now would be a good time.'

'This is a travesty,' fumed Best. 'I refuse to be a party to it.' He rounded on his ex-wife. 'Surely you haven't forgotten your role in this affair and the solemn undertakings you gave. If you go back on your word, that's the end of it. I'll wash my hands of you.'

'It ended a long time ago, Roger,' she said calmly. 'And if it wasn't for this affair, as you call it, you would've washed your hands of me then.'

She resumed looking out of the window. Best glared at her, his clenched fists vibrating. Ihaka sensed a history of violence.

'Damn you.' Anger clogged Best's voice. 'Damn you to hell.' He waved his arms at Ihaka, a rich old man feeling his control slip away. 'What lies has she told you?'

'None that I know of,' said Ihaka. 'But then she hasn't really said anything about that night. And all she's told me about your son is that he's kept busy down on the farm.'

'I don't believe you,' said Best.

'I don't give a shit,' said Ihaka.

Tina's snort of amusement coloured Best's cheeks like a slap. 'You're a disgrace,' he raged. 'You were a disgrace as a wife, now you're a disgrace as a mother.' To Ihaka: 'I'm off to see my lawyer. You're going to find you've bitten off a lot more than you can chew.'

'I've heard that before,' said Ihaka. 'People keep underestimating my capacity.'

Best left, slamming the door behind him. Ihaka sat in the vacated chair. 'Are you OK?'

'I'm fine, thank you,' said Tina.

'I need your son's address.'

'I can never remember it, but it's in the address book on the bedside table. Under J for James.'

Ihaka jotted down the address, then went back to the chair. 'That wasn't strictly true what I said. About you not telling me anything. The story about your mother and brother and the stepladder wasn't really about them, was it? It was about you and James. And that photograph you gave me, how old were you then?'

'Seventeen.'

'The same age Polly was. James killed her, didn't he?'

Tina nodded.

'Thinking she was someone else?'

Tina closed her eyes and leaned back, her expression almost serene. 'Yes.'

'Lucy Barton told him you were upstairs with Johnny. He went up there crazy drunk looking for you, wanting to hurt you. He bumped into Polly in the dark and strangled her, thinking she was you.'

'James didn't really believe Lucy,' she said. 'But then he found Roger outside, in tears, with vomit down his shirt. Roger told him it was all true. By the time James got upstairs, I'd already gone back down.'

'Polly would've waited for you to leave, would've been coming out as James came in. She probably walked right into him. When did you find out?'

'The next morning. When we heard about Polly, James told Roger what he'd done. Roger said it was my fault. He said we'd both committed sins but mine was worse because it made James do what he did. We couldn't bring her back, so it was our duty as parents to protect our son. He made me promise never to breathe a word.' She gripped Ihaka's arm. 'They weren't the same. I know I did a dreadful thing, but James took that poor girl's life.' She released Ihaka's arm and sat back. 'And he meant to take mine. That didn't seem to trouble Roger.'

Ihaka stood up. 'Are you going to be all right?'

She nodded. 'I feel better now. I've paid my debt.'

When Ihaka looked back at her from the doorway, she said, 'Thank you, Sergeant.'

'What for?'

'For hearing what I couldn't say.'

Ihaka nodded. 'Thank you for wanting to be heard.'

On his way out Ihaka stopped by Beatrice's office to tell her that on no account should Tina's ex-husband or son be allowed anywhere near her. Then he rang Central to organise uniformed protection for Tina and arrange for detectives from Hamilton to bring in James Best. Then he rang Finbar McGrail.

A few minutes after Van Roon was seated at a corner table, Eddie Brightside walked into Café Mirabelle. He had a backpack slung over his shoulder and was wearing a baseball cap and aviator-style dark glasses even though he'd come in out of the rain. He peeled off the sunglasses and looked down at Van Roon with his wise-guy smile. 'How're you doing?'

'So-so.'

'Well, let's see if we can do something about that. Although I realise I'm behind the eight ball on account of being me, as opposed to the divine Ms S.'

Van Roon shrugged. 'When it comes to women, I'm nothing if not a realist.'

'It pays in the long run,' said Brightside. 'Ever had cassoulet?'

'Not that I'm aware of. What is it?'

'A French peasant dish – bit of duck, bit of pork, bit of sausage, a shitload of beans. The version here's a little peppery for my taste, but you won't find it in too many other places in Aotearoa.'

'I'll give it a go,' said Van Roon, getting to his feet.

'You stay there,' said Brightside. 'This is on me. A glass of Rosé de Provence to wash it down?'

'Why not?'

Brightside went to the counter to order, returning with a bottle of rosé and two wine glasses. After he'd poured and they'd raised glasses, he said, 'How goes the investigation?'

'No idea. I told Ihaka you didn't do it. That wasn't what he wanted to hear, so I haven't seen or spoken to him since.'

'Well, that's a good note on which to get down to business: I have a proposition for you.'

'Great,' said Van Roon. 'I could do with one.'

Even though the other diners were several tables away and not paying them any attention, Brightside leaned forward, lowering his voice. 'You know Gerry Waitz has a house not far from here?' Van Roon nodded. 'In that house is a safe. Waitz would regard it as a secret safe, but he'd be labouring under a misapprehension because I know where it is and how to get into it. Waitz being paranoid, the safe is chock-full of rainy-day money – cash, uncut diamonds, bearer bonds. I propose that you and I gain access to that safe and help ourselves.'

'Why do you need me?'

'I'll get to that. Based on what I observed unbeknownst to Waitz – admittedly it was quite a while ago,

265

but the leopard won't have changed his spots – there could be a mill five, maybe two mill. Your share would be one third.'

'And what would I have to do for that?'

'Terminate the son of a bitch.' Van Roon's expression made Brightside chuckle. 'Did you think I'd cut you in for that sort of dough to hold my coat? No such thing as a free lunch, buddy.'

Their meals arrived. Brightside peered at his boeuf bourguignon, exchanging rapid-fire French with the proprietor. When the proprietor withdrew, Van Roon hissed, 'Why don't *you* kill him?'

Brightside ate, nodding approval. 'Tried it once, didn't agree with me.'

'Good answer.'

'You, on the other hand…'

'What about me?'

'Some people aren't that bothered by it. That's just the way they're wired. I have the feeling you're one of those people, and I have good instincts in these matters.'

'Let's leave my wiring and your instincts out of it, shall we?' said Van Roon. Now that the shock of the second part of Brightside's proposition had worn off, deflation was setting in. He should've known it was too good to be true. 'Why do you want him dead?'

'Remember me telling you I disappeared because I figured Waitz might try to get rid of me? The truth is, I knew for damn certain he wanted to get rid of me. Fortunately, the first guy he offered the gig to, an old CIA hand, owed me one. So then Waitz put out a contract: bring me the head of Eddie Brightside. I had to disappear; I had no goddamn choice in the matter. And he's still after me – that's why his proxies hired you to find me. As long as Gerry Waitz is above ground, I have to stay out of sight – and I've had a gutsful of it. It's time to kick it in the head.'

'And get rich in the process?'

'The way I see it,' said Brightside, 'Waitz owes me for twenty-seven years of elaborate, expensive and inconvenient security measures and the stress of having to constantly watch my back. I regard it as fair and reasonable compensation. Besides, it's no good to him where he's going.'

'I see a major problem in terms of my involvement,' said Van Roon. 'In fact, I'd go so far as to say it's insurmountable.'

'I don't like the sound of that,' said Brightside. 'What is it?'

'The money trail. The minute I come into money I can't account for, my ex-employer is going to be all over me like a rash.'

Brightside poured himself another glass of wine. 'You had me worried for a moment there. The third part of my proposition is that you become my organisation's New Zealand representative. We'll set you up with a home office, meaning you can get out of that shithole into somewhere decent, and you can do as much or as little actual work as you want. Who knows, you might even enjoy it. If not, your contract, which I have in my backpack, contains a clause stating that in the event that we pull the plug on the New Zealand operation, you'll receive an extremely generous payout. So the timing is up to you: a year from now you could have your full share, all shipshape and above board. Of course you'll have to pay tax on it, but you can't have it both ways.'

'So you'll take everything in the safe and drip-feed me my share in the form of a salary?'

'Exactly.'

'How will you get it out of the country?'

'You let me worry about that,' said Brightside. 'I've been moving money around the world for donkey's years.'

'Well, you've solved one problem,' said Van Roon, 'and I have to admit that's a nifty solution, only to raise another.' Brightside smiled as if he knew where this was going. 'Waitz is dead; I'm here with nothing to show for it; you're off in the wild blue yonder with all the money. What's to stop you deciding to keep it all? And what could I do about it if you did?'

'There's no guarantee I can give you that gets around that,' said Brightside. 'But frankly, Johan, if we're going to do this thing, there has to be some mutual trust. Ann will be joining me in the wild blue yonder, but first she's got to sell her cottages. That'll take a few weeks, possibly months, and I wouldn't dream of exposing her to risk by welshing on the deal.'

Van Roon stared. 'What risk? What do you think I am?'

Brightside shrugged unapologetically. 'I think you're someone who wouldn't take kindly to being shafted. Hell, as fastidious as I am, if I was in your shoes under those circumstances, I'd be out for blood. And, as I said, I have the sense you don't share my fastidiousness.'

'OK. I assume that once it's done, you'll be off in a cloud of dust, whereas I'm not going anywhere. That being the case, I'm wondering what you've got planned to steer the investigation in some direction other than mine?'

'How's the cassoulet?'

'Different.'

'Not too peppery?'

'I wouldn't want it any more peppery.'

'Yeah, I see you've got a bit of a glow on. What you mean is, a compelling theory?'

'What I have in mind,' said Van Roon, 'is a theory that's so fucking compelling the investigators won't feel the need to pursue other lines of enquiry with any great vigour.'

Brightside grinned. 'Great minds think alike. I've been planning this for a long time. Believe me, I've got my ducks in a row. Waitz's demise will be big news in the States. It'll also trigger a spate of revelations about his shady business dealings with various shady characters, the sort of guys who don't phone their lawyers when the other party doesn't live up to their side of the bargain, if you get my drift. The compelling theory will be that Waitz stiffed one of his shady associates, whose response was to send a pro down here to put him out of business permanently. The beauty of it is that the more the media digs into Waitz's business activities, the more potentially shady shit they'll come across. And if the working premise is that it was a hit initiated in some faraway place, there's not a hell of a lot your former colleagues can do except accumulate air points.'

'That sort of guy would have some pretty serious security, wouldn't he?'

'He would,' said Brightside, 'and when he's most other places in the world, Waitz does. But he feels completely safe here. That's why he comes here, to get away from all that shit. And bear in mind the picture of Waitz that emerges post-mortem won't be entirely accurate: there'll be hype, embellishments, false trails. But a man could spend a fair while establishing that. Hopefully assorted assholes here and elsewhere will.'

'You've got it all worked out, haven't you?' said Van Roon.

'As I said, years in the planning.'

'So what's the time frame?'

'It goes down tomorrow night.'

'Jesus.'

'The day after tomorrow Waitz flies out to Europe,' said Brightside. 'He won't be back for months. Tomorrow is his annual open day when he lets the public take a nosy around his house and grounds for a couple of hours. There's no way he'll be sticking around to meet and greet the rubes – he'll go for a drive or play golf or something. I'll take the tour and find a hiding place – I know that house very well. Around six a chef from one of the vineyard restaurants will arrive to prepare dinner. He or she will be gone by 7.30 at the latest. After dinner Waitz will settle down with a Cuban cigar and a bottle of five-hundred buck cognac to watch Fox News or porn, depending on his mood. At nine I'll let you in the back door and we'll get to it. I don't know what Waitz has got lined up in Europe, but there's a pretty good chance the alarm won't be raised till after the weekend, or maybe not even till his property manager checks the place in a week or so.'

'Weapon?'

Brightside mopped up the remnants of his stew with a piece of bread, then sat back chewing contentedly. 'That's your department. Shit, man, I can't do everything.'

Van Roon pushed aside his plate. 'I accept you've done all the work so far, but that still leaves the hard part.'

'Hard but well rewarded,' said Brightside.

'It's almost thirty years since you had eyes on that safe. What if Waitz has changed his MO? What if there's nothing there?'

'Trust me, there will be. But in the extremely unlikely event the cupboard is bare, you hand me the weapon and go on your merry way. Then it's up to me. Either way, it won't affect you.' He poured the last of the wine. 'So, Johan, do we have a deal?'

Van Roon didn't answer straight away because he was thinking of the pistol that wasn't at the bottom of Lake Taupo. The one he'd helped himself to when he and his partners in crime turned over a couple of ram raiders who'd cleaned out a Queen Street jeweller. The one he'd carefully wrapped in plastic and buried at one of his stashes dotted around rural Wairarapa. The question was: which one?

'I'll think about it on the way home.'

Brightside kept his expression neutral, not wanting to telegraph that he knew what the answer would be. 'I'll call you tonight.'

After the phone call from his father, James Best used a stepladder to get his double-barrelled shotgun and a box of cartridges down from the top of the wardrobe. He scribbled a few lines on the back of a begging letter from his old school (he hadn't read far enough to find out what they wanted money for this time), folded the piece of paper and slipped it in his hip pocket. Then he went outside and got in his ute.

He drove to the edge of his property where a deep, wooded ravine separated flat pasture from bush-covered hills. He stopped the ute on the lip of the ravine. He spread the note out on the passenger seat. He loaded the shotgun, put the butt on the floor between his feet and the muzzle under his chin, hooked his thumbs over the triggers and jammed down.

They found him next morning. The note said:

Every day of my adult life I have reflected on the irony of our family name.

My father was a rotten husband.

My mother was a rotten wife.

I was a rotten son.

I killed an innocent person. I meant to kill someone who wasn't innocent but was entitled to think I'd be the last person on earth to do her harm.

I should have done this years ago.

22

The next morning, Saturday, Ihaka went to Auckland Hospital to see Miriam Lovell. As he approached her cubicle, the voice he hadn't expected to hear again floated over the plastic curtains, a murmur of mock-protest prompting warm male laughter. He peered through a chink in the curtains. Miriam's bare ankles and feet protruded from a blue smock but the rest of her was obscured by her partner, Barry Shanklin.

Ihaka backed off and sought out the red-headed registrar who looked less exhausted but no older. She said it was too early to tell whether Miriam would have ongoing issues as a result of her injuries, but the indications were positive.

'How's her memory?' he asked.

'She doesn't remember anything about the attack itself, but that's to be expected. Otherwise it seems to be intact.'

'Can we talk to her?' The registrar made a discouraging face. 'It'll only take a couple of minutes.'

'Well, all right, but please take it very gently. If she doesn't want to do it, don't start. If she becomes disoriented or distressed, don't continue.'

'Her partner's with her now,' said Ihaka. 'I'll send Detective Constable Pringle over this afternoon. It'll be short and sweet. One question, one answer, then we're done.'

It had been brightening up since early morning. As Ihaka drove over the Harbour Bridge the remaining cloud broke up. Suddenly the sun glowed in an empty sky, turning Waitemata Harbour from battleship grey to chemical blue.

Ihaka parked in the courtyard in front of Willie Smaile's house. The garage door was up and the garage was empty, but as he got out of the car Smaile called down to him from the first-floor balcony: 'Go and harass someone else, copper. It's over. I've got nothing more to say.'

Ihaka smiled up at him. 'I have.'

Smaile turned his back and disappeared from view. Ihaka let himself in, climbed the stairs and went out onto the balcony, where Smaile was stretched out on a recliner with a rug over his legs even though it was pleasantly warm.

Ihaka took in the scene: the sun-trap balcony, the privacy, the sea view, the old man taking it easy.

'What do you want, Ihaka?' said Smaile, barely glancing up from his newspaper. 'My time is too precious to waste on you.'

'Well, we might have to get a second opinion on that. I mean, it'd be embarrassing all round if you're still kicking back out here three years from now.'

'That's a pretty transparent bluff,' said Smaile, not entirely confidently. 'I've no doubt you'd do it in a flash if you could get away with it. But you wouldn't – I'll give your superiors that much credit.'

'We'll see. Did you have my father killed?'

'Oh, so that's what this is about?' Smaile fast-forwarded through the paper. 'I thought he had a heart attack – apparently he was a prime candidate. That's all I have to say on the subject.'

'That's what we all thought. But Miriam Lovell showed me something she found in Ethan Stern's papers. I know you got the diaries, but you missed some other stuff. Like a note saying he wouldn't be surprised if Jimmy Ihaka met with an accident, in inverted commas, one of these days. And guess what? A few days later he did. And guess what else? A few days after that, so did Stern.'

Smaile's derisive laugh came out as a dry rattle. 'That has no legal weight whatsoever. Like many of his kind, Stern had a flair for the melodramatic. But if we're going to talk about deaths, mysterious and mundane, let's talk about Wayne Mowbray's. That reeked of the old "died while attempting to escape police custody" manoeuvre as practised by fascist regimes the world over. Why don't you tell me what happened to him?'

Ihaka leaned against the balcony rail. 'I can, as it happens, because I was there. He certainly wasn't trying to escape – he was absolutely poked – but he wanted to go down swinging. He hit me, I gave him a shove, he fell over and hit his head. Goodnight, nurse.'

Smaile propped himself up on his elbows. 'You killed him, didn't you? I know you did. I can see it on your face. And you have the bare-faced gall to come into my house —'

'Well, the thing is, Willie, your boy Wayne went out of his way to piss me off. He bloody near killed Miriam, who's a friend of mine, and he was all set to kill me. That's fairly provocative, wouldn't you say? But it raises the question of who sent Wayne out to do that shit, because we both know he was a fucking wind-up toy. And if the bloke who did that is the same bloke who had my old man knocked off, well, all I can say is I wouldn't want to be in that old cunt's slippers.'

Smaile's eyes darted to the mobile phone on the side table. He made a grab, but Ihaka beat him to it. Smaile joined the long list of those who'd found out the hard way that, measured in reaction time, Ihaka's appearance was deceptive.

Ihaka tossed the phone aside. 'Let's just keep this between the two of us. As I was saying, Willie, you've gone right to the top of my shit-list. And as if I didn't have enough reasons to give nature a hurry-up, your little bitch Tom Murray came up with another one. You've got some dirt on him, right? That's the only thing keeping him from telling me everything. The minute you croak, he'll blab his head off. When I think of all the years you took from my father and I look at you sitting here in the sun like a good citizen in well-earned retirement, I say fuck it. Time's up, old man.'

Smaile threw off the blanket and struggled to his feet. 'You stay away from me.'

In one fluid, effortless movement, Ihaka grabbed Smaile by the scruff of his neck and the belt holding up trousers that were now too big for him, hoisted him off his feet and launched him head-first over the balcony. Smaile hit the concrete forecourt like a sack of old bones.

Ihaka wiped down Smaile's phone and the balcony rail and went downstairs. Smaile was face down in a pool of blood, a jumble of oddly angled limbs. Ihaka took a photo of him on his phone, then rang Central.

On his way back to town, Ihaka rang Tom Murray to say something had come up and they needed to talk. They arranged to meet at Murray's office that afternoon.

Ihaka did some shopping and made himself lunch. As he was on his way out to meet Murray, Pringle rang. Miriam Lovell had confirmed that Stu Boyle had taken her to Karekare on the pretext of meeting an ex-SIS man and left her to Wayne Mowbray's tender mercies. Ihaka told him to bring Boyle in.

Murray was waiting in the ground-floor foyer. He let Ihaka into the building and they took the lift to his floor, Murray at ease in country-club casual: dark-green corduroys, Argyll sweater, tasselled loafers. When they were sitting down in his office, Murray said, 'OK, so what am I giving up my round of golf for?'

'Willie Smaile's dead.'

'What?' Murray shuffled expressions from shock to disbelief to hope. 'Since when?'

'Since this morning. I found his body. Looks like he took a swan dive off his balcony. Sorry, off your balcony. I took a snap for you.' He passed Murray his phone.

Murray glanced at it and handed the phone back. 'How can I tell if that's him? I can't see his face.'

'You wouldn't want to. If you don't believe me, check the *Herald* website. There's probably something up by now.'

Murray went to his computer. After a minute or so, he said, 'Well, happy days. The wicked wizard is dead.'

Ihaka looked over Murray's shoulder.

BROWNS BAY MAN IN FATAL FALL IDENTIFIED
Police have confirmed the identity of a man who fell to his death at his Browns Bay home this morning. He was Wilfred 'Willie' Roy Smaile.

A retired trade union official, Smaile was a significant

figure in the union movement and left-wing political circles from the 1960s until the dissolution of the Workers' Vanguard Party, which he founded and headed, in the early 1990s.

Police are still at the scene and refusing further comment, but the Herald *understands Smaile, who was 82, was seriously ill with an untreatable condition.*

Murray glanced up at Ihaka. 'That's two down in a matter of days. You're a health hazard, Sergeant.'

Ihaka went back to the sofa. 'I'm a cop. We go where the bodies are.'

'Yes, but those two were alive until —'

'Until they weren't,' said Ihaka. 'That's how it works: one minute you're alive, next minute you're not.'

'You make it sound like they died of old age.'

'No, they died of karma. You want to die in bed, don't get blood on your hands. Now you made me a promise: the day Smaile died, you'd tell me the whole story.'

Murray squinted suspiciously. 'How do I know you haven't got some sort of gadget on you, like the other night?'

Ihaka held out his arms. 'Feel free to search me. I'm not trying to catch you out here. I just want to know what happened. For personal reasons.'

Murray patted him down, Ihaka obligingly peeling off his hoodie and lifting his T-shirt.

'What about indemnity?' said Murray.

'What about it?' said Ihaka. 'You said you couldn't talk while Smaile was alive. Well, he's dead, so whatever he had on you doesn't matter a fuck any more. And anything you say now, it's not like an official statement in front of witnesses. You can just deny you ever said it.'

'All right,' said Murray. 'I guess you're entitled to know.'

Smaile saw possibilities in the young Tom Murray. Between them, Smaile and his KGB handler at the Soviet Embassy came up with the idea of turning him into a sleeper.

The first step was to get Murray out of the WVP and set the stage for his ideological conversion, hence the stage-managed falling out with Smaile and expulsion from the party. Step two was for Murray to establish his capitalist credentials. The KGB provided start-up capital and a business plan concocted by some closet Marxist moneymaker in the UK. Murray often wondered how many other members of the Moscow Millionaires Club there were, and what had become of them.

The master plan was supposed to unfold this way: Murray would become an active member of the National Party, get selected as a candidate, enter Parliament, specialise in defence/security issues (the handler would tutor him on that stuff), and work his way up to Cabinet level, where he'd have access to classified information of interest and value to Moscow. Murray was sceptical, but Smaile assured him they were following a blueprint that had worked in several West European countries. The key was patience: they were playing a long game.

But before he was cut loose, Murray had one final assignment that doubled as a test of his commitment: getting rid of Ethan Stern, who had undermined the cause and betrayed Smaile's trust by leaking information to the obstructionist saboteur Jimmy Ihaka.

Smaile and Jimmy had been at loggerheads for years, but in 1986/87 it went to another level of bitterness. Someone inside the WVP fed Jimmy details of the Soviet

Embassy's funding and tactical support for the campaign being waged by the unions and their left-wing allies to keep the US navy out of New Zealand waters. There were confrontations, Jimmy threatening to tell the media that the anti-nuke movement was being manipulated by an unfriendly foreign power for its own geopolitical ends. He didn't have an issue with the campaign itself or with New Zealand getting offside with the Yanks, but he wasn't going to stand by while the Soviet Union, the other nuclear-armed superpower, used Kiwi working people as useful idiots in pursuit of strategic goals that had nothing to do with nuclear disarmament.

Smaile's handler supplied potassium cyanide, a poison used in the 1982 Tylenol murders in Chicago, which caused cardiac arrest. The task of administering the poison was given to the one WVP member Jimmy wasn't averse to eating with, drinking with and generally letting his guard down with: Stu Boyle.

'Stern was the leaker?' said Ihaka. 'I wouldn't have thought he was privy to that sort of stuff.'

'That was the word that came down from on high,' said Murray, 'but Smaile was adept at putting a big-picture gloss on his self-interest. If you want my opinion, Smaile hated your old man's guts and wanted him dead, end of story. But he needed his handler's buy-in. My guess is Smaile leaked it himself, then went to his handler and said, this guy Ihaka knows what we're up to, he's got to be stopped before he exposes us. Stern had to go because the leak had to be plugged, but again it suited Smaile to make Stern the fall-guy. He knew too much, which was Smaile's fault for allowing him inside the tent.'

'So to sum up: Boyle poisoned my old man, you shoved

Stern down the bank, and Mowbray beat the hell out of Miriam – all on Smaile's say-so?'

'Yes.'

'What happened to the sleeper operation?'

'Oh, that went out the window along with everything else when the Soviet Union collapsed,' said Murray. 'I didn't hear a peep from Smaile for ten years. The business took off and my political views changed accordingly. As they say, a neo-conservative is a lefty who's been mugged by reality. Then one day, out of the blue, Smaile came to collect: either I became his private ATM or he told the world that my business was built on red roubles. So there was the house, which you know about, the trips to various people's paradises – Cuba, Venezuela – and lately some very expensive medical treatment. So however you managed it, Sergeant, I'm extremely grateful to you for getting that evil old monkey off my back.'

Johan Van Roon walked up the seashell drive, his footsteps crunching in the echoing silence of the countryside at night. He felt detached, almost disembodied, as if he was perched in one of the hundred-year-old oak trees that lined the drive watching his double trudge through the moonlight towards the point of no return.

He rounded a corner and there was the house, a great, graceful, wooden relic of a bygone era, like the sailing ships that brought the first Europeans to New Zealand. As Eddie Brightside had promised, no sensor lights came on as he crossed a wide stretch of lawn and negotiated formal gardens on his way to the rear of the house.

He went up the steps to the veranda on tiptoe. The illuminated display on his digital watch said 20.59. As it switched over to 21.00, the back door quietly opened.

281

Brightside, wearing surgical gloves, held an index finger to his lips as he beckoned Van Roon inside with his other hand.

They were in the kitchen, a state-of-the-art fit-out in a nineteenth-century space.

Brightside whispered, 'Stay close and stay quiet. We don't want to spook him. I probably don't need to say this, but don't touch anything. Are you ready?'

'I'm ready now,' breathed Van Roon, 'but I don't know how long I can stay that way. Let's get it done.'

'Roger that,' said Brightside. 'But there'll have to be a bit of banter.' He flashed a cold grin. 'I mean, we can't just hit and run.'

He led Van Roon down a long wood-panelled corridor, plush rugs muffling their footsteps. They came to an octagonal entrance hall dimly lit by wall-mounted lamps. Brightside pointed to the crack of light at the foot of a door. Crossing the hall, they could hear the feigned ecstasy and heaving exertion of performance sex.

Brightside gave Van Roon a nod and eased the door open. They slipped into a high-ceilinged room furnished in the style of a gentlemen's club: leather sofas and arm-chairs, heavy silk curtains, a blazing open fire, the walls hung with paintings of naval battle scenes from the age of cannons and grappling hooks. Waitz was sprawled on a sofa with his back to the door. On the large screen against the far wall, a white woman was being roughly used by a quartet of muscular black men.

Brightside said loudly, 'Black on white gang-bang porn – the last refuge of the sick fuck.' Waitz's head whipped around. Van Roon registered orange-tinted glasses, bushy grey hair, a salt-and-pepper beard and a horse-collar double chin. 'Good to see you've stayed classy, Gerry.'

Waitz zapped off the porn and got to his feet. He was huge, over 1.8 metres tall and at least 120 kilos, dressed in a tent-like white T-shirt, light tracksuit pants and jandals, sensible attire given the heat the fire was throwing out.

'Holy shit, look at the size of him,' said Brightside. 'You need to put a padlock on the fridge, pal. Like Marlon Brando.'

'Yeah, I'm a glutton,' said Waitz, his voice a bass rumble. 'No two ways about it. But at least it's all gourmet. Brando ate himself into the grave on hamburgers and ice cream. You want to know what the real problem is? When you're really fucking loaded, it doesn't matter what you look like. There's never a shortage of twenty-five-year-old hotties wanting to keep you warm at night. So after a while you kind of think what the fuck and have that third helping of crêpe Suzette.'

Brightside scanned the room. 'I don't see any twenty-five-year-old hotties. All I see is a fat man getting ready to jerk off.'

Waitz ducked his head, acknowledging Brightside had a point. 'Well, here's the thing about your twenty-five-year-old hottie: after a time, and it's generally not that long, her conversational limitations combined with the fact she's incapable of shutting the fuck up – a trying combination, I think you'll agree – induce a craving for solitude. You called tonight's sociological study the last refuge of the sick fuck. I prefer to think of it as the last refuge of the solitary man.' He took off his tinted glasses and picked up his brandy balloon. 'So, Eddie, where the fuck have you been, amigo? Did it never occur to you that your old buddy might appreciate a lousy fucking postcard every once in a while?'

'I've been underground, Gerry,' said Brightside. 'Down in the tunnels and the sewers. See, you made one mistake when you decided you'd sleep easier if E. F. Brightside was six feet under: you tapped the wrong guy. Bobby G happened to be beholden to me at the time so he felt kind of obliged to check if I had any objection to going in the hole. But I knew you wouldn't be deterred by Bobby turning you down, just as I knew there'd be plenty of guys who'd be only too happy to execute the contract. So I ran. And I've been channelling Doctor Richard Kimble ever since.'

'Who?' said Van Roon.

'*The Fugitive*,' said Waitz. To Brightside: 'Who's the dimwit?'

'My associate.'

'Come on, Eddie,' said Waitz, 'I was just covering the bases in case it all turned to shit. It was hypothetical. I never actually authorised anyone to clip you.'

'Now you're making the same mistake all over again, forgetting I was just as well connected in that world as you were.'

Waitz threw back some cognac. It seemed to make him angry. 'Well, so fucking what?' he boomed. 'Frankly. You fucked off without a word, leaving an unholy goddamn mess. What was I meant to do?' He drained his glass, refilled it from a crystal decanter and drank some more. This time it had the opposite effect. 'But fuck it, man, that was then and this is now. Let's start over in a spirit of constructive engagement. You want me to make it up to you? You want redress? I can do that. That's what this is all about, isn't it?'

'Well, yeah.'

'OK,' said Waitz. 'Let's have a drink and work something out.'

'Hey, I appreciate the offer, Gerry,' said Brightside, 'but I'm going to be driving all night so I need to keep a clear head. As for the redress, I can save you the trouble of arranging a bank transfer or any of that shit. How about we just take what's in your safe and call it quits? That way, there are no electronic footprints. No one's any the wiser.'

Waitz and Brightside eyed each other through a silence filled by the crackling of logs on the fire. Eventually Waitz said, 'What safe?'

'The one in the library,' said Brightside. 'Behind the bookshelf that swings out from the wall when you press the button behind the Dostoevsky section. That safe.'

Waitz looked into his glass. 'Assuming there is such a safe, how do you propose to get into it?'

'Well, we're not going to chop off your fingers, starting with this little piggy' – Brightside waggled a little finger – 'and working our way up till you spill the combination. We're not that sort of people.'

Waitz jerked his chins at Van Roon. 'Does that go for him?'

Brightside smiled thinly. 'More or less.'

'So what exactly is he doing here?'

'Think of us as a mutual admiration society,' said Brightside.

Van Roon said, 'Can we just get on with it?'

'But if he has a fault,' said Brightside to Waitz, 'it's impatience. He couldn't give a shit that we've got a lot of catching up to do. To answer your question: one night, back in the day when I was a frequent guest in this house, I heard noises from downstairs as I was drifting off to sleep. I felt obliged to investigate. It was coming from the library, so I stuck my head around the door and saw you pull out the Dostoevskys, press the button and open sesame. You were pissed to beat the band, Gerry, all thumbs, so it took you a few goes to get the safe open. And as you fumbled away, you were talking to yourself, repeating the numbers out loud. There was a pen and paper on the sideboard just inside the door, so I took dictation. When you finally opened the safe and I got a look at what was in there, I thought, there's my superannuation, right there. I would've helped myself years ago, but circumstances didn't permit. Now they do. So let us go then, you and I, and see what we've got.'

The library, which was also off the entrance hall, continued the gentlemen's club theme. There was more leather seating, floor-to-ceiling bookshelves, a full-size billiards table and paraphernalia, and an even bigger fireplace but no fire. Waitz hugged himself, slapping his arms. 'Son of a bitch, it's freezing in here. Let's hurry this up.'

'It'll be over soon enough,' said Brightside. 'Gerry, why don't you do the honours?'

'Fuck you,' said Waitz. 'This is your show.'

Brightside shrugged. 'If you insist.'

He went to the bookshelf furthest from the door, pulled out several books and reached into the gap. After a series of clicks and accompanied by whirring noises, the bookshelf slowly came away from the wall, like a door opening. Van Roon glanced at Waitz. He'd dropped a buttock on the arm of a sofa, trying to look bored.

The bookshelf swung through 180 degrees, revealing a wall safe that to Van's Roon's untrained eye looked as old as everything else in the room. Brightside produced a sheet of paper, Blu-tacked it to the wall above the safe and went to work. After ninety seconds or so, he gave the others an over-the-shoulder wink, turned the dial one more click and pulled the safe door open.

Brightside was blocking Van Roon's view. 'Well?'

Without turning his head Brightside said, 'Welcome to El Dorado, baby.'

After half a minute's silent contemplation, Brightside was all business. 'We need a receptacle.' To Van Roon: 'As you might expect, this place has a room whose sole purpose is storing Gerry's Louis Vuitton suitcases, which come in all shapes and sizes. I'll pop upstairs and grab one.' To Waitz: 'Don't do anything silly, Gerry. My associate came prepared for that eventuality. Besides, you'd probably just do yourself an injury.'

As soon as Brightside was out of the room, Waitz said, 'Two things. Whatever he's paying you, I'll treble it. And if you stick with him, he'll double-cross you. Eddie can't help himself. Even if there was nothing to be gained by it, he'd double-cross you. It's just the way he is.'

'You on the other hand,' said Van Roon, 'are Mr Integrity, right?'

'I wouldn't say that,' said Waitz, 'but I'm rich enough not to have to scoop the pool every time. Eddie doesn't have that luxury.'

Van Roon pointed at the safe. 'If money's no object, why do you care?'

'It's the principle of the thing.'

Brightside reappeared with a mid-sized suitcase. He looked from Waitz to Van Roon. 'Let me guess. He said I'll double-cross you.'

'Yep.'

'And offered to quadruple whatever I'm offering?'

'Treble.'

'Jesus, Gerry,' said Brightside, 'you've turned into a tightwad.'

Waitz said, 'It's all coming back to me why I went off you. Take it and fuck off. It's only been half an hour and I'm sick to death of you already.'

'That's an unfortunate choice of words,' said Brightside.

Waitz stood up. 'What do you mean by that? You're not going to kill me, are you?' When he thought it was just a shake-down, Waitz had alternated between man-of-the-world nonchalance and bluster. Now that it was dawning on him that maybe the money wasn't the only thing they'd come for, all he could do was plead. 'Eddie, please, don't do that. There's no need.'

'Beg to differ, Gerry,' said Brightside. 'Whichever way you look at it, it's the sensible thing to do.'

Van Roon pulled the Colt Woodsman .22 from his overcoat pocket, extended his arm and shot Waitz in the chest. He staggered back, collided with a chair and toppled over.

'Put one in his head,' said Brightside. 'That's what the pros do.'

Van Roon stood astride Waitz and shot him in the back of the head. When he looked up, Brightside was already filling the suitcase.

'You had me lined up for this all along,' said Van Roon. 'That's why you got me up to Fiji.'

Brightside closed the suitcase and the safe and pushed the bookcase back into position. As he walked past Van Roon, he tossed him a thick bundle of notes. 'A bit of pocket money to tide you over.' He stopped at the doorway, waiting for Van Roon. 'Based on what Ann told me, I was pretty sure you were the one, but I needed to see you up close. You're a man who appreciates irony, Johan, so get a load of this: Waitz's proxies found you for me. When they hired you to track me down, they sent me the killer I'd been looking for.'

EPILOGUE

A year or so after Polly Stenson's death, her parents moved to the Bay of Plenty where they'd thrived, getting into and out of the kiwifruit industry at the right times. They'd retired to Mount Maunganui, an apartment on Marine Parade. Cross the road and you were on the beach, looking straight out to Mayor Island.

When Finbar McGrail rang to say he was coming down to update them, Gordon Stenson was understandably surprised to hear from him and, less understandably, not particularly keen to see him. 'Can't you just tell me over the phone?' he asked.

'I really think it should be done face to face,' said McGrail. 'I can assure you I'm not proposing to come down just to tell you there've been no developments.'

'I see,' said Stenson. 'That sounds like it could be upsetting.'

'I don't imagine there's anything very much I could tell you that wouldn't be.'

'Yes, well, that's why I'd rather you do it over the phone,' said Stenson. 'That way I can filter it for my wife. I don't want to make it sound as if we're past caring, because that's certainly not the case, but it's been a long time – years in fact – since we've heard from you people. I suppose we'd reached the point of accepting we were never going to have closure. That's hard to live with, but you find a way. So for it to come up out of the blue like this, well, I just don't think it'll do my wife any good to have to go through it all over again.'

'This will be the last time you hear from us,' said McGrail. 'We're closing the file.'

The conversation went on like this for a few more minutes, Stenson putting up barriers, McGrail bypassing them. Eventually Stenson got the message that McGrail wasn't going to deliver the update over the phone and wasn't getting off the phone till he received an invitation.

McGrail drove to Mount Maunganui and found Marine Parade. The Stensons received him in their front room, a sunny spot where you could sit and gaze at the Pacific Ocean and empty your mind of dark memories. They'd aged better than McGrail had expected, but that might have had something to do with their tans. When he declined the offer of tea or coffee, they sat down, their silence his cue to say what he'd come to say, their expressions an indication they didn't expect much good to come of it.

McGrail told them who killed their daughter and why. Barbara Stenson watched him intently, imploring him, he felt, to invest her daughter's death with a meaning that set it apart from the random erasures that lead the nightly news. When he'd finished she said, 'So you've come down from Auckland to tell us Polly was murdered because she got dragged into these high-and-mighty people's disgusting games?'

'Yes.'

Her eyes burned through welling tears. 'How do you think that makes us feel?'

'You can't blame the Superintendent, dear,' said her husband. 'He's just doing his job.'

'Now there'll be a trial,' she groaned. 'We'll have to relive the whole —'

'There won't be a trial,' said McGrail. 'When James Best realised we were on to him, he took his own life. As I told your husband, we've closed the file. There's nothing more to be said or done.'

Anguish wrenched Barbara Stenson's face. She muttered something McGrail didn't pick up and hurried out of the room.

'This is exactly what I was afraid of,' said Stenson. 'You reach a stage of thinking, it's not going to bring Polly back so what's the point?'

'Nothing was ever going to bring her back to this world,' said McGrail. 'All we could do was keep her in our hearts and refuse to let whoever took her from us get away with it.'

Stenson insisted on accompanying McGrail to his car. As they left the apartment building, McGrail handed him the photograph of Polly taken on the day of her death. 'Your wife gave me this when she asked me not to forget Polly. It certainly helped in that regard.'

Stenson stared at the photograph. When he looked up, McGrail's car was pulling away from the kerb.

Icy rain fell on Lake Taupo that night. When Johan Van Roon got back to his car at 4.30 am after disposing of the Colt Woodsman .22, his teeth were chattering and he couldn't feel his hands or feet. He sat in the car with the heater on full bore for five minutes, then rolled slowly out of Hatepe. When he hit State Highway 1, he switched the headlights on, turned left and headed for Auckland.

When Ihaka showed up at Central on Wednesday morning to resume normal duties, she was waiting for him:

tiny, sombre, silent, a fish out of water but a resolute one. Willie Smaile's widow.

'She came in first thing Monday morning, Sarge,' said Detective Constable Joel Pringle. 'Once we got it through to her that you were having a couple of days off, she was out of here. Wasn't interested in talking to anyone else. When I got in this morning, she was already here.'

Ihaka went over to her. As he was asking what he could do for her, she stood up, pulled an unaddressed padded envelope from her handbag and thrust it at him.

'For me?' he asked.

She nodded vigorously.

'From your husband?'

Another flurry of nods.

The envelope contained a folded sheet of paper and an audio cassette tape. She gestured at the sheet of paper, indicating that he should open it. It was a letter.

To whom it may concern

The fact that you are reading this means I'm dead, but not of natural causes. That being the case, the enclosed audio tape is almost certainly pertinent.

It records a conversation which took place on 19 June 1987 concerning the death, a few hours earlier, of Ethan Stern, an American academic who worked in the University of Auckland's Political Studies Department. Stern's death was found to be an accident: he'd slipped while jogging in the Waitakeres and died of injuries sustained as a result of falling down a steep slope.

The participants are myself (New Zealand accent) and Tom Murray (Scottish accent; these days a well-known businessman) in our respective capacities of General Secretary and member of the Workers' Vanguard Party.

My wife is entrusting you with this tape in the hope and expectation you will appreciate its significance and act accordingly.

And below, an almost childishly legible signature:

W.R. Smaile
Browns Bay
January 1st, 2010.

Ihaka slipped the letter back into the envelope. 'Your husband told you to give this to me?'

Her head shakes were as brisk as her nods. 'No. I decide that.' She pointed at the envelope: 'You understand?'

'Yes,' said Ihaka. 'Completely.'

Her business concluded, she gave Ihaka one last nod and headed for the lifts.

He found a tape deck, inserted the tape and pressed play.

There's a knock on a door.

SMAILE: Enter. Ah, Comrade Murray. Bearing good news, I trust.

MURRAY: Yeah, it all went as planned, Comrade Secretary. Stern's dead.

SMAILE: Sit yourself down, Comrade, and tell me exactly what happened.

MURRAY: Well, I waited for him at that spot we chose, where it's really slippery and there's a hell of a drop. It was perfect – I could see him coming but he couldn't see me. I timed it dead right, sent him flying. You should've heard the racket he made on the way down, bouncing off those bloody big branches. I scuffed up the ground to make a mess of the footprints, then doubled back and went looking for him on the lower trail.

SMAILE: Anyone else about?

MURRAY: Hardly another soul, as we thought being a Friday morning. I heard voices at one point but didn't see anyone. They must've been on a different trail; it's amazing how voices carry in the bush. It took me a while to find him because he hadn't gone all the way down; he got snagged on a branch. He was dead, though. No doubt about it.

SMAILE: So you didn't have to administer the coup de grâce? That must've been a relief.

MURRAY: Christ, yes. I was a bit nervous by then anyway, thinking my luck's going to run out and there'd be a bunch of schoolkids on a field trip round the next corner. I made my way to the pick-up point and stayed out of sight till Comrade Mowbray turned up. I got changed in the car so I assume he's thrown my gear in the incinerator by now.

SMAILE: I think we can rely on him to perform that undemanding task. Excellent work, Comrade. Once again you've lived up to our high expectations.

Smaile probably recorded the conversation to give them a hold over Murray if he tried to backslide on the sleeper operation, thought Ihaka. When Smaile started ratcheting up his extortion demands, it must have occurred to him that one day Murray might decide he'd had enough and do what Smaile himself would do if the boot was on the other foot.

Ihaka's first instinct was to head straight out to Ellerslie and watch Murray squirm. On the way down to the car park, he had second thoughts: let's run it past Charlton; that's what he's always telling me to do. Besides, this would be the last thing he wants to land in his lap right now.

* * *

Shortly before midnight on a mild early summer's night four months after Tom Murray was charged with the murder of Ethan Stern, Tito Ihaka drove to the bottom floor of a virtually empty downtown underground car park, swung into a parking space and turned off the engine. As he waited for the meeting to convene, he sat stock-still, staring straight ahead, deep in thought.

Shortly after midnight, a brand-new black Range Rover pulled up alongside. The man who got out of it and into Ihaka's passenger seat was forty years old, round-faced and pink-complexioned with a ginger scalp stubble. His beer belly tended to distract attention from his powerful upper body, just as his permanent half-smile encouraged strangers to assume he was one of those cheerful fatsos who always look on the bright side and don't have a bad word to say about anyone.

His name was John Scholes, although the Auckland underworld knew him as Johnny B Bad. He ran a criminal gang called The Firm. The fact that it was named after the outfit headed by the infamous Kray twins which operated out of the East End of London in the 1950s and 60s said pretty much all there was to say about the gang and a fair bit about John Scholes.

'Mr Ihaka,' said Scholes, his accent as unmistakably Cockney as the day he jumped ship in Auckland, a seventeen-year-old tough who'd sailed around the world looking for a place to call home. 'How's it going. All right?'

'Yeah, Johnny. Yourself?'

'Can't complain. Well, I could, but most people I come across have got more to worry about than me so it don't seem right to bleat, you know what I mean?'

'What can I do for you, Johnny?'

'I'm going legit, Mr Ihaka. It won't happen overnight,

but eighteen months from now I aim to be out of the game completely.'

'Jesus. What brought this on?'

'My kids,' said Scholes. 'They're growing up faster than I can keep up with. Of course, they know I've done bird, but that was for giving a filthy raping piece of shit the seeing-to he richly deserved, as opposed to what you might call everyday professional villainy, so they think I was hard done by. My eldest, the girl, she's sharp as a fucking tack. She knows her old man's not your usual businessman, but she hasn't joined the dots yet. Before she does, I want to be able to give her an honest answer when she asks, Dad, what do you really do?'

'Well, good for you, Johnny.'

'It'll be a tricky business, mind, extricating myself from my current situation. It'll have to be handled delicately and timed just right.'

'Yeah, I can see that.'

'You know what my worst nightmare is? I'm just about to leave the life behind and I get done on some technicality. Your colleagues in Waitemata are still spitting blood over that deal we did to get me out of the cage.'

'You earned your way out, Johnny. The boys out west just have to wear it.'

'Where do we stand now then?' said Scholes. 'Am I still in credit?'

'You mean if you slip up, will McGrail tell Waitemata our arrangement still stands?'

'I won't slip up, but there are things I can't control.'

'If you walk a reasonably straight line, Johnny, we'll be there for you. If they catch you with a bloodstained axe in one hand and the mayor's head in the other, we probably can't help you.'

'Can't say fairer than that. Thank you, Mr Ihaka, that's a load off my mind. Now is there anything I can do for you?'

'Actually, there could be something. A strange thing happened to me a few months ago: I found out my old man was murdered.'

Scholes stared. 'What the fuck?'

'The family had always assumed he'd had a heart attack, but it turns out he was poisoned. This was back in 1987, trade union bad blood.'

'Fucking hell. Who did it?'

'Well, the bloke who ordered it killed himself – around about the time I found out.'

'Saw you coming, did he?'

'Let's say he joined the dots. And just last week the one who actually administered the poison pulled four years in Mt Eden for being party to causing GBH with intent. Fella by the name of Stu Boyle.'

Scholes nodded thoughtfully. 'Fond of your old man, were you?'

'Shit, yeah. Sometimes it feels like my whole fucking life is about trying to fill the hole he left.'

'I know what you mean, although my experience was somewhat different. My old man was a crim, of course, a hard nut and a nasty piece of work. When I was seven, he got himself in the shit, biffed my mum one last time and took off, never to be seen again. There was talk he joined the French Foreign Legion. If so, let's hope some fiendishly cruel ragheads or big black lads with machetes got hold of him. On the other hand, I do have kids and if anyone so much as harmed a hair on their heads, I'd track them down, cut them into bite-sized pieces and feed them to my dogs. So while I'm coming at it from a different perspective, I can put myself in your shoes.'

Scholes' half-smile disappeared altogether. 'I have some influence in that institution you mentioned, so put your mind at rest. It'll be taken care of. If that fucking slag Boyle knew what was in store for him, he'd drown himself in the nearest bog.'

DEATH ON DEMAND

Paul Thomas

Maori cop Tito Ihaka, "unkempt, overweight, intemperate, unruly, unorthodox and profane", is a stubborn investigator with an uncanny instinct for the truth.

Ihaka is in the wilderness, having fallen foul of the new regime at Auckland Central. Called back to follow up a strange twist in the unsolved case that got him into trouble in the first place, Ihaka finds himself hunting a shadowy hitman who could have several notches on his belt.

His enemies want him off the case, but the bodies are piling up. Ihaka embarks on a quest to establish whether police corruption was behind the shooting of an undercover cop and – to complicate matters – he becomes involved with an enigmatic female suspect who could hold the key to everything.

PRAISE FOR *DEATH ON DEMAND*

"Big, bruising police procedural set in New Zealand. Excellent."
Ian Rankin

"Welcome return of Tito Ihaka, a maverick Maori cop. The unfamiliar locations are as compelling as the actions." *Sunday Times*

"A splendidly written, constantly engaging, deliberately puzzling, always gripping story. Ihaka is wonderful, his fellow-cops and the crims well delineated, and the women both femme and fatale."
Crime Time

"A twisty plot and an unusual lead combine to make this a winner by Ned Kelly Award–winner Thomas."
Publishers Weekly

www.bitterlemonpress.com